TERRAIN OF TERROR

Benjy looked at a mat hanging on the wall of the underground room. Kenny nodded and opened fire with his silenced Swedish-K.

Small holes appeared in the mat. A soft grunt filtered back into the room, followed by a thud.

Benjy pulled away the mat, and Kenny beamed his flashlight through the hole. The body of one VC lay spread out on the tunnel floor, but his surviving partner opened fire. The roar of the AK-47 filled the tiny chamber as he fired blindly into the bright light of the flashlight. Kenny pulled the trigger on his Swedish-K and the VC dropped down dead next to his comrade.

"Hell. That was close," Kenny said. What he didn't say was that the worst part of the tunnels still lay ahead. . . .

FIELDS OF HONOR #3

THE SILVER STAR

Donald E. Zlotnik
Major (Ret) U.S. Army Special Forces

A SIGNET BOOK

SIGNET
Published by the Penguin Group
Penguin Books USA Inc., 375 Hudson Street,
New York, New York 10014, U.S.A.
Penguin Books Ltd, 27 Wrights Lane,
London W8 5TZ, England
Penguin Books Australia Ltd, Ringwood,
Victoria, Australia
Penguin Books Canada Ltd, 2801 John Street,
Markham, Ontario, Canada L3R 1B4
Penguin Books (N.Z.) Ltd, 182–190 Wairau Road,
Auckland 10, New Zealand

Penguin Books Ltd, Registered Offices:
Harmondsworth, Middlesex, England

First published by Signet, an imprint of New American Library, a division
of Penguin Books USA Inc.

First Printing, May, 1991
10 9 8 7 6 5 4 3 2 1

PUBLISHER'S NOTE
This is a work of fiction. Names, characters, places, and incidents either
are the product of the author's imagination or are used fictitiously, and any
resemblance to actual persons, living or dead, events, or locales is entirely
coincidental.

ARMY REGULATION (AR) 672-5-1
Section II, Criteria

2-10. Silver Star

The Silver Star is awarded to a person who, while serving in any capacity with the Army, is cited for gallantry in action against an enemy of the United States while engaged in military operations involving conflict with an opposing foreign force, or while serving with friendly foreign forces engaged in armed conflict against an opposing armed force in which the United States is not a belligerent party. The required gallantry, while of a lesser degree than that required for the award of the Medal of Honor or Distinguished Service Cross, must nevertheless have been performed with marked distinction.

—Extracted from the regulation

CHAPTER 1

○○○○○○○○○○○○○○○○

PISGAH NATIONAL FOREST

April 1965

She lay on the outcropping and watched the squirrel dig in the soft humus at the base of the limestone den where she had wintered with her clan and a few copperheads and large rat snakes. The winter-thin squirrel found a cache of shagbark hickory nuts he had hidden the previous fall and sat back on his haunches to tear the thick shell off the nut. A large rat snake slithered over the rotting leaves near the den and stopped to sense the air twenty feet away from the squirrel. The warm-blooded animal saw the long black snake and froze. The sun-heated limestone outcropping saved the squirrel from detection by the snake's heat sensors. The squirrel waited a few seconds until the predator was out of sight before biting into the sweet meat of the hickory nut. He knew that with the warming sun came many more dangers. During the winter he could dig through the snow and leaves with only a late hunting owl or maybe a fox to fear. But now that the season had changed, snakes would be leaving their dens and be ravenous. He stretched up on his haunches to make a final check for the rat snake, and his upper body extended over the lip of the limestone ledge.

She struck.

The two boys were dressed almost identically in well-worn Levi's and high-top leather hunting boots. The only difference in their dress was that one wore a Black Watch tartan flannel shirt and the other boy wore a faded Royal Stewart pattern. They were identical twins.

The first boy dropped down and looked at the deep hoof marks in the soft earth of the narrow deer trail. He could see that the big buck was dragging his left rear leg, and that made him frown. He knew that he was a better shot than that; he had hit the buck near its heart. He glanced over his shoulder at his brother and used the barrel of his over-and-under shotgun-rifle to point toward the limestone outcropping that capped the end of the ridge line they had been tracking along. The deer couldn't be much farther ahead of them on the trail.

A soft clicking alerted the twin in the lead that something was wrong, and he slowly started lifting his rifle to his shoulder as his eyes swept the forest. His eyes followed his brother's gesture toward a spot about thirty feet ahead of them on the trail. A seven-foot rat snake was watching them, trying to decide if the boys were a threat. The boy in the lead nodded and started approaching the limestone ledge with a great deal more caution. It wasn't the lone rat snake he was concerned about, but the company the snake kept during the winter months. The south-facing limestone outcropping made a perfect place for a rattlesnake den. It was late April, but the winter cold had lingered this year and had slowed the awakening process of the hibernating snakes. Old Hillard Green had taught them about rattlesnake dens the very first time he had taken them out on a hunt in the mountains when they had just turned nine years old.

The boy in the lead spotted the deer as soon as they reached the limestone ledge. The buck had died and fallen down the back side of the outcropping. The twin smiled to himself; he could see the small red mark near the deer's heart where the .22 long rifle round had entered. The deer had been dragging his hind leg because he had lost so much strength. The boy had made a good shot, but next time he was going to aim for the head so that they wouldn't have to track so far away from their cabin.

"Snake! Back off, Benjy!" The boy bringing up the rear used the barrel of his rifle to point at a large timber rattler, the squirrel sticking halfway out of her mouth. She was stretched out on the limestone ledge less than three feet away from Benjy's legs.

"She's a big bitch, for sure!" Benjy stepped back off the trail and unlocked his over-and-under so that he could exchange the slug he had in the twenty-gauge chamber for a number-six birdshot.

He always hunted with a .22 long rifle in the upper chamber and a heavy slug in the shotgun barrel, just in case he ran into a bear.

"Take care, Benjy!" The boy kept the barrel of his rifle pointed at the huge snake. "Watch her an' I'll get a snake stick!"

"What for?"

"She can't bite with that squirrel stuffed in her mouth like that!" The boy looked around for a forked stick on the ground. "Hillard Green can git good money for her." He located an appropriate tool and tested it against the ground to make sure it wouldn't break under pressure before shoving the forked end behind the rattler's neck. Benjy reached down and grabbed her as close to her head as he could. He held her until his brother could tie a piece of rawhide around her neck and bind her head to the pole so that she couldn't strike.

Benjy hefted the snake. "She must be twenty-five pounds, Kenny!" He shook his head. "We can't carry her and the buck back home." The conflict was sharp; the venison was food for their table, the rattlesnake would bring cash. Both were important.

"Le's tie her up agains' the tree"—Kenny nodded at a nearby sapling—"an' come an' git her tomorra."

Benjy nodded in agreement and tied the stick and the timber rattler's head up against the side of the small tree, using the remainder of the long rawhide lace.

"Le's butcher." Benjy looked over at his kill.

"Shit!" The cliffs were alive with rattlesnakes. Now that he had attuned his eyes to the pattern of the snakes' markings, it was impossible to miss them.

"Damn! They's all over here!" Kenny who had been bringing up the rear spoke up loudly; there was no more need for quiet now that they had found their deer.

"Be careful, Kenny. . . . You can't see 'em in the leaves!"

Kenny looked down around his feet and started backing off the trail down the side of the mountain.

"No!" Benjy's voice stopped his brother. "Don't get off the trail or they'll bite us for sure!"

"Why aren't they singin'?" Kenny's eyes scanned the rocks and paused each time he located a snake.

"Damn if I know. Probably too cold yet." Benjy pointed back the way they had come. "Le's backtrack an' come up from th' north side, where it's still shady."

"You sure you want to come back at all?" Kenny wasn't happy about lingering around the snake den.

"That's good meat, Kenny, an' I ain't goin' back to Ma empty-handed!"

"Fine! But I don't wanta get snakebit either!"

"C'mon, jus' be careful!" Benjy led the way around the back side of the shaded limestone cliff until he could see the buck. He approached the deer cautiously and tied another piece of rawhide around the buck's rear legs and started pulling it away from the cliff. Kenny helped and they dragged the deer two hundred feet before risking a stop.

"Here, carry my gun." Benjy handed his brother

his over-and-under and lifted the buck up over his shoulders. He bounced it a couple of times, testing the weight. "Winter's been hard on him. He's not as fat as he looked."

"Still got some nice back meat." Kenny patted the hindquarters of the deer.

"Le's get over t' Mr. Harley's place an' spend the night."

"I don't like dead places." Kenny was referring to the Harley family cemetery that was near the old mountain cabin.

"Kenny, I ain't carryin' this buck all the way back home today! 'Sides, we kin butcher it on Harley's old hog rack and carry the meat home in pieces."

Benjy was making good sense and Kenny nodded in agreement. The cabin was less than a mile away and the walk was mostly downhill. The buck had run farther away from their cabin than they had counted on. "Do y'think Ma'll fret?"

"Naw, she knows we went after the buck." Benjy started walking flat-footed with the deer balanced across his shoulders.

The smell of jet engine exhaust filled the ready area next to the ramps where the two Special Forces training teams were waiting to board their aircraft. All twenty-four soldiers were starting their final phase of the long Special Forces training cycle. The men had been formed into two twelve-man A-Detachments for their last month of field training.

Now they were going to make a night infiltration jump. Only the four instructors who were going to jump with them knew where they were going. The two A-Detachments had been designated as the guerrilla forces for the exercise, and the only thing they knew was that a battalion from the Eighty-second Airborne Division would be hunting them down.

A Special Forces jumpmaster approached the waiting men and signaled them to stand for a final equipment check before boarding the aircraft. Strain showed on all their faces. Passing this phase in guerrilla warfare was important to all of them; there was a twenty-eight-percent failure rate during this portion of training.

Sergeant Bradshaw looked over at his junior radio operator. "I've never liked night jumps all that much."

The trainee smiled. "Me neither, except the part where my feet touch the ground."

"I don't mind night jumps on Bragg's DZ's, but I heard we're jumping into a *two*-second drop zone . . . fuck!"

"That's at least five or six passes . . . shit, I hate it when they make sharp turns in those damn planes!"

"It's all in a day in the life of a paratrooper, Rickman." Bradshaw tried smiling out of the corner of his mouth as he lifted his arms and laced his fingers together behind his helmet. The jumpmaster flipped open the flap that covered the ripcord pins on his reserve parachute and checked to ensure they were properly seated. He slapped the side of the parachute when he had finished, and Bradshaw turned to his right so that the jumpmaster could inspect his waist strap and quick-release lace in his buckle. The jumpmaster slapped his side again and Bradshaw presented his back to the jumpmaster. The senior NCO inspected his static line and handed the snap-link end of the bright yellow cord to him over his left shoulder, which signaled that he would be jumping out of the right exit door as he faced to the rear of the aircraft.

The rear ramp of the C-130 was lowered and the trainees boarded the aircraft in reverse order. Bradshaw unbuckled his seat belt and adjusted it so that it would fit around his waist before settling in to the red nylon seat. Specialist Rickman buckled into the seat next to him. The rucksack he carried between his legs rested on the aircraft floor and took the weight off his harness. Rickman sighed and leaned against the netting. He could feel the sweat break out over his forehead the instant he sat down in the confined space. The roar coming from the four engines made talking impossible, and he watched the rest of the trainees load up and take their seats. A friend of his at base operations had told him that his aircraft's scheduled flight time was only three hours, which meant they would probably start jumping in about an hour and a half. That was good news, because it meant their training area was going to be somewhere on the east coast. He had heard that some of the training missions were as far away as Utah and the Special Forces trainees had to find their way back to Fort Bragg without being caught by the local and state police, who had been alerted about them. The trainees had been warned during long hours of briefings that all of the local police departments were working for the opposing forces, but a local guerrilla force would meet them at their DZ and guide them to their first rendezvous site. Then they would turn in their parachutes and receive their special instructions and field maps.

Sergeant Bradshaw rested the back of his helmet against the frame of the aircraft and closed his eyes. He tried getting his mind off the strong odor coming from the engines by thinking about the mission. He was the trainee team leader for the three-week exercise and was responsible for one of the A-Detachments. If he screwed up and made a bad decision, the whole team could fail the course. If it wasn't a big error, they would only be recycled to another class, but if it was an honor violation, the whole team would be failed and thrown out of Special Forces. He opened his eyes and glanced over at the men sitting across the narrow aisle; all of them had been in the training group for over a year and had survived at least four extremely difficult training phases for their particular Special Forces occupational specialties. They were putting a lot of faith in him.

Bradshaw closed his eyes again and felt the C-130 start to taxi down the runway. The pilot tapped his brakes too hard and the large cargo plane jerked to a halt, causing the jumpmaster, who was standing up in the rear of the aircraft, to stumble and fall against Bradshaw.

"I can see this is going to be a fucked-up flight

already!" The master sergeant cursed above the roar of the engines as the pilot revved the engines for takeoff. The jumpmaster buckled himself in on the seat that had been reserved for him and chewed the wet end of his unlit cigar.

The bright lights from the military jeep spread out over the tall meadow grass, sending long shadows back over toward Harley's cabin. Kenny stood up from where he had been squatting next to the large fire he had built and looked over to see who was coming down the rarely used lumber trail that passed within a few yards of the cabin.

"Seems we've some visitors." Benjy took advantage of the extra light to skin a large section of hide off the deer that was hanging from Harley's old chestnut hog-butchering rack.

The Army jeep turned into the overgrown front yard and then backed up when the driver saw the fire burning back near the unoccupied pigpen. Bull thistles had grown to heights of nearly eight feet in the rich soil the summer before, and the yard was a solid wall of prickly brown leaves and stems.

The man sitting on the passenger seat spoke to the boys when the jeep pulled to a stop with its lights shining on them. "Y'all been huntin'?"

"Suppose so," Benjy answered the familiar voice, but he couldn't see the man because of the bright lights in his eyes. Kenny reached over and pulled his 30-30 lever-action Winchester across his lap.

"No need for that." The voice was directed at Kenny. "Your Ma'll be madder'n hell if y'shoot me!" The man chuckled under his breath. Kenny could see that the driver had left his seat and was walking out in front of the headlights where they could see him.

"Is that you, Mr. Ledford?" Benjy lowered the hand that was holding his skinning knife.

"Sure as hell is!" The middle-aged man stepped out where the boys could see him. "Whatcha doin' huntin' so damn far from your cabin?"

Benjy went back to skinning the buck in the headlights of the jeep. "Made a bad shot an' he ran aways 'fore he fell."

"I'll say! Two . . . maybe three miles!"

Benjy changed the subject. He didn't want to talk about the poor shot he had made. "Whatcha all doin' up here?"

"Playin' war." Ledford spit out a brown stream of tobacco juice.

"With this Army man?" Kenny nodded at the sergeant major standing to one side of the jeep. He had moved away from the headlights so that Benjy could have more light to work by.

"Yep." Ledford stopped spitting long enough to answer, and then started chewing slowly again on the fresh tobacco he had added to his chew. "Paratroopers are comin' in here tonight."

"The kind that jump outta airplanes?" Kenny glanced over at his brother.

"For sure." Ledford was acting important. "This is Sergeant Major Yates from Fort Bragg down on the piedmont."

"Hi, boys." The sergeant major smiled and nodded at each boy. "They're due in here in three hours. How would you kids like to make ten dollars apiece?"

"Doin' what?" Benjy was suspicious.

"Helping me set up a drop zone so that the pilot in the airplane can find this spot on the mountain."

"Whose side?" Benjy used the back of his bloody hand to scratch an itch at the tip of his nose.

"I don't understand what you mean." The sergeant major frowned.

"He wants t'know if you're workin' for the guerrillas or the town folks," Ledford said.

"We're setting up this drop zone for two guerrilla teams tonight." The Special Forces sergeant major smiled. "It's easy money, setting up a couple of fire pots around the meadow."

Benjy looked over at his brother. "Sorry, mister. We can't help you."

"Why? Did I say something wrong?"

"Nope . . . just that my mother's friend is the sheriff an' he don't like the guerrilla soldiers very much. We don't need trouble with our mother."

"Ten dollars apiece is good money anyways y'look at it." Ledford helped out the sergeant major again.

Kenny looked over at his brother. It was good money for only a couple hours' light work. "Can y'keep it secret from our mother?"

"Sure."

Benjy hesitated and then nodded in agreement. "First I gotta finish dressin' this buck."

"No problem, we've got plenty of time." The sergeant major pointed at the headlights. "Do you want me to leave them on for you to work by?"

"It'd be appreciated." Benjy started back on the deerhide again and worked faster under the bright lights.

Kenny wandered around to the small trailer the jeep was towing and lifted the canvas flap. He could see a number of round five gallon cans that had their tops cut off and were filled a third of the way with loose sand.

"Those are fire pots. We'll pour a little diesel fuel on the sand and light it so that the people in the airplane can see it from above, but there won't be much of a fire to see from the ground." The sergeant major had followed Kenny around the jeep. He reached farther back under the tarp and pulled out a cardboard case. "You kids hungry?"

"A bit. Soon's Benjy finishes the buck, we're goin' t'roast some in the fire."

"Here." The sergeant major handed Kenny a smaller box from the larger container of C rations and removed three more. "You like beans and franks?" He was talking to Benjy.

"Sure." Benjy stopped working just long enough to see what the Army man was doing.

Yates used one of the small P-38 can openers that came with the rations to open the can of beans and franks. Kenny watched how the sergeant major did it and copied him.

The Special Forces NCO folded back the top of the can and bent the edges down, making the lid into a handle before he set the rations down in the hot coals at the edge of the fire to heat.

"Hey, Benjy! Smells good!" Kenny used one of the white plastic spoons to stir the can of beef and potatoes he had opened.

"I'm almost finished here." Benjy had smelled the food and was hurrying to finish on the deer. He hadn't realized how hungry he was.

The sergeant major watched the boys devour the rations and went back to get a couple more boxes for them to eat. "You kids hurry up and finish eating so we can get started on the drop-zone lights."

Benjy shoveled down the warm rations and nodded at the sergeant major. The cans of Army food were a lot better than the stuff the church people brought by their cabin for Thanksgiving and Christmas.

The jumpmaster leaned out of the open side door and looked down at the black masses of trees that covered the mountains. Streams and rivers shone up as silver threads down below and large meadows would reflect the soft moonlight and show up as light tan patches on the mountainsides. He pointed to the row of fire pots that formed an arrow on the ground and then over at the marked DZ in the distance. He turned to face the seated paratroopers and gave hand signals for them to stand up.

The C-130 made a slow banking turn to the left and lined up for its approach on the small drop zone. The pilot figured he would have to make six or seven passes to get all of the men out safely. The DZ was tiny compared to the large DZ's at Fort Bragg, where major course errors didn't make much of a difference to the jumpers except that they would have to walk a little farther to the pickup point. Here a miss by only a hundred yards could put the jumper in a hardwood tree that could tear a parachute apart, not to mention the jumper.

Sergeant Bradshaw watched the jumpmaster and then switched his attention over to the flashing green light attached above the doorframe.

"Go!" The jumpmaster pointed out the open door. The jump stick obeyed and the men started shuffling forward with their heavy rucksacks bouncing against their legs. Two men exited each door and then the jumpmaster stopped the stick while the plane banked slowly and lined up for another pass. The jumpmaster leaned out of the door attached to his safety strap and located the landing paratroopers. They had hit the meadow area almost perfectly. He pointed at the next two men in the stick and yelled again, "Go!"

Bradshaw felt his parachute jerk open. He released his rucksack and let it drop below him on the rope attached to his harness. Landing with the heavy cargo bag still attached to his body could cause severe injury and it was necessary to let the rucksack hit the ground before the man landed to reduce the man's weight on impact. A soft mountain breeze came up out of nowhere and started changing Bradshaw's course. He could see Rickman's parachute off a little to his left rear and he corrected for the wind, using his right toggle line.

Kenny stood in the shadows next to the pigpen and watched the dark shadow coming down out of the moonlit sky. The paratrooper landed on the tin roof of the pigpen and slid down in the old pig yard.

"Fuck! *Damn!*" Rickman had landed right in the middle of the bull thistles.

"Need some help?" Kenny couldn't help laughing at the struggling paratrooper.

"Yes! Collapse my parachute before it pulls me through this shit!" Rickman whispered.

Bradshaw landed softly in the middle of the meadow and was instantly up on his feet and out of his harness. He ran around and collapsed his chute and started coiling it up in his arms before he realized that the silk was filled with thousands of small crickets. The folded parachute wouldn't fit in his B-4 bag and he would have to drag the cricket-filled chute over to the blinking flashlight that signaled the team's assembly area near the cabin. Bradshaw looked up and saw the next two men preparing to land in the meadow. He hurried to get off the small meadow and out of their way.

"Do y'need some help?" The voice came from out of a small stand of trees near the edge of the meadow.

"Sure, if you can carry my rucksack until I drop off this parachute, I'd appreciate it." Bradshaw stopped walking and watched the small shadow leave the protection of the trees. "You look awful young to be working with the guerrilla force."

"We're just helpin' out tonight."

"What's your name?"

"Benjy Kingston." He looked over toward the assembly area for the team. "My brother Kenny is over there."

Bradshaw handed the small teenager his rucksack and watched the boy lift it almost casually over his shoulder, using only one of the straps. The boy was thin, but had the wiry build of the Appalachian mountain people. Bradshaw adjusted the B-4 bag on his shoulders and started walking toward the red light coming from the military flashlight.

The sergeant major watched the two A-Teams assemble from his seat on the hood of the jeep. There was only one man absent. "What happened to our missing man?"

One of Bradshaw's team members spoke up. "I think it was Koski. He slipped with the wind and landed a little off the drop zone. His chute might have gotten hung up in a tree."

Sergeant Major Yates looked over at Bradshaw. "You the team leader?"

"Yes, I am, Sergeant Major."

"Take a couple of your men and go help him. We don't need to turn in a torn parachute and go through all of that paperwork, do we?"

"No, Sergeant Major." Bradshaw's voice reflected the respect he had for the senior Special Forces NCO.

"Take the boys with you; they know this mountain better than anyone." The sergeant major nodded over at the twins, who were sitting next to each other watching all of the Army men.

Bradshaw beckoned. "Come on, Benjy, let's find my missing man."

Once their eyes adjusted to the moonlight, it was easy to see as they walked across the meadow. The trainee who had spoken up earlier was in the lead until they reached the edge of the woods, and then Kenny slipped up front and disappeared into the dark mass of trees.

"Ahhh . . . help me."

Bradshaw looked up and saw the dark shape hanging in the the tall black locust. The soldier's parachute was tangled up in the dense network of branches. "You all right?"

"No . . . I think a branch broke and I'm caught on it."

"Hang on, we'll come up there and help you down." Bradshaw walked around the tree, looking for a low branch he could use to pull himself up on, but all the branches were too high.

"Give me a boost up that tree an' I kin cross over to his tree." Kenny pointed to a five-inch sapling growing next to the giant locust.

Benjy and the sergeant helped him get started up the trunk and Kenny shimmied up the sapling until he reached a solid branch where he could cross to the locust. He moved through the branches faster than a raccoon chased by a pack of hounds. The soldier hung from a broken branch and Kenny could see in the pale moonlight that the man's right side was covered with blood.

"You all right, mister?"

The soldier lifted his head. "I think I'm caught up on my harness."

"You're bleedin' some." Kenny moved around the trunk of the tree and looked to see where the broken branch was hooked to the man's webgear and saw that the limb had hooked on the man's thick harness, but the sharp tip of the broken hardwood limb had gone through the soldier's left lateral muscle and had the man hanging. The harness strap had taken most of the load off the man's flesh, or his own weight would have torn the muscle out of his body.

"I think I broke a rib or something."

"Prob'ly." Kenny looked down at the ground and called to his brother. "Benjy, get up here and give me some help."

Benjy followed his twin brother's path up the trunk and was standing on the limb next to the trapped soldier in a matter of seconds. He saw instantly what his brother was pointing at and removed his skinning knife from its sheath on his hip and cut through the strong nylon suspension lines of the parachute that were attached to the soldier's harness.

The man's weight shifted and he screamed. The sergeant major looked up from his seat on the jeep's hood and then sprang into action. "Medics, grab your kits and get in!" He started the jeep and backed it up until he reached the meadow, and then slipped it in first gear for the ride across the clearing to the forest.

Bradshaw had the wounded Special Forces trainee down on the ground and was trying to stop the flow of blood from the torn flesh. Benjy and Kenny were standing to one side watching.

Sergeant Major Yates parked the jeep as close to the injured man as he could and left the engine running. The medics jumped from the vehicle and rushed over to where Bradshaw was kneeling.

"You're lucky, Koski, not everyone has *four* Special Forces medics looking after him." Bradshaw patted the injured trainee's leg.

"Shit! I hope this doesn't mean I'll be recycled to another class!"

"Let me run you in to the hospital in Morgantown and we'll decide there how bad that wound is." Yates could see that the man would require a number of stitches to close the hole, but his prime concern was how much damage had been done to the muscle.

Bradshaw walked over to where the boys were standing and watched the medics load up the trainee. "You did good work up there in that tree. If it wasn't for you kids, we would have had a hell of a time getting him down."

"I think I hurt 'im." Benjy sounded worried.

"You did *right*, boy! There was no other way to get him off that branch." Bradshaw patted Benjy's shoulder. "I'm damn proud of you!"

Benjy smiled shyly and glanced over at his brother.

"As long as we're heading into Morgantown, I'll take you kids home." Sergeant Major Yates used his thumb to point at the jeep.

"Thanks for th' offer, but we still have somethin' in the woods t'get." Kenny remembered the rattlesnake. "But, we sure could use a ride in the mornin'."

Yates chuckled. "I'll be back to get you. Stay near the cabin."

The twins nodded in unison.

Nights got cold up in the Appalachian Mountains and the Special Forces trainees had brought their sleeping bags. Bradshaw noticed that the boys were banking the fire and Kenny had cut some pine boughs to sleep on. "Do you boys have blankets?"

Kenny shook his head. "We didn't think the buck was goin' t'run far."

"Use Koski's sleeping bag." He handed the injured trainee's rucksack to Kenny and looked over at Benjy. "You can use mine tonight. We have to pull guard duty, so there's going to be an extra one."

Benjy looked sheepishly at the sergeant. "I can't take your beddin'."

"It's fine, believe me." Bradshaw handed the boy the light brown down-filled sleeping bag.

The twins laid the bags on the boughs next to the fire and removed only their boots before slipping into the warm covers. Benjy looked over at his brother and smiled; neither of them had ever slept in something so fine in all their lives.

The sun started breaking over the tops of the trees at almost the same time the sound of an approaching vehicle reached Bradshaw. He glanced over at the men sleeping around the fire. The boys had moved their sleeping bags next to each other sometime during the night and Benjy slept with his arm over Kenny's shoulder and his head tucked against his brother's back. Bradshaw thought that it was a little strange that the two brothers would sleep so close to each other, but the thought was cut short when Benjy shifted his position and Bradshaw could see both of their faces as they slept. He did a double take and stared. They were identical twins. He had known they were brothers, but the darkness had prevented his getting a good look at the boys.

Kenny opened his eyes and caught Bradshaw staring at him. He rolled over on his side and touched Benjy's shoulder. "Time to get up."

Bradshaw was still a little shocked over how much the boys looked alike; even the way their hair dropped down over their right eyes was identical. "You're twins," was all that he could think of saying to them.

"Yep . . . been twins all our lives." Benjy started rolling up his sleeping bag while Kenny slipped on his boots.

"I think the sergeant is comin' back." Kenny looked over to see if the jeep was coming up the timber trail. "We'd better get over and get that snake before he gets here."

"Snake?" Bradshaw folded his poncho liner and shoved it down in his rucksack.

"Yep, big'un too." Benjy handed the sleeping bag to the sergeant. "Thanks."

"Where's it at?" Bradshaw was interested in the snake.

"We's got 'em tied up t'a stick." Benjy nodded back towards the woods.

"Do you mind if I come along?"

Benjy shrugged and picked up his over-and-under from the pine boughs.

Bradshaw brought up the rear of the three-man formation, with Benjy taking the lead. The boy moved down the trail at a slow jog without looking back. Bradshaw noticed that the boys were running in perfect step, and when Benjy looked to the right side of the trail, Kenny glanced to the left. They were a perfect hunting pair. Benjy stopped after they had gone a half-mile and held up his rifle. "Snake den."

Bradshaw stared at the limestone outcropping and didn't see anything but leaves and stone.

"Kenny, untie her." Benjy kept scanning the rocks with his eyes.

"Holy shit!" Bradshaw saw the timber rattler tied to the sapling. "That's a fucking monster."

"Yup, she's a big'un for sure." Benjy kept his eyes on the ground. "Careful round here, could be more."

Bradshaw watched Kenny grab the six-foot rattler

behind her neck and lift her off the ground. She was still cold from the long night and didn't resist his handling.

"Le's get back." Benjy turned and started walking back toward the cabin, carrying Kenny's 30-30 in one hand and his over-and-under in the other hand. Bradshaw brought up the rear, wearing a stunned look.

Sergeant Major Yates looked up when he heard the group approaching, and quickly concealed the look of surprise on his face. "You've got a dandy there, kids."

"Fair size." Kenny smiled, showing his pride in capturing such a trophy snake. "Should get twenty dollars for her."

"You're selling it?" Bradshaw stood next to the fire and felt a shiver ripple along his back.

"Yep." Kenny looked over at the sergeant major. "You don't have a spare poke in your jeep, do you?"

The rest of the trainees formed a semicircle around the jeep trailer and stared in awe at the huge poisonous reptile the small teenager was holding almost casually in his hands.

Sergeant Major Yates flipped back the tarp on the trailer and looked behind the cases of C rations. "I've got a couple of sandbags back here, but I don't think that rattler will fit in one!" He shuffled through the gear and finally stopped when his hand rested on the wooden toolbox. "I guess we could empty this and use it until we can find something better."

Kenny dropped the snake into the box and Yates slammed the wooden cover closed. "You boys had better get your venison so we can get you home." Yates looked over at Bradshaw. "Clean up this site and be ready for your briefings when I return. It shouldn't take more than an hour."

"We'll be waiting, Sergeant Major." Bradshaw started turning away, but stopped. "Sergeant Major, do you think we could use those boys as recon scouts?"

A small smile slipped over the senior NCO's face. He had been thinking the same thing. "It can't hurt asking them."

The team leader for the other A-Team spoke up. "I could use one of the boys for my team."

Benjy and Kenny returned to the jeep carrying the sections of plastic-wrapped venison on their shoulders. Bradshaw was the first one to speak. "How would you kids like to work for us as scouts?"

"I don't think the sheriff would like that. He's always with the townfolk."

"It would be fun and we'd pay you twenty-five dollars a week. You could meet us after school and guide for us until dark."

"We don't go t'school."

"How old are you guys?"

"Fifteen."

Bradshaw caught the sergeant major's look and nodded. "Well, then, you can spend all three weeks with us. It's good money and the food is free."

Kenny glanced at his brother. Benjy shrugged. "We'll have to ask our ma."

"Good, one of you can scout for each of our teams." Bradshaw pointed at the other team leader.

Benjy's answer was quick. "Sorry, we have to stay together." Kenny nodded in agreement.

"You asked first, Sergeant Bradshaw, so they'll stay with you if their mother approves." Yates slid behind the wheel of the jeep. "Let's go, boys."

The boys' cabin was only three miles through the woods over the animal trails, but it was closer to fifteen miles by road. At the end of a rarely used lane that led back to the Kingstons' cabin, Yates brought the jeep to a stop only a couple of feet from the front porch of the building. He could see that the cabin had been built near the turn of the century, and would bet money that it had a dirt floor. A woman opened the door and stepped outside, holding the hand of a small boy.

"Hey, Ma!" Kenny hopped out of the jeep, followed closely by Benjy.

The woman looked hard at the uniformed sergeant and spoke in a soft voice. "They ain't in some kind of trouble, are they?"

"No, ma'am! You've got a pair of fine boys there!" Yates had worked the Pisgah National Forest area as a cadre instructor for over three years, but he had never seen people living poorer than what he was looking at. "In fact, we'd like to hire them to work for us."

"Work?" She glanced over at her sons.

"Yeah, Ma! Scouts!" Kenny couldn't contain his excitement. "Army scouts!"

Fear flashed across the woman's face. "They's too young t'be in the Army!"

"No, ma'am . . . we're not taking them in the Army. We just want to hire them to help us train some new soldiers up here. We met them back in the woods." Yates nodded at the venison in the jeep trailer. "We can't pay much, only twenty-five dollars a week."

"Each?"

"Yes, ma'am, plus we'll see that they get fed."

She could see the excitement in her sons' eyes and smiled. "Well, I guess it's all right. How long?"

"Three weeks."

"Git that meat in the smokehouse first, 'fore you go!"

"Yes'm!" Benjy ran over to the jeep and grabbed the hindquarters of the buck.

"Have a seat, mister." She pointed to the edge of the porch.

"Thanks." Yates took the offered seat and winked at the shy little boy peeking out at him from behind his mother's skirt. The boy had black hair. "Have you been living up here long?"

"Since my husband off'n left us . . . eleven years ago. This was my daddy's cabin. He built it hisself."

"Well, I'm mighty proud you're letting the boys work with us for a while. I'll make sure they get back here to visit regular."

" 'Ppreciate that." She smiled when she saw her sons approaching from behind the cabin.

Yates thought for a couple seconds and then went over to his jeep and removed two cases of C rations. "Ma'am, I don't know if you can use these, but I know your boys liked some of the canned goods." He set the cases down on the porch. "There's some coffee and cocoa in there."

"Coffee?"

"Yes, ma'am, not a lot, just little packets."

"I ain't had coffee in a while."

"It's yours if you want it."

"Thank you."

The twins had traded places in the jeep for the ride back to Harley's place on the mountain without even discussing it. Yates noticed that each boy always seemed to know what the other was thinking. When it had been mentioned that they serve as scouts on separate teams, it was as if they had been asked to commit an unmentionable crime.

"What kind of scoutin' do you want us t'do?" Benjy spoke up above the wind noise.

"Mostly finding trails and taking the team from one place to another without getting caught."

Benjy glanced over at his brother and smiled. "That's all?"

Sergeant Bradshaw had his team waiting when the sergeant major returned with the two boys. He was happy that they had agreed to join his team as scouts; it would make his job a lot easier and give him more time to plan for their missions.

Yates slipped off the driver's seat and handed Bradshaw and the other team leader their sealed packets of instructions. "Go ahead and look at them." He glanced down at his watch. "You're about sixteen hours behind schedule and I'm afraid that you're going to have to make up the time before the end of the week."

The second A-Team leader glared over at Bradshaw. He was jealous that neither of the boys wanted to scout for his team.

"Bradshaw, seeing that you've got the scouts . . . I'm going to send your team across the Linville Gorge to link up with the guerrilla band near Tablerock Mountain."

The second A-Team leader smiled. Linville Gorge had a reputation for burning a team out very fast; it was extremely difficult to negotiate.

Bradshaw nodded and picked up his M-16 off his rucksack. He had opened his instruction packet and had located his first checkpoint. "We're ready to move out now, Sergeant Major." The whole team was anxious to get the field problem started and to get away from the training-group cadre so they could relax a little.

"Fine! I'll see all of you again at your first objective, I hope." Yates grinned and tilted his head.

"We'll be there, Sergeant Major!" Bradshaw took the lead of his formation, followed closely by the twins, who were carrying their own weapons. The only difference between the twins' guns and the Special Forces trainees' M-16's was that the twins' guns were loaded.

CHAPTER 2

○○○○○○○○○○○○○○○○○○○○○

THE LINVILLE GORGE

Late April 1965

Sergeant Bradshaw had used his military 1:25,000-scale map to guide his team to the south entrance of Linville Gorge park. He had followed a gravel road until he had reached the ranger station, and then he had taken the team through the thick woods until they reached one of the cleared sleeping areas the park service had cut out of the forest. Linville Gorge was designated a national wilderness, and all of the trails leading down into the gorge were very rugged, with only small orange strips of plastic to mark the way. People using the park were supposed to check in with the rangers, but Bradshaw knew the ranger station was probably being watched by the conventional forces, so he sneaked his team into the park.

"The way I figure it . . ." Bradshaw unfolded his map and rested his back against his rucksack on the ground. ". . . we can take this trail down to the river and cross over somewhere along this narrow stretch." He tapped the map with his finger. "The problem is that once we get to the other side of the gorge, the going will be very tough. There aren't any trails over there." He looked over at the twins. "What do you kids think? Do you know a way out of the gorge from the other side of the river?"

"Sure. We know lots of 'em," Benjy said.

"Are they on this map?" Bradshaw held the map out for the twins to look at.

Kenny took the map and politely looked at it, but he couldn't understand any of the symbols.

Bradshaw saw the puzzled look on the teenager's face and felt like a fool for thinking the boys would know how to read a military map. "Sorry, Kenny . . ." He took the map back from the boy. "I just assumed that you would know how to read a map."

Kenny was embarrassed. "I can read a gas-station map some."

"These are special maps. I forget that you kids were only our scouts. You're so good in the woods, I thought you were one of the team." Bradshaw's comment cheered Kenny up a little.

"There's bear an' deer trails all over the gorge." Kenny pointed off toward the water.

"Bear?" Bradshaw looked over at his teammates.

"Sure." Kenny grinned. "Best bear huntin' in the whole state of North Carolina!"

"Y'got bullets fer your guns?" Benjy hefted his over-and-under.

"No," Bradshaw replied.

"Why carry guns without bullets?"

"We're training, Benjy. Besides, this is a national forest, and carrying weapons is against the law. We needed special permission just to carry our M-16's while we train."

Benjy stuck his lower lip out and shrugged; everybody he knew carried a gun in the woods, and it didn't matter if it was federal land or not. "We're Americans."

Bradshaw smiled over the boy's answer and changed the subject back to getting his team across the gorge. "So you know a trail we can use?"

Kenny looked around the campsite to orient himself to his exact location before speaking. "We're goin' to have to backtrack for a ways."

"How long do you think it'll take us?" Bradshaw lifted his rucksack off the ground and dreaded putting it back on again.

"We should be up on Tablerock by campin' time." Benjy looked up at the sun through the trees. "Maybe sooner if the river isn't runnin' high."

Bradshaw was shocked. All of the stories he had heard of A-Teams going through the gorge were horror stories about days of hard traveling, especially when they tried climbing back out of the steep-walled gorge. He looked at his watch. "Benjy, you're talking about crossing the gorge in six hours!"

"Yep." Benjy slipped the rucksack Sergeant Major Yates had given him over his shoulders and bounced a little to settle the pack on his back. "Le's get goin' so we don't lose good daylight."

Benjy led the way back out to the gravel road and started walking at a brisk pace. The Special Forces trainees tightened their belly straps and leaned forward with their heavy loads. None of them would ask the teenager to slow down, but there wasn't a man in the group who didn't wish for a much lighter rucksack.

Kenny took the position behind his brother and the two boys started walking as if they were hunting; very little escaped their searching eyes. A mile up the road, Benjy veered sharply into the woods and broke a new trail. He went about a hundred meters and stopped in the center of a well-used but narrow path. Bradshaw moved forward and dropped down on one knee to whisper in Benjy's ear, "Why didn't you tell me this trail was here before?"

Benjy's expression was blank when he answered. "You're the boss. We figured you was goin' where you wanted t'go."

Bradshaw was angry at himself for not asking the boys to begin with which was the best way down into the gorge. He wouldn't make that mistake again. "Go on."

Benjy hefted his gun and started moving downhill along the trail that hairpinned down to the floor of the gorge. The old trail had been used by hunters for well over a hundred years and had been originally a deer trail. Animals always found the best way down to a water source. It might not be the fastest way or a scenic route, but an animal trail always provided cover and escape routes and normally led to water.

Bradshaw checked his map as they walked along the path and couldn't find the trail marked anywhere on it. His rucksack brushed the thick undergrowth on both sides of the trail, but the footing was smooth. A rock wall appeared out of the woods and wound around a granite cliff that had bushes and small trees growing out of the cracks on its face. A sheer twenty-foot drop-off to their left ended in a moss-covered boulder graveyard. The sound of fast-running water reached the team as soon as they had turned around the corner of the cliff. They were within a few hundred meters of the river.

Benjy stopped and raised his hand over his head. He nodded at a herd of deer drinking from a small flood pool near the river. The herd buck snorted and tapped the ground with his right front hoof as a warning to the intruders. Kenny snorted back and the buck took off down the floor of the gorge, followed by his does.

"Unbelievable! Absolutely unbelievable!" Bradshaw shook his head. "We're going to make up the sixteen hours we fell behind back at the meadow." He pointed at what looked like a random scattering of large flat rocks that lined the river bottom. "We can probably ford that without even getting wet."

"Ther's a better place a little further downstream." Benjy tilted his head. " 'Sides, y'want t'get up to Tablerock, don't y'all?"

"Right. Lead the way, scout!"

Kenny grinned and shook his head for his brother to see. The flatlanders got excited over such little things. "Y'want me to take the lead for a while?"

Benjy nodded and dropped back behind his brother. Bradshaw watched the boys slip quietly down the trail. It didn't make a difference which one was in the lead, they moved at exactly the same speed.

Kenny stepped out onto the large rock in the river and balanced himself before jumping over to the next rock. The white water between the car-size boulders varied from a couple of feet deep to ten feet of dangerous rapids where the water was channeled between huge boulders. The team followed the teenagers in single file out onto the rocks and moved cautiously across the hundred-meter stretch of fast-moving water and wet boulders surrounded on both banks by old evergreens and tall hardwood trees. A light mist hung over the gorge, filling the air with a damp mountain scent.

Sergeant Bradshaw paused on one of the larger boulders in the middle of the watercourse and looked upstream at the white water and sun-filtered mist. He felt the cool air rushing down over the water and made a mental note to come back and visit the beautiful mountain ravine when his children were old enough to enjoy it.

The climb up out of the gorge was tough, but again the twins had selected a winding trail that made the task a lot easier than trying to climb straight up the sheer sides of the ravine. The team paused often because of the seventy-pound rucksacks they were carrying, but they still were making excellent time. Bradshaw smiled to himself as he thought how surprised the sergeant major was going to be when they radioed back to the headquarters that they were at their Tablerock Mountain rendezvous site almost two days ahead of schedule.

Specialist Rickman set his rucksack down next to the base of a black walnut tree and rolled his shoulders, trying to work out the pain in his joints. The radio operators on the team had the heaviest loads. Their hand-operated generator weighed over forty pounds by itself. Rickman had spent almost a year in the Special Forces communication course and could send and receive twenty-six words a minute in Morse code.

The evergreen boughs parted five feet in front of Rickman and the very worried face of a twelve-year-old boy stared at him. "Am I glad to see you!"

"What are you doing over here on this side of the gorge?" questioned the startled radio operator.

"My family's camped near the river and I was hopping on the rocks and got lost." The boy's cheeks were tear-streaked, but he wasn't crying now.

"How long you been walking around out here?"

"Since yesterday."

"Come on, we'll get you back to your parents." Park rangers and probably a number of the locals would be out searching for the boy in the gorge and they would probably recruit one of the infantry companies from the Eighty-second Airborne Division, who were playing the conventional forces against them. The gorge would be crawling with searchers, and that wasn't good for them.

Bradshaw looked up from his map when Rickman walked up with the lost boy. "What's this?"

"Lost kid." Rickman nodded at the boy, who was staring at the team.

"You Army guys?" The boy's eyes rested on the twins.

"Naw, scouts," Benjy answered.

"We're a Green Beret team and we're training here for a couple of weeks." Bradshaw frowned. "We've got a problem here."

"What's that, Sarge?"

"If we take him back, we can get nabbed by the CI force, but if we keep him with us, his parents will be worried sick."

"He's already been alone in the gorge all night." Rickman reached over and rested his hand on the boy's shoulder. "I think we should risk taking him back."

"Why not take him up to the ranger station on Tablerock?" offered Kenny.

"That's a good idea." Bradshaw looked at Rickman. "Instead of taking him back across the river, we can just leave him at the station here." Bradshaw addressed the lost boy. "If we drop you off with the rangers, will you do what I say?"

"Sure!" The boy took the offered can of fruit cocktail one of the team members held out for him and started eating it as he talked. "I'll do whatever you say."

"We're on a secret training mission over here and we can't get caught or we'll flunk our training."

"I won't tell on you!"

"Benjy, I want you to run him up to the ranger station and drop him off. That should get the search parties called back, and then you can rejoin us at our overnight site."

Benjy nodded and picked up his gun. "Le's go, before it gets dark."

Kenny paused for a second and spoke to Bradshaw. "If you follow the trail for maybe an hour, there'll be a big flat place next to the cliff and a cave. It's a good place to camp for the night. Benjy and me'll meet you there."

"Why don't you stay with us, Kenny? Benjy can take the boy up." Bradshaw nodded at the lost kid.

Kenny smiled, but didn't answer the sergeant. He balanced his rifle in his hand and followed behind the twelve-year-old as his brother led the way up out of the gorge.

Rickman waited until they were well out of hearing range before he risked making a comment. "I think they shit together!"

"Aw . . . I can understand why they're so close, living up here in the mountains, especially back there in the woods. Twins are normally extremely close to each other, and this kind of setting probably makes them even closer." Bradshaw leaned back against his pack. "We'll be moving out in fifteen minutes." He kept his eyes on the trail where the teenagers had disappeared.

The twins moved down the dark path slowly so that they wouldn't trip over roots and loose rocks. It had been a while since they had hunted this side of the gorge, so they took their time. Benjy stopped and sniffed the air. He could smell the campfire smoke but couldn't see the light from the fire. He started moving again along the narrow trail, and the friendly scent of the campfire became stronger until they made a turn in the trail and the campsite appeared directly in front of them.

"They're back." Rickman had been pulling guard and called to warn the rest of the team that the twins had returned. The fire was safe down in the gorge as long as the light was blocked. Bradshaw had the fire built next to the cliff under an overhanging rock. The cliff was black from the numerous other fires that had been built there by hunters and probably Indians before them. The place was a natural area for a rest site, with water close by and protection from the wind by the trees and cliff.

"How did it go?" Bradshaw was heating up a can of C rations near the fire.

"Fine. We just left him near the ranger cabin. He promised not to tell how he got there." Kenny's white teeth flashed in the firelight.

Bradshaw opened the code book and wrote a message for Rickman to send back to their operations base. The words were coded and then placed in five-letter groups to be sent by Morse code. The twins watched Rickman slip his knee set on over his lower thigh and test the Morse code key. The radioman adjusted his headset and sent out his call sign. He was answered almost immediately by the base radioman and then Rickman let the message flow in a rapid Morse code. The whole sequence only took a couple of minutes, since the highly trained Special Forces men wasted no time on the air.

Rickman reached up and removed his headset. "It's sent and received, Sarge."

Bradshaw looked at the fire. "Good. Get some rest, we have a long day ahead of us tomorrow."

Sergeant Major Yates took the decoded message the radio operator handed him. A huge smile broke out over his face and he slowly shook his head. He knew that this was going to be a good field exercise, just from the way it was starting out. Bradshaw's arrival so early at his first site was impressive, but the twins were what really had him excited. He read the short message again:

XXX BT XXX
2DT BT
LOCATION BT TABLEROCK SITE BT 256987
MSG FOLLOWS BT LOCATED A LOST BOY RE-
TURNED HIM TO RANGERS BT SCOUTS HAVE
BEEN WORKING OUT EXCELLENT BT
2DT OUT

CHAPTER 3

CAVALRY CHARGE

Early May 1965

Kenny opened his eyes and listened to the night sounds surrounding him. The team was camped in the woods near a large pasture.

"Chuck-will's-wid-ow . . ."

Kenny turned his head and tried locating the bird in the woods.

"Chuck-will's-wid-ow . . . Chuck-will's-wid-ow . . ."

A branch cracked over at the edge of the pasture and a soft snort reached the teenager.

"Croak!"

The loud froglike sound came from only a few feet away from the sleeping team.

"What in the hell was that?" The man on guard spoke to himself and stirred the small night fire with a stick.

"It's a chuck-will's widow . . . he's catchin' moths." Kenny couldn't believe how little the Special Forces men knew about the woods. "It's about the same as a whippoorwill, 'ceptin' it's a bit bigger."

"You awake?" The guard adjusted his poncho liner around his shoulders, glad that he wasn't awake by himself during the early-morning hours.

Kenny nodded. Of course he was awake or he would not have answered. He had been lying there awake, and just from the sounds around him he could tell what was going on in the woods. The croaking had told him that the night hunting bird was flying through the woods and the breaking stick had told him that a deer was walking along the edge of the woods and had been looking at something out in the meadow.

"Sun should be coming up soon." The guard looked nervously at the fog rolling in over the pasture.

A soft moan came from the other side of the clearing. Kenny lifted up on his elbow and saw that Benjy was sitting up too. The moan sounded again, but a lot louder.

"Sounds like someone is having a nightmare." The guard stood up and looked over at the circle of sleeping bags.

"It's Sergeant Bradshaw." Benjy spoke from his sleeping bag with his eyes still closed.

"He was in Vietnam before coming to the training group." The guard kept his eyes on the NCO's outline in the dim light coming from the fire.

A muffled scream came from Bradshaw's location. Benjy got out of his sleeping bag and went over to where Bradshaw lay on the ground. He could see that the sergeant's face was covered with sweat and the man's hair was matted down like he was just stepping out of a swimming hole. Benjy reached over and shook the sergeant's shoulder until the man opened his eyes. "Y'all right?"

Bradshaw struggled to his feet before he was completely awake and turned in a circle a couple of times before his eyes focused. "Uh . . . yeah, Benjy . . . I'm fine." He reached up and wiped the sweat off his face with the palm of his hand and mumbled, "Shit! Hot fucking shit!"

"Something don't seem right, Sergeant. Y'look like y'got the fever." Benjy remained standing near the NCO.

"Bad dream, Benjy . . . just a bad dream is all." Bradshaw opened his rucksack and pulled his olive-drab towel off the top of his gear to dry his face and hair. "You'd better get back in bed, morning comes early." He looked at his watch and read the luminous numbers even though he knew already that it was minutes away from three o'clock in the morning. The dream always came at that time.

"You all right, Sarge?" The guard remained sitting near the warm fire; a chill in the air had swept in with the fog.

"Yeah, keep it down so we don't wake everybody up." Bradshaw dried the sweat off his upper body and slipped on his clothes. He laid the towel out on his rucksack to dry and removed his canteen cup and filled it with water for coffee. He knew from experience that he would not dare go back to sleep again that night. He carried the metal cup over to the fire and banked a small pile of red coals to set the makeshift coffeepot in before leaving to take a seat on the fieldstones that bordered the meadow.

Kenny pretended that he had fallen asleep, but he could smell the strong smoke from Bradshaw's cigar. He opened his right eye as he lay on his side and saw the faint red glow coming from the tip of the cigar and then a bright red as Bradshaw inhaled. Kenny could see that the man was smoking too fast and knew that something was bothering the sergeant. Kenny got dressed and went over to the fire to mix the instant-coffee packets with the hot water for Bradshaw. The sergeant drank his coffee very black and strong, without sugar. Kenny had watched the NCO go through his coffee-making ritual every morning now since they had been working for his team as scouts. Kenny felt a strong sense of loyalty to the NCO and wanted to help him. He and Benjy had been scouting for the team for almost three weeks, and Bradshaw had treated him and his brother like they were his kin.

Benjy appeared next to Kenny, carrying both of their canteen cups and four packets of C-ration cocoa. He set the cups down in the hot coals and tapped the packets against his thigh to get all of the cocoa powder down at the bottom before tearing the tops off. "I sure like this stuff. I don't know what we're goin' t'do when they leave."

Kenny smiled at his brother. He had gotten used to drinking hot cocoa and eating C-ration cookies himself.

Bradshaw sat on a smooth fieldstone and looked out over the open pasture. A riding stable and horse ranch was at the other side of the large opening in the forest and was their next-to-last rendezvous site. For some reason, the strong odor of horses on the mountain breeze relaxed him a little. The fog prevented him from seeing the barn, but Bradshaw knew it was nearby. The fog shifted and rolled in front of him, and the firelight to his rear acted like the bulb in a movie projector. Small figures started appearing in the fog: little children running down a jungle road. One of them was burning from the jellylike napalm that covered her back. All of the children were crying and screaming for their parents. The Vietcong had used the montagnard as a screen for their advance against the Popular Force Company of local villagers. The MAG chief had called for a napalm strike against the VC position and it had landed on the children. The screams echoed off the fog. Bradshaw inhaled the cigar smoke deep into his lungs and wished he had brought a bottle of whiskey with him on the field trip, even though he knew that if he were caught with it, he would be thrown out of the training group. That had been his biggest worry before the field exercise—having the dream reappear while he was out in the woods. Getting sloppy drunk had been the only way he could get rid of the nightmare.

"Here's your coffee." Kenny set the hot canteen cup down on a rock so Bradshaw could pick it up by its handle.

"Shit!" Bradshaw almost knocked over the coffee. "You scared me!"

"Sorry 'bout that. I didn't mean to." Kenny took a seat on a nearby rock and looked out over the mist. "Sure is pretty and peaceful, isn't it?"

Bradshaw sipped from the hot lip of the cup. "This is good! You make a fine cup of coffee there, boy!"

"Thanks." Kenny saw Benjy coming, carrying their cocoa. "Do ya mind some company?"

Bradshaw was about to say that he wanted to be alone, and then smiled at the teenager. "Sure . . . stay for a while, but come noon, you're going to be wanting to take a nap."

"Prob'ly." Kenny didn't fight the statement.

"I'm proud of the way you and Benjy have worked out for us. At first I didn't think it would be a good idea, bringing two fifteen-year-olds along, but you boys have proved me wrong."

Kenny nodded his head and asked directly, "Do all the soldiers coming home from Vietnam have bad dreams?"

"Some do and some don't . . ." Bradshaw took a bigger sip from the hot coffee and intentionally let the lip of the cup burn his mouth. "It all depends on where you were and what you did . . ." Bradshaw shrugged. "Sometimes you don't have much control over either one."

"If it's so bad over there, why are you taking this training and wanting t'go back?" Benjy finished the sentence with a bite from a vanilla-filled cookie.

Bradshaw looked out over the fog and took a

long time to answer the boy's question. "Someone has to get good at it or a lot of innocent lives are going to be lost."

"Sun's coming up." Kenny stood and arched his back. He had gotten stiff sitting on the rock. "That cocoa hit the spot, Benjy. It's chilly this early in the morning."

"Being able to have a night fire is a luxury." Bradshaw knew that it would be impossible to have a fire at night if it weren't for the twins and the local people who kept a lookout for the team. The conventional forces hadn't been able to come within a mile of them without the team knowing about it. The other team that had been inserted with them had spent their whole field trip one step ahead of the paratroopers from the Eighty-second. Bradshaw had been monitoring their radio messages and felt sorry for the team leader. They had been on the run for the whole three weeks without even a single night going by when they didn't have to break camp and run from the enemy. Bradshaw knew that he would have been in exactly the same position if it hadn't been for the twins.

"Do y'want us to wake the team?" Benjy asked.

"Sure, we'll be moving out as soon as we see some activity over at the ranch." Bradshaw looked at Kenny. "I want you to come with me to recon the area before the team breaks camp." He winked at Benjy, knowing full well both of the boys would go. He had been playing games with them in a joking way ever since the twins had taken the lost boy back to the ranger station. The whole team had teased the boys about being so close to each other.

Benjy walked over to wake the rest of the team. Kenny rinsed out their canteen cups and put them away before joining Bradshaw for their recon of the horse ranch. Benjy met them at the edge of the pasture and they set off.

Benjy led the way around a huge haystack to the back side of the horse barn that couldn't be seen from the main road. The conventional forces normally used jeeps to scout the main highways and gravel roads early in the morning. The tactic would catch a lazy team or a team at the end of the three-week program that was so worn-out humping the woods that they would try taking shortcuts.

The Dutch door at the back of the horse barn opened and a young man stepped out into the barnyard wearing rubber boots up to his knees. As soon as he saw Benjy he smiled. "Hey, Benjy! What brings y'up here?"

"Scoutin' for the Army."

"Scoutin'?" The boy leaned against the weathered fence and rested the toe of his right boot on the bottom rail.

"Yep. Workin' with the guerrillas." Benjy looked up at the horses coming out of the barn, followed by the sister of the boy he was talking to. "Hey, Beth!"

She waved shyly and followed the horses over to the watering trough and turned on the faucet. "What can we do t'help you?"

"We was wonderin' if y'could hide us in the barn till dark."

"Fine, so long as y' don't mess with the horses." The boy looked at Bradshaw. "Just three of you?"

"Fourteen in all." Bradshaw answered.

"Pa won't mine. Bring 'em up on that side of the road." The boy pointed to the front of the ranch, where the country road passed.

Bradshaw didn't like the idea of having to cross over the road twice, but having the protection of the barn for his team would be worth the effort.

Benjy saw the jeep come down the road and pass by the horse ranch. He also saw the Army helicopter following it and watched it circle when the sergeant major pulled into the trees a half-mile down the road and parked. Benjy waited until the sergeant walked back to his observation post and then whispered from the shadows, "Sergeant, you'd better turn around and go on back. A helicopter followed you here."

Yates stopped walking along the road and looked up in the empty sky. "You sure, Benjy?"

"Yep."

"Damn, we'd better warn the team to get out of here. The area will be buzzing with conventional forces shortly." Yates started running back toward the horse barn.

Bradshaw looked up from his seat on the stacked bales of hay. "Hello, Sergeant Major. What brings you out here?"

Yates leaned against the sliding main door and

struggled to catch his breath. "That's it! I start running again as soon as we get back to Fort Bragg!"

"A little out of breath there, Top?" Bradshaw smiled.

"Don't forget that you're a trainee!" He tried acting angry, but smiled instead. "Don't forget, you've still got one more objective before this phase of your training is over."

"I know, Sergeant Major."

"Look, a CF helicopter followed me out here and I'm sure that this area is going to be crawling with paratroopers within a couple of minutes."

Bradshaw hopped off the hay and called out to his resting team, "Saddle up!"

The men jumped into action. Yates noticed that none of them had their rucksacks with them and they carried only their weapons and webgear. He smiled when two of the team members pushed the small double doors open that separated the hay from the stables, revealing a row of saddled horses waiting for the team. Seven horses had been rigged as packhorses and carried the team's rucksacks and gear.

"What do you think?" Bradshaw smiled at the senior NCO.

"Remarkable!" Yates was impressed. None of the other teams had ever thought of using the horses to carry their gear through the woods.

"We've got the horses on loan until we reach our last objective." Bradshaw waited and then asked, "If you please, Sergeant Major . . . ?"

"Oh, I almost forgot." Yates handed Bradshaw

the sealed packet that contained the orders for the team's last objective.

Bradshaw read the cover letter quickly and looked up at his waiting men. "As we suspected, it's the bridge over the river. We have to cross to the other side without using the bridge itself and rig it for demolition." He looked at the team's two Special Forces engineers.

"Great! It's about time we had a chance!" The senior engineer slapped his partner on the back. "Let's kick some ass!"

"There're instructions in there that tell you where to find your cache of C-4 explosives and fuses." Yates looked at the twins. "Your mother said to tell you boys hi and that she misses you."

"How's she doing?" Kenny asked the question but was checking the saddle on his horse at the same time.

"Good. Your little brother has rickets, but not a bad case. I think we've caught it early enough to prevent any real damage."

The sound of helicopters filtered into the barn.

"They are efficient, I must say." Yates looked out through a crack in the barn wall and watched the four Huey choppers touch down in the pasture and the paratroopers unload.

Bradshaw mounted his horse. "Benjy! Kenny! Do what I told you! We'll meet back at that old campsite in two hours!"

The twins mounted and took the packhorses out of the barn and circled around the corral of riding horses to the narrow trail that led up to the still. The ranch owner's son rode with them.

"This is some excitin' shit!" The boy's face gleamed with the challenge of escaping from the Army men.

"Quiet!" Benjy warned.

Bradshaw had his twelve-man team mounted inside the barn, and Beth stood next to the doors waiting for the signal to pull them open. The helicopters lifted off from the pasture and the paratroopers started spreading out for their sweep of the area to search for the guerrilla team.

Yates had climbed up in the hayloft and taken a seat in the loading window to watch.

"All right! Let's go!" Bradshaw leaned forward in his saddle to clear the low doorframe and then stayed low in the saddle so the paratroopers couldn't see him lead his team out of the barn. Three of the team members had never ridden before, so they were going around the corral and were going to follow the tree line around the pasture and meet up with the team on the other side. Bradshaw led the other nine members of his team around the barn and waited until they had spread out and lined up in the dark shadow of the huge structure. The paratroopers couldn't see them from their positions crossing the sun-filled pasture.

Bradshaw waited until the conventional-forces platoon started condensing to enter the barn area from the pasture. The paratroopers were relaxing after their walk in the open pasture; they had expected the guerrilla force to open fire on them as soon as the choppers left.

"Charge!" Bradshaw lowered his M-16 and dug the heels of his boots into the side of his horse. The line of nine Special Forces cavalrymen charged out from the shadows of the barn directly at the paratroopers.

"What the fuck is that!" The airborne lieutenant looked up too late and was nearly run over by two horses.

"It's the fucking guerrillas! Shoot!" The platoon sergeant gave the order too late. The cavalry unit was three-quarters of the way across the pasture and the two men in the lead were already entering the woods.

Sergeant Major Yates leaned back on a bale of hay and laughed so hard that he cried. He had never seen anything so funny in his whole life.

CHAPTER 4

∞∞∞∞∞∞∞∞∞∞∞∞

THE BRIDGE

Mid-May 1965

The water was very cold as the two Special Forces engineers, along with Bradshaw and Rickman, slipped into the river upstream from the bridge. Bradshaw had formed two small teams to set the charges on the huge stone center supports that went down to the bedrock under the river. Each of the engineers swam with one of the two logs that carried their fake explosive charges. The team needed to place the devices on the bridge in order to get credit for the mission, and it was important that the engineers do their jobs well, or they would receive only partial credit for the team and failing grades for themselves.

Bradshaw let the strong current pull them toward the bridge and used his feet for rudders to steer one of the logs toward the left-center support. Rickman and the other team engineer steered toward the other main support.

Benjy and Kenny waited until they were sure the demolition teams were near the bridge before riding their horses from the cover of the trees. The boys had changed into their own clothes so that the paratroopers who were guarding their end of the bridge wouldn't be alarmed. The bridge symbolized the borders of two nations for those who were participating in the program, and once the guerrillas reached the opposite side of the river, they were safe and the training exercise would be over.

Kenny rode ahead of his brother next to the road and eased over to the dark structure after checking to make sure there weren't any cars coming. It was well before midnight and there was still some light traffic using the bridge.

"Hey! What in the hell do you kids think you're doing!" The voice caught the twins by surprise because it came from the woods bordering the road across from the bridge entrance.

Kenny brought his horse to a halt and leaned forward in his saddle. "Lookin' for a couple of lost dogs."

"Black-an'-tans. Have you seen 'em runnin by?" Benjy picked up his brother's story instantly.

"No . . . we haven't seen any dogs." A lieutenant stepped out from the trees. "It's a bit late to be looking for dogs, isn't it?"

"Depends on what y'consider they's worth. Now, in our case, we like our dogs a lot an' we don't need 'em gettin' killed by some old Army truck!" Kenny played the civilian part to the hilt.

"Whatcha doin' on the bridge?" Benjy stood up in his saddle and rubbed the seat of his Levi's.

"We're playing a war game and we're expecting some of the guerrillas to try to cross the river here tonight."

Benjy watched the guards on the bridge entrance. Both of them were watching the lieutenant talking to them.

Kenny rubbed his neck and looked down at the lieutenant. "You're the second bunch of Army men we've seen lately."

"Second?" The lieutenant became very interested.

"Yep."

"What do you mean, second? Were they dressed like us?"

"Nope." Kenny was stalling for as much time as he could give the demolition teams.

"How were they dressed?"

"Funny. They had different colors on their faces and were all dressed up in suits thet looked like the woods."

"Guerrillas!" The lieutenant looked back over his shoulder at someone in the dark. "Sergeant! Get the platoon ready." He returned his attention to Kenny. "Where did you see them? Can you remember?"

"Sure."

"Well, where?"

"I figure that might be worth somethin'?"

The lieutenant reached in his back pocket and removed his wallet. "How about ten dollars?"

Kenny held out his hand and took the money.

"We saw 'em all goin' into a garage behind the restaurant in Linville."

"How many? Did you count them?" The lieutenant's voice was rising.

"Twenty . . . maybe twenty-five."

"*Both* teams! Do you hear that, Sergeant! They've combined their teams to try to cross the river together!"

"Not so fast, Lieutenant. We don't know who these kids are." The sergeant stepped out of the woods and looked up at the teenagers. "What're your names?"

Kenny smiled down at the tough-looking NCO. "Our daddy is the sheriff."

"He's on our side," the lieutenant said with no attempt to hold back his excitement. "I've attended meetings at headquarters with the sheriff. He's a staunch supporter of the conventional forces during this exercise."

The sergeant relaxed a little. "I'll get the captain on the horn and find out what he wants us to do."

The young lieutenant's face darkened. "That's *my* job, Sergeant!"

"Fine, call him, *sir*."

The lieutenant disappeared back into the woods.

"We gotta be gettin' along . . ." Kenny nodded at the sergeant.

"You kids wait here until we've talked to the captain!"

" 'Fraid not. We've gotta find our dogs 'fore they get out on the roads." Kenny spurred his horse.

The sergeant started to reach up and grab the bridle, but changed his mind.

"Y'all have a fine time playin' war," Benjy called back over his shoulder, and followed his brother away from the bridge.

Bradshaw's lower body had become numb from the cold water as he hung on to the log with one arm and the edge of the stone support to the bridge. The engineer had crawled out of the water, using the steel rods anchored in the stone for inspectors to use and had placed the charges up high on the support near the top of the bridge. The teenagers had given them excellent cover. Bradshaw had hoped for just enough time to place the charges at the bases of the supports and not way up on top. The team would receive excellent marks if they could get safely away.

The current tugged at the log and nearly pulled it free from Bradshaw's grip only seconds before the shaking demolitions sergeant returned and slipped back into the water. All four of the men had been wearing only their olive-drab underwear. Bradshaw heard the horses leaving and pointed for the sergeant to grab the log for their ride downstream, where they were supposed to meet the rest of their team and get into dry clothes.

A voice filtered down from the bridge to the four Special Forces men drifting away. "Keep a sharp lookout for any guerrillas! This bridge was on their objectives list!"

Rickman ignored the cold water and let the excitement of the mission keep him warm. He had provided a little extra touch to the demolition charges that would add something to the guards' night. The C-4 charges were only blocks of wood painted tan to look like the high explosive, but he had rigged a tiny air horn to each of the charges with a timing device that would activate the devices in three hours. The small air horns, which would fit comfortably in a pocket, were popular with city hunters afraid of getting lost in the woods.

The river suddenly widened and Sergeant Bradshaw felt his toes touch rocky bottom. The twins had told them that the river would widen and shallow out for about a half-mile, but then quickly narrow again and turn into a rapids.

Bradshaw called to Rickman and the other engineer, "Over here!"

Rickman let go of his log and started swimming toward his team leader, followed by the junior engineer. The mission had been more successful than any of them could have hoped for, and Rickman's teeth shone brightly in the faint moonlight. "I love it! I damn near came in my pants! Did you hear those kids talking to the CF lieutenant?"

"They're good!" Bradshaw struggled to wade over to the shoreline. "We've got to make them honorary Green Berets!"

"You've got my vote!" Rickman slipped into a hole over his head and drank a mouthful of water before struggling back to the surface. "Shit!"

Bradshaw was the first one to reach the riverbank, and stood shivering in his soaked underwear.

"Sarge?" a voice whispered from the undergrowth.

"Yeah!" Bradshaw struggled over the muddy riverbank to the voice. Kenny was waiting for him, holding the reins of his horse. "Y'look cold, old man."

"I don't need any shit out of you, boy!" Bradshaw grabbed for his towel and removed his wet shorts at the same time. "I *know* for sure my best friend isn't going to ever be the same again!"

Rickman pulled himself out of the river laughing. "The first good-looking woman you see will solve that problem for you."

"Shit! He's shrunk up so small that I'll have to squat like a woman to pee!" Bradshaw used the towel to dry off.

"It *is* small, isn't it, Kenny?" Benjy was getting even with Bradshaw for teasing him about always staying so close to his brother.

"Now, *you* had better shut up or I'll have your skinny ass shot before a firing squad!"

"Now, don't pick on them, Benjy! Not everyone can have a big'un like us mountain boys!" Kenny started laughing.

"That's *it*! I'm recommending both of you for fucking courts-martial! Harassing a noncommissioned officer under combat conditions!"

The engineers and Rickman joined the twins in laughing at the goose-bump-covered Bradshaw. They weren't much better off, but the tension from the mission was over and they needed a good laugh.

The team removed their rucksacks from the packhorses and stacked them on the rafts they had made earlier in the day for the night crossing of the river. A section in their special instructions had prohibited their crossing the bridge after it had been blown up, which made sense even though the structure would still be there. Bradshaw didn't like the idea of getting back into the cold water, but he was getting excited about ending the field program and returning to Fort Bragg, where they would receive their Green Berets after more than a year of difficult training.

"Someone's coming!" Kenny had been standing guard.

"Take cover!" Bradshaw felt the fear welling up inside him. They were too close to their goal to be captured now.

Rickman recognized the first man that came out of the woods and stepped onto the road that paralleled the river. "It's Hopper's team!"

Bradshaw stayed in the shadows and waited until the other guerrilla team leader came abreast of his position. "Hey, Hopper, how's it going?"

"Shit! This field program has kicked our asses! We couldn't keep the CF units off our backs!" The team sergeant glared at Bradshaw. "You've been fucking lucky!"

"How's that?"

"Man, they've been chasing us and have left your team alone!"

"You're right about that." Bradshaw wanted to add that Hopper could have used his head a little bit better, so his team wouldn't have been running for three weeks straight, but he kept his mouth shut.

"Those kids have saved your ass." The cutting remark was directed at Bradshaw's ability to lead his team.

"Could be." Bradshaw tried avoiding an argument. "Are you planning on crossing over the river here?"

Hopper glared at Bradshaw in the dark. "Fuck! The water's freezing! I'm taking my team across at the bridge, fuck the conventional forces. We've scouted this area for the last couple of hours and there ain't anything guarding it."

"We just saw a whole bunch of paratroopers down there a little while ago." Kenny volunteered the information.

"Look, *kid*, I asked for your help at the beginning of this fucking field maneuver, but you were too much of a fucking baby to leave your brother!" Hopper's voice was extremely cutting.

Kenny felt his face starting to burn and turned to leave the NCO's.

"That was a shitty remark, Hopper!" Bradshaw pointed his finger at his fellow NCO.

"Fuck him!"

"He was trying to do you a favor, but if you want to get yourself kicked out of training group this late in the game, be my guest!"

"I plan on it!"

"At least give your men the choice of coming with me and making a river crossing like we're supposed to. If they don't want to, they can risk sneaking across the bridge with you."

"What the fuck are you trying to do, Bradshaw, take over my team now?"

"We've all worked too hard to screw up now." Bradshaw looked over at the dark figures resting on the ground with their packs still on their backs. "Any of you who want to make the river crossing with us are more than welcome. Throw your rucksacks on one of the rafts and get your gear off. We're crossing naked and dressing on the far bank." Bradshaw risked a look over at Hopper, but could make out only his shadow. "The water here is fairly shallow, and for the most part, you'll be able to touch bottom."

Hopper lit a cigarette.

"I'd appreciate it if you'd put that thing out!" Bradshaw was becoming very angry. "You can still join us, Hopper, but none of that kind of crap!"

"Fuck you, Bradshaw. You've been kissing the cadre's asses since we started training group, and I'm sick of your shit!"

"Later, Hopper. Right now I've got to take care of my men, but if you want to meet somewhere back at Bragg to settle this, just say the word."

"I will." Hopper turned his head to speak to his team. "If any of you are candy asses and want to cross over with asshole here . . . stay behind!" Hopper signaled for his team to move out, and seven shadows followed him.

The four remaining shadows waited until Hopper

was out of hearing range before one of them spoke. "He's fucking crazy, Sergeant Bradshaw!"

"He's probably tired." Bradshaw was still trying to cover for his fellow NCO, even after what Hopper had said.

"The guy's a fucking idiot! He kept the CF teams on our asses because he was too lazy to hump the woods for a couple of days so that we could shake them." The soldier's voice sounded exhausted. "I don't like the idea of getting in that cold water, but I hope you understand that graduating from Special Forces means a lot to me and these other guys."

Bradshaw nodded in agreement. "Let's do it the right way, and if there's nobody guarding the bridge, we're going to look like wet fools . . . but if there *is* someone still there . . ."

"Let's go!" Rickman spoke up. A huge cloud mass had covered the moon and made the whole area pitch black.

Sergeant Hopper looked back over his shoulder and counted the men following him. He flexed his jaws but didn't say anything. The training exercise would be over officially as soon as they crossed the bridge, and then it was only a matter of a short walk to the assembly area to load up on the waiting trucks for their ride back to Fort Bragg. The outline of the bridge structure loomed up ahead, and he signaled his team to take cover. Hopper had personally reconnoitered the area and found that the CF platoon had left and had taken the bridge guards with them. He signaled for his team to cross over immediately, before any of the CF paratroopers returned.

The bridge was only two hundred yards across, and was just wide enough for two lanes of traffic. Hopper stayed in the shadows of the steel buttresses and moved swiftly toward the far end and safety. He heard a soft tapping sound coming from up in the crossed steel beams of the converted railroad bridge and stopped moving. Hopper's eyes searched the structure, but a dark cloud passing over the moon made the task of finding what made the noise impossible. He started moving faster across the bridge, using the dark clouds as cover.

The bright beam from a five-cell flashlight caught Hopper in mid-stride.

"Are you taking a shortcut, Sergeant Hopper?" Sergeant Major Yates's voice filtered down to the bridge's deck from his perch in a V section of the gridiron fifty feet above Hopper and his teammates.

"Motherfuck!" Hopper placed his forehead against the nearest steel support and gently started tapping his head. "I can't believe this shit! I've had the worst damn luck!"

Yates dropped down to the bridge's surface and leaned over to adjust the tops of his pants in his highly shined jump boots. He removed his swagger stick from the back of his belt where he had tucked it for his climb down and started tapping it against the side of his leg. "This is a sad way to end a year's worth of training." Yates scanned the dark figures standing near him.

"Can't we work something out, Sergeant Major?"

one of the trainees who had followed Hopper over the bridge said in a voice on the verge of breaking. "I mean . . . we were just following orders."

"You son of a bitch!" Hopper took a threatening step toward the trainee and felt Yates's swagger stick pushing against his chest.

"Easy there, Sergeant Hopper." Yates looked over at the dark shadow that had spoken. "You're partially right, but there are such things as lawful orders."

A loud noise interrupted Yates and scared the trainees on the bridge who weren't still in shock from being caught by the sergeant major.

"What the fuck is that!" Hopper held his empty M-16 up as if he were going to shoot at something.

"That was a simulated detonation, Sergeant Hopper. Now you know why the bridge was off limits. Your fellow teammates were assigned to destroy this bridge, and if you had taken the time to break the coded messages between Sergeant Bradshaw's team and guerrilla headquarters, you would have known that."

"Bradshaw!" The name seemed to burn Hopper's tongue. "He's caused me a lot of grief on this training exercise!"

"How did he do that?" Yates couldn't believe that Hopper was blaming his misfortune on his fellow NCO.

"If he had carried his share of the load with the conventional forces during the program, my team would have had some time to break those messages!"

"Hopper, you're the kind of lazy son of a bitch

that gets a lot of people killed in combat. That's the purpose of this field exercise—to weed out assholes like you before we ship you to Vietnam, where you can do *real* damage!" Yates glanced over at the men with Hopper and added, "It's a pity that these men have to suffer for your mistakes, but it looks like some of the others were smart enough to try a river crossing on their own!"

A wistful voice from the back of Hopper's team whispered, "They went with Sergeant Bradshaw's team."

"I'll meet you back at the assembly area." Yates left the team and walked over to where he had parked his jeep.

Bradshaw felt the gravel under his feet and used the traction to push the raft up against the riverbank. The team members grabbed their clothes and rucksacks and scurried into the woods to dry off and get dressed. Bradshaw took a couple of seconds to look back across the river. He knew that the twins were still there watching from the woods. Bradshaw lifted the waterproof flashlight he had worn on a cord around his neck for the crossing and signaled to the twins that they had made it across.

Yates and the training-group staff were waiting for the two guerrilla teams to assemble for their ride back to Fort Bragg in the back of two-and-a-half-ton trucks. Hopper and his eight men were sitting under the roof of a roadside picnic-table shelter, smoking quietly.

"We can't afford to lose eight men, especially two of our medics, Sergeant Major. I would have agreed with you a year ago, but the Vietnam war is starting to pick up, and we need every single fully qualified Green Beret that we can get." The training-group commander stood in the jeep lights with his hands on his hips. The headlights reflected off the white flash sewn on his beret and off the silver eagle.

"I think that's what we're talking about, sir—the meaning of 'fully qualified.' I say Hopper is *not* fully qualified."

"I understand where you're coming from, Sergeant Major, and I respect your old-school philosophy, but we need to graduate men for the new A-Camps."

"You're the boss, sir." Yates wasn't about to agree with the colonel, but he would support the senior officer's decision even though he didn't like it.

The colonel walked over to Hopper and his men, followed by the sergeant major. "Sergeant Hopper?"

"Yes, sir!"

"I've decided to give you and your men a second chance. If you want to volunteer to be recycled through this phase of training again, we'll give you another chance at graduating."

"Thank you, sir!"

"I also want you to know that the sergeant major doesn't agree with my decision and he will still be the NCOIC for this phase of the training. I assure you that I will not intervene to save your asses again if you fail!"

"Yes, sir!"

The colonel glared at the eight men. "Do any of you want to get on the trucks and go back to Bragg?"

Hopper looked puzzled. "Sir, when do we start this new phase?"

Sergeant Major Yates grinned. It was the only concession he had won from the colonel. "Monday morning. You can have the weekend to get your gear back in shape."

One of Hopper's teammates looked over at his buddy and then spoke up. "Sergeant Major, I don't think I can go through three more weeks of this with—"

"Before you say something you might regret"— Yates looked over at Hopper but continued talking to the young trainee—"Sergeant Hopper will be transferred to another team and will not be in a leadership position. We'll give you a new leader."

The trainee looked over at Hopper and saw the hate in the man's eyes. "Fine . . . then I don't have anything else to say. I'll stay."

The sign in the restaurant window said it was closed, but all the lights were on and most of the booths were filled with civilians and uniformed soldiers. Sergeant Major Yates and the rest of the cadre for the guerrilla training team were hosting an end-of-the-training-cycle party for the people in the community who had supported their teams during the exercise. The party was traditionally held in the restaurant that housed the headquarters for the guerrilla forces.

Yates set his glass down on the countertop and stood up so that everyone could see him. He waited until the room became quiet before beginning his speech. "I don't plan on taking up much of your time, 'cause there's some *serious* drinking to be done tonight." Most of the men in the booths started cheering and then quieted down when their wives glared at them. "I would like to say that I think this was the best training cycle we've ever run through the Pisgah National Forest area, and it wouldn't have happened if it weren't for all of you."

Kenny glanced over at Benjy, who was sipping from his Coke.

"I would like to make a special presentation tonight." Yates reached behind the counter and picked up something from a shelf. He kept the two boxes down at his side as he continued talking. "Kenny and Benjy Kingston have worked for us for only one training cycle, but their dedication and outstanding woodsmanship have impressed all of us!"

The boys looked over at their mother, who was sitting across from them in a booth with their little brother. They could see the pride in her eyes.

"Benjy and Kenny, would you boys mind stepping up here for a minute."

Everyone in the room started clapping as the

twins left their booth to go up to the sergeant major and the training-group colonel.

Yates handed each of the boys a box. "Go on and open them."

Kenny lifted the lid and looked down in the box. His breath caught in his throat.

"Oh, man!" Benjy set the box down on the counter and held the green beret up so that everyone in the restaurant could see it and the embroidered word "honorary" on the white training-group flash.

"Bradshaw and Rickman donated those berets for you guys. They spent three months shaping them, so they should fit pretty damn good!" Yates knew how hard it was to shape a new beret so that it fell perfectly along the side of the wearer's head. It took dozens of shrinkings in hot water, with the still-warm wet beret placed on the man's head so that it would form perfectly. Usually a trainee would purchase a beret and start shaping it when he was halfway through the training group, but he wasn't allowed to wear it in public until he was officially presented it after his last phase of training. It was a generous gesture for Bradshaw and Rickman to donate their first berets to the twins. "Well! Go on, let's see what they look like on." Yates watched the boys slip the berets on and then check with their fingers to make sure that the flashes were lined up perfectly over their left eyes.

The colonel started laughing. "You boys know how to do that better than I do!"

"The bar is open and the smoking lamp is lit!"

Yates waved with his hand over at the bottles of whiskey and the tubs filled with beer and ice.

Kenny slipped behind the bar with Yates and fought back the tears. "Tell Bradshaw and Rickman we said thanks."

"They're the ones who came up with the idea, but you boys *earned* the right to wear them."

CHAPTER 5

FLATLAND TRAINING

August 1967

The air conditioner in the window ran constantly, even with the door closed in the small office and the drapes pulled tightly shut. The old World War II buildings on Smoke Bomb Hill had been built as temporary troop barracks during World War II, before insulation and air conditioning were used in construction.

A soft knock on the door brought Yates out of his deep thoughts. "Come in!"

"How ya doing there, *Command* Sergeant Major! Congratulations." Staff Sergeant Rickman stepped into the dark office. Only the small lamp on Yates's desk was on.

"There's no more money in it, but I like the title a little bit better than 'staff sergeant major.' "

"You busy?"

"No . . . have a seat. Let me run in the back and

get us some coffee." Yates dropped his feet down off his desk.

"I've got one of the clerks bringing us some in already." Rickman winked. "So tell me what's going on. I hear you've got orders for the big Nam."

"Yes, that's why I asked you to stop by. Since you've just returned from there, you might be able to fill me in a little."

"Sure, Sergeant Major . . ."

The door opened and a clerk brought in two cups of coffee. He set them on the edge of the desk and left without saying a word.

"I just left Bu Dop. Talk about a fucking mess! They decided to build the camp like an old American fort—you know, with logs for the berm—and then they came up with the bright idea of making a second row of logs fifteen feet behind the first and roofing and sandbagging the whole thing so the commandos and their families could live there right on the fighting perimeter."

"That doesn't sound too bad to me." Yates shrugged. They had to provide quarters for the dependents of the commandos, and what better place than near their men."

"Good idea, except fighting bunkers are no place for little kids to grow up."

Yates instantly saw what Rickman was driving at. "I didn't think of that."

"Neither did the engineers and the team leaders. After a half-dozen kids blew themselves and their parents all to hell playing with hand grenades and flares, we had to redesign the whole damn camp!"

"At least we learn." Yates smiled and drank some of his coffee. "What do you know about B-32?"

"Not much, but I've stopped by there a couple of times, just passing through, and they seem like a tough group of guys. A lot of the old-school types are there who are three-qualified and are rangers."

Yates frowned. Rickman was referring to the old Special Forces standard of being qualified in at least three occupational specialties before you won your green beret. The expansion of the Vietnam war had lowered the standard to one MOS and very little in addition to that. After 1966 the floodgates had been lowered and a lot of men got into Special Forces who didn't even go through the training group but were "skill-transferred" to the groups. The old-timers were pissed and had formed secret cliques to protect the standards, and they shunned the "idiot bars" and instant beret wearers.

Rickman continued, "It's really beginning to pick up over there. When I first arrived in Nam, we would run into VC platoons with a company, but now we're running into NVA regular battalions with our commando companies and getting our asses kicked. Shit is really hitting the fan up in II Corps around Duc-Co and Plei-Me."

"Yeah, but we both know all that can change overnight." Yates finished his coffee and set the cup on his desk blotter.

"I was wondering, Sergeant Major, whatever

happened to those two kids who worked as scouts for us during my last phase of training here?" Rickman rested his head against the seat. "I've thought about them a couple of times in Vietnam. I really felt sorry for them."

"Well, you don't have to!" Yates's eyes lit up and his grim expression disappeared. "Those boys are doing fine, just fine! I don't know if you know about it, but there was a special fund established in training group for the boys and their family, and it has done quite well. We kept the twins on as scouts for other guerrilla teams and put them on flat salaries; they're making five hundred dollars *apiece* for each cycle they take through the training, and I've heard—mind you, I've just *heard*—a rumor that the teams pitch in on a kitty that the twins get to keep if they take them through the training without the CF teams finding them. I want you to know that has caused us a number of serious problems!"

"How's that?" Rickman was smiling. He was proud of the twins, and because they had been with his team first, he felt a special bond with them.

"Well, what happened was, the guerrilla teams would disappear for three weeks. The only way we'd know they were still in the area was that they performed their assigned missions. The CF units were becoming totally demoralized and all of the local people were starting to side with the guerrilla forces and sabotage the CF teams."

Rickman slapped his leg and started laughing. "Two kids! Just two teenagers made all the difference."

"We moved a part of our operation out to the twins' cabin. We set up a house trailer to use as a forward support base and control that sector. Of course, in the winter we just left the trailer out there rather than haul it back to Bragg."

"And the twins had a key . . . right?" Rickman shook his head. He was happy that the training group had adopted the twins and their family.

"Someone had to maintain the facility for us and keep an eye on all of the supplies that were stock-piled out there for our operation come spring." Yates looked sheepishly out of the corner of his eye.

"Right!" Rickman inhaled a deep breath. "How old are they now?"

Yates slapped the top of his desk. "Seventeen! They just turned seventeen, and you'll get a chance to see them soon!"

"How's that, Sergeant Major?"

"They've joined the Army and will be taking basic training here at Fort Bragg in exactly nine days!"

"How in the hell did you pull that one off?" Rickman was impressed.

"Those boys have one fine reputation here at Bragg, and I don't think there's a paratrooper in the Eighty-second or a Special Forces man who hasn't heard of the exploits of the Kingston twins. Getting them here was easy. The hard part is going to be getting them into Special Forces after their training is over. That might be impossible, but wherever they end up, some NCO is going to have a pair of military jewels—cut, polished, and ready to shine!"

"What about their mother?" Rickman knew how close they were to her and how much she had depended on them.

"She's the secretary for our forward operations." Yates raised his eyebrows. "From the way she talked, you'd think she was a little slow, but once she had been given a chance, she picked up things faster than the twins. Believe me, Rickman, you won't recognize them! They've grown into a pair of handsome young men, healthy as young bulls. My God! After having at least a hundred Special Forces medics watching out for them and pumping vitamins into them, they've grown like weeds!"

"That's good news, Sergeant Major. I'm glad to hear they've done well." Rickman finished his coffee. "I've got to in-process. I've been assigned to the Sixth Group."

Yates stood to shake hands with Rickman. "I'll give you a call when the twins arrive and get settled in."

Kenny pushed open the door to the house trailer and stuck his head inside. "Ma, we're back! Benjy and I are going to clean up and change clothes."

She looked up from the papers she was filing and called back to her son, "Check on your little brother for me, will you, Kenny?"

"Will do!" Kenny carried his rucksack loosely in his hand and went over to check on his little brother before going around to the addition that had been built on the back of their cabin to take a shower and clean the camouflage paint off his face. He heard the shower running inside and took a seat on the back step to wait for Benjy to finish. The cabin had changed a lot since they had started working for the Special Forces group. Team engineers had installed a deep water well for the cabin, as a training project, along with the new addition that contained two bedrooms and a modern bathroom and laundry area. The cabin itself had been renovated with a new turned-tin roof that matched the additions and the small one-car garage that was detached from the main structure. The Special Forces teams had also built a gravel road to the cabin from the main highway, another training project, so that they could bring in the house trailer for their forward headquarters. Everything had been done legally, but always in the best interest of the Kingston family.

The shower stopped running and Kenny went inside. Benjy stood with a towel wrapped around his waist in their bedroom. "You'd better hurry with your shower or they'll be here before you're done."

Kenny gave his brother one of his rare exasperated looks. If there was one thing the twins fought over, it was who took the longer shower. One of them always ended up with cold water. "I'll be ready!" Kenny threw his dirty tiger suit in the clothes hamper and stepped under the refreshing hot water. They had just finished their final cycle with the training group as scouts and were going to be picked up that afternoon by their recruiter for the ride to Fort Bragg's Basic Training Reception Center.

Benjy was out in the garage looking at their jeep when Kenny joined him. The used CJ-5 was the first thing they had bought with the money they had made scouting.

"Help me slip the cover over it." Kenny threw a corner of the light canvas over to his brother.

A horn honked outside.

"That must be him." Benjy looked out of the door. "Yep! Let's get our stuff and say good-bye to Ma."

Kenny paused in the garage doorway and looked back at the mound under the tarp. He loved that jeep and would miss driving it. He cheered himself up with the thought that it would only be a couple of months, maybe only a few weeks before they would get their first leave. They could always hitch a ride with one of the Special Forces trucks that came and went from the cabin all summer and fall.

A dark green military sedan was parked next to the house trailer. Benjy was already sitting on the front seat when Kenny locked the garage door. He ran over to the trailer and slipped inside to give the key to his mother.

"Now, you make me proud, y'hear? Give me a kiss before you go." She fought hard not to cry. "You know I love you, Kenny."

"Love ya too, Ma." Kenny hugged his mother and gently broke away before he started crying. "See you in a couple of weeks."

" 'Bye, Kenny!" Little Harley ran over and gave his half-brother a hug. "Bring me back something!"

Kenny shook his head. "Ma, we've got to do something about that kid!" He looked down affectionately at the six-year-old dressed in an exact replica of the Special Forces tiger suit, complete with hat and webgear.

"Y'd better get, before they leave without you!" She walked behind her son to the door and watched as he ran to the waiting sedan. She was proud of her boys. They were growing up to be fine young men.

The twins talked constantly all the way to Fort Bragg. They had made the trip a couple of times before with Sergeant Major Yates and knew the way there. It wasn't like they were going to a strange place. They had been briefed about the reception center and had been given a detailed day-by-day description of what would happen during their basic training. Yates had given both of them good advice about not bragging about their Special Forces scouting up in the mountains because there were a large number of officers and NCO's in the training center who were extremely jealous of Special Forces. At Fort Bragg a person who was not airborne-qualified was at the very bottom of the social ladder, and most of them resented it.

The sedan approached Fort Bragg from the west and passed through the golfing resorts of Southern Pines and Pinehurst. The wealth displayed there in Moore County was in direct contrast to its neighboring county of Hoke, where poverty was the norm.

"What's that over there?" Kenny pointed to the huge open expanse of plowed sand.

"That's a drop zone for paratroopers and heavy equipment." The captain quickly returned his attention to the narrow road.

Benjy recalled the tiny drop zone up in Harley's meadow and shook his head. "How much longer until we're there?"

The captain looked at his watch. "About a half-hour." He suppressed a grin. The twins were anxious to get started with their army career, but even though they had been briefed on what to expect, he knew that the first couple of weeks were going to be a shock to them.

Benjy and Kenny quieted down when they started passing buildings and finally reached the main post area of Fort Bragg. To them the pale yellow stucco senior officers' quarters looked like lined-up mansions. The car stopped in front of the training center, which had formerly housed the Eighty-second Airborne Division.

The reception station in-processing was well-organized, and the twins took less than three hours to hit all of the stations and receive their assignments to Alpha Company. They would be returning to the reception area the next day for a series of placement tests, but their company cadre would pick up them and the rest of their company at four-forty-five, just in time to keep the second lieutenant from having to find billets for all of them for the night.

Sergeant First Class Watts sat on the front seat of the fifty-passenger military bus, being very careful not to stub the toes of his highly shined boots on one of the seat legs. He could see the new recruits sitting on the benches that lined the back of the reception station when the bus turned the corner of the building. Watts was a very close friend of Sergeant Major Yates, and their paths had crossed numerous times since they had first met in Korea. Yates had asked him for a favor and Watts had agreed to do it. Luck had been on their side, because the twins would automatically be assigned to his platoon on an alphabetical basis.

Sergeant Watts was the senior NCO representing the company and had been sent with five other junior cadre to bring the new trainees back to their company area. He inspected the area closely before stepping off the bus. The wide brim of his campaign hat shadowed his face and his mirrored sunglasses prevented anyone from seeing who or what he was looking at. Watts inhaled a deep lungful of air and sighed; another cycle had begun.

The junior NCO's waited until Watts stepped down from the bus and sprang into action. They decended on the unsuspecting recruits like a flight of killer bees, roaring out orders, stinging and shocking their victims.

Watts watched the recruits panic. Nothing ever changed from cycle to cycle. The game was played to perfection and had been developed and passed down from training cycle to training cycle. Watts noticed the twins immediately, not because they looked identical but because out of the hundred and twenty new recruits, they were the only ones not in shock. They stood near the wall of the building holding their Adidas bags, waiting for instructions. Watts smiled. Yates had told him that these boys were special.

"Get your damn asses moving! Line up down there on the fucking numbers!" A small buck sergeant screamed first at Kenny and then over at Benjy. The yelling lost most of its effect because he changed victims. "I said move it! Assholes!"

Watts blinked his eyes slowly behind the cover of his sunglasses. Sergeant Hoitt had found the twins. Hoitt was the worst training NCO in the battalion and had been shifted through a half-dozen committee-group assignments before ending up with the troops. There wasn't any doubt in Watts's mind that Hoitt had a major inferiority complex.

Hoitt followed the twins over to the white lines and screamed at them constantly. Benjy glanced over at his brother and smiled.

"What are you smiling at, recruit?" Hoitt locked in on Benjy.

"Nothing important, Sergeant!"

"Everything's important to me, recruit!"

"I was smiling over how worked up you're getting over nothing."

Hoitt's face turned red and the veins on each side of his neck stood out. "Nothing! You call my correcting your sorry asses *nothing*!"

"No, Sergeant!" Benjy stood at rigid attention. Kenny was struggling not to burst out laughing.

Sergeant Watts held the clipboard out in front of him and spoke in a soft voice. Compared to the screaming band of junior NCO's, he sounded like an angel. "Listen up!"

Hoitt had been standing on his toes screaming in Benjy's face, and dropped back down on his heels. "You're mine, recruit! Do you understand me! Mine!"

"Yes, Sergeant!" Benjy sighed. He was glad to have the man out of his face, because his breath stank.

"Sergeant Hoitt, would you please let me call roll?" Watts waited until the junior NCO moved out of the ranks and stood in the back of the formation. "When I call your name, I want you to fall in line. Number one will be the first man whose last name begins with an A, and so on until we reach Z, which should be number one-twenty or near there."

Benjy moved over to his number, and Kenny waited until the sergeant called his name before moving, even though he knew that he would be standing next to his brother. It was a smart decision, because Hoitt had been watching the twins like a hawk waiting for any excuse to attack them. He hated the self-confidence he saw in their eyes and he hated their good looks and everything else about them.

Sergeant Watts had the recruits loaded on the buses and supervised the unloading at the company area. He made sure the twins were put in his barracks, but it was done low-key. The recruits were fed in the mess hall and then taken back to the barracks for their last free night. Technically, none of the recruits was fully in the Army until he received his UCMJ briefing the next day. The Uniform Code for Military Justice was presented to them by a military lawyer in an hour-long class. After the briefing they would be held liable for their conduct.

Benjy and Kenny had drawn their bedding and had lucked out and gotten a double bunk at the end of the squad bay near the NCO rooms, where they had the most privacy. The small NCO room on their side of the aisle was empty, and Watts used it for his office during the day. There were still a dozen men taking showers when the duty NCO came through the barracks and turned out the lights in the squad bays. The twins lay on their bunks with the windows open and listened to the night noises coming from outside. They could hear firing coming from the ranges and the sound of flares popping even closer to their barracks.

The door to the barracks opened and a dark shadow entered, wearing a helmet liner. Only the senior instructors who had gone to drill sergeant's school were allowed to wear the coveted campaign hats. The shadow walked slowly down the center of the dark aisle and stopped. "Kingston! Kenny and Benjy!"

"Here . . ." Benjy didn't know what to call the

shadow, and figured overranking it would be better than underranking. ". . . sir!"

"Grab your gear, you're being transferred to the Fourth Platoon!" The voice seemed to hiss the words. "Move it!"

The twins slipped into their clothes and shoes and grabbed their Adidas bags.

Kenny paused. "Should we take out bedding, sir?"

"Yes!" The voice didn't correct them for addressing it as "sir." When they reached the lit entranceway to the barracks the twins could see that the shadow was the small buck sergeant who had harassed them at the reception station.

"Follow me!" Hoitt led the way over to the Fourth Platoon barracks and went over to the lower bunk closest to the entrance light and pointed. "You will sleep here." He pointed at Benjy and started walking up the stairs. "Come on!" He took Kenny to the double bunk at the top of the stairs that was directly above Benjy's. At both bunks the entrance lights would shine all night in the faces of the occupants. "This is yours! Put your bedding and gear on it and follow me!" Hoitt waited only a second or two before going back down the stairs and beckoning for Benjy to follow him with his brother.

Kenny flashed a look at Benjy that told him exactly what he feared the most. He didn't mind the poor location of his bed; it was the fact that he was going to be so far away from his brother that bothered him. Benjy returned the look.

Hoitt led the twins out behind the company area

to a large circular pit filled with sawdust. The bayonet pit smelled good to the twins and reminded them of the woods.

"Start running around the edge of the pit . . . on the inside." Hoitt stood in the dark with his hand on his hips.

"Did we do something wrong, Sergeant?" Benjy asked the question in a neutral voice.

"I didn't ask for you to talk! Start running!"

The twins obeyed the sergeant and got in the pit and started a slow jog around the inside edge of the pit in the loose sawdust. They were both in superb shape and the light exercise felt good.

Hoitt watched the twins jogging and could see from the tilt of their heads in the moonlight that they would wait until they got to the side of the pit away from him to whisper to each other. He let them run for an hour at their pace before he screamed for them to run faster. The twins obeyed, and Hoitt lit a cigarette and adjusted the sandbags he was sitting on. He let them run for fifteen minutes and then stopped them. They were breathing deeply, but not winded. Hoitt hated them even more.

"Take your shoes and socks off and run." Hoitt curled his lip when he spoke. He planned on breaking them before morning. He would show everyone in the company that no damn recruit could make a fool out of him.

The small pieces of wood mixed with the sawdust cut into the twins' feet. Both of them were drenched in sweat. August in North Carolina at night was still very warm, and down on the piedmont the temperature hovered in the mid-seventies.

Hoitt saw that the twins were slowing down after running for an hour and a half and smiled. He stopped them and made them stand at attention for a few minutes while he smoked a cigarette and blew smoke in their faces. "You boys look a little hot."

"Yes, Sergeant!" Kenny could feel the sweat pouring down his chest in streams. "We could use a drink of water, Sergeant!"

"So could every GI in Vietnam, but you've got to learn how to sweat and *not* drink any water." Hoitt grinned out of one side of his mouth. "I'll tell you what I'll do to be nice. You can take all your clothes off and run."

"Thanks anyway, Sergeant. We'll pass on that one." Benjy's voice was filled with sarcasm.

Hoitt flew to a spot only inches away from Benjy's face and hissed, "I'm not *asking* you, recruit! That's an order. I don't want you getting heat exhaustion and dying on us."

Kenny slipped his soaked shirt off over his head and laid it on the sandbags that bordered the pit. He looked around in the dark to see if anyone else was watching, and slipped off his Levi's. He stood there in his white briefs waiting for Benjy. "Come on, Benjy . . . it's no big deal."

Benjy glared at the sergeant and followed suit. He stood next to his brother wearing only his white underwear.

"That won't do, recruits! The NVA could see your white shorts five miles away! Take them off too!" Hoitt's voice had lost all control and climbed the scale. "Now, run! Damn you! *Run!*"

The twins started jogging naked around the pit. Kenny waited until they were at the far side before whispering to his brother, "Don't forget what the sergeant major told us." Kenny was referring to the tips Yates had given them on cooperating and making it through the training. "He'll lay off us once he gets it out of his system."

"I don't think so, not this guy, Kenny. He has a funny look in his eyes when he looks at us." Benjy stopped talking as they drew near to where Hoitt was sitting on the sandbags.

Hoitt watched the twins run naked for another twenty minutes before stopping them. "Go clean up and get ready for the morning formation!"

The twins picked up their clothes and walked back over to the barracks naked. Both of them went into the latrine and turned on the cold water in the sinks to drink from. Kenny was the first one to stop drinking. "He's crazy."

"I told you . . ." Benjy gasped for air.

"At least we didn't quit." Kenny turned off his faucet. "Let's shower."

Hoitt had been the CQ for the night and had used that opportunity to switch the twins over to his platoon. He didn't think anyone would notice, because the recruits blended in with each other the first couple of days. He had given the armorer who was pulling duty as his runner fifteen dollars to cover for him while he harassed the twins, but he didn't figure that the armorer would report him to

Sergeant Watts. Hoitt had told him not to tell the CO or the first sergeant but hadn't mentioned anything about Watts. The armorer had kept his word.

Watts left the orderly room at a fast walk and headed over to the mess hall where he knew Hoitt ate breakfast. He could feel his face burning from the rush of blood. Never in his life had he wanted to kill someone as much as he wanted to kill Hoitt. It wasn't simply the matter of the twins, but the fact that what Hoitt had done to them answered a number of questions Watts had about other recruits who had suddenly left the company and refused to speak about it to anyone.

Hoitt was sitting with two of the company officers when Watts entered through the side door of the mess hall. He scanned the recruits eating breakfast and saw the twins sitting at a far table wolfing down huge helpings of SOS—the Army's version of chipped beef on toast but affectionately known as shit-on-a-shingle. The twins looked a little worn but all right.

"Sergeant Hoitt, I would like to have a word with you." Watts struggled to keep his voice level.

"Later, Watts . . . I'm briefing the lieutenant on last night's CQ."

Watts looked at the company executive officer. "Sir, will you excuse us for a minute?"

The officer could see that something was bothering Watts. "Sure . . . we were done anyway."

"Hoitt, let's go outside."

"I'm not finished eating." Hoitt flashed a hate-filled glance over his shoulder.

Watts grabbed the buck sergeant by the back of his collar. "Now! Or I'll drag you outside!"

The lieutenant looked alarmed, but he didn't interfere. Sergeant Watts was the company's best drill sergeant, and if he wanted to talk with Hoitt in private, then as far as he was concerned it was NCO business.

Hoitt looked across the table at the officer for help.

"Go with Sergeant Watts and see what he wants. You can always get a fresh tray of food." The lieutenant smiled. "It looks like it might be something important."

Watts half-dragged the junior NCO out of the building and let go of him under the overhead parallel bars next to the mess hall. "You little son of a bitch! Don't you ever go into my platoon again and steal *my* trainees so you can fuck with them!"

"They're not *your* trainees, Watts! I was short men in my platoon and I just balanced out the barracks a little." Hoitt smirked.

Watts grabbed Hoitt by the front of his shirt and slammed him up against the side of the building so hard that the trainees near the wall looked out the window. "I am taking those boys back to my platoon after breakfast, and if you so much as even *look* at them for the next eight weeks, I'm going to kick your dick so far up into your throat you'll end up squatting to pee!"

Hoitt's face turned white.

Sergeant Watts dropped Hoitt down on the ground and left him there gasping for air. He waited outside the exit door until the twins left the mess hall. "You two . . . come with me!"

Kenny looked at Benjy and sighed. Benjy shrugged; he didn't know what they had done to deserve this kind of treatment.

Watts led the boys over to Hoitt's barracks and stopped as soon as he entered the building. "Get your gear and be back here in one minute."

The twins didn't have to be encouraged, and they ran to their bunks and returned to the waiting NCO in seconds. Watts took them back over to the second platoon and stopped in front of the empty double bunk they had selected the night before. "Now, listen closely to me . . . these are your bunks and this is your platoon. *I* am your drill instructor . . . do you understand?"

"Yes, Sergeant!" the twins answered in unison.

"If Sergeant Hoitt tells you to do *anything*, you tell him that you have to clear all orders from him with me first. Do you understand?"

"Yes, Sergeant!" The twins smiled.

CHAPTER 6

❀❀❀❀❀❀❀❀❀❀❀❀❀❀❀❀❀❀

GLORY CALL

February 1968

Benjy used his duffel bag as a backrest and had his fatigue cap pushed down over his eyes to block out as much of the hot sunlight as he could while Kenny kept watch for the battalion's S-1 NCO. They were part of a group of replacements who had been waiting outside the tin-and-plywood building all night.

A volley of heavy artillery being fired a few hundred meters away made the replacement sitting across from Kenny jump to his feet and look around. "What the fuck is going on?"

"Just our artillery firing in support of our guys out in the boonies. Relax, man." The young buck sergeant who spoke up moved a toothpick from the left side of his mouth to the right side and grinned. The sergeant's eyes were hidden behind a pair of mirrored sunglasses.

Benjy used his index finger to shove the brim of

his hat up high enough to see the NCO. He hadn't spoken to the sergeant, but he sensed that the man didn't like him and suspected the junior leader was a dopehead from the way he acted.

"You got a problem, stud?" The sergeant saw Benjy looking at him.

"Nothing that can't be handled." Benjy took a seat on the duffel bag and smiled over at the sergeant.

"You've got an attitude problem, fella." The buck sergeant chewed the end of his toothpick and switched it rapidly from side to side in his mouth. "You'd better hope that your sorry ass isn't assigned to my fire team."

Benjy was about to answer the cocky NCO when the screen door to the S-1 building opened and the assignments sergeant stepped outside. "Circle around." He held his clipboard out in front of him like a royal herald who was about to announce a decree.

Kenny could feel the sweat running down his chest. He felt his heart beating in violent thuds in his chest and wondered if anyone standing around him could see it.

The NCO read off each name on the replacement list and told them their unit assignment. The buck sergeant had been assigned to the Second Battalion, Twenty-eight Infantry. Kenny hoped that Benjy and he wouldn't end up in that unit. They didn't need the hassle. The sergeant looked up at the circle of tense faces. "Have I called everyone's name?"

"No, Sergeant." Benjy spoke up. "You missed my brother and me."

"Oh, yes!" The sergeant flipped over the sheet of names and read off another piece of handwritten paper. "Kingston, Benjy . . . you're assigned to the First Battalion, Eighteenth Infantry, and Kingston, Kenny . . . you're assigned to the Second of the Twenty-eighth Infantry."

The twins reacted immediately. "Sarge . . . you can't do that. We came in under the buddy plan and we're supposed to stay together," Kenny said.

"What the fuck is your problem?" The toothpick-chewing buck sergeant's voice carried halfway across the battalion compound. "This is Vietnam, asshole, and you do what you're fucking told!"

Benjy whirled around and faced the junior NCO. "I've had enough of your shit, *Sergeant*. The next word out of your mouth is going to cause you a great deal of pain."

"Oh? And what the fuck are you going to do, Private First Class?"

"I'll tear your fucking face off and shove it up your ass—*try me!*"

The buck sergeant saw the glare in Benjy's eyes and knew the young soldier would do it.

Kenny pleaded with the NCO. "Sarge, it's important that my brother and I stay together . . . we're twins."

"We know that, soldier." The sergeant's voice was sympathetic but resigned to enforcing the orders. "Sorry, but that's exactly the reason why we have to split you up. The colonel doesn't want both of you in the same battalion, just in case of . . ." He let the statement finish itself.

"*We* don't mind that!"

"Well, the problem is that the two of you shouldn't have gotten this far *together*. Regulations state that brothers cannot be in the same unit in combat." He shook his head. "And when he saw that you were *twins*, the colonel hit the roof!"

"Let us talk to the colonel!" Kenny pleaded.

"That would be impossible . . . he was pretty pissed that the two of you got down to brigade level together. I'm positive he isn't going to change his mind."

Kenny looked over at Benjy with a look of total panic. They had made it all the way through basic and advanced training together, and had even received their orders for Vietnam at the same time.

A voice spoke through the screened window from the hutch next to where the group of replacements were standing. The roof overhang prevented the replacements from seeing who had spoken, but the administration sergeant knew the voice. "Sergeant, bring the Kingston brothers over to my office."

"Yes, sir!" The sergeant glanced at the twins and beckoned with his head for them to follow him. He whispered under his breath so that only the twins could hear him, "We're in some serious trouble. This colonel is a basket case! He has the reputation of being the meanest officer in the First Division, ever since he was passed over for brigadier general."

"It can't get any worse for us." Benjy glanced

over at Kenny and shrugged; they had nothing to lose by seeing the colonel.

The S-1 NCO opened the colonel's door and led the twins into the small office. "Sir . . ."

The colonel turned away from the long screened window and looked at the twins for a long time before speaking. He had casually returned their salutes and walked around from behind his desk and leaned his buttocks against the front edge. "You can leave us, Sergeant."

The NCO left the room and shut the door behind him.

"You boys present a real problem for me. I don't know who in the hell allowed the two of you to get this far together—"

"Sir . . ." Benjy cut into the colonel's sentence.

He raised his eyebrows and tilted his head slightly. "Yes, soldier."

"Sir . . . we know all about the military regulations and what they say about brothers being assigned in combat, but *we* don't care if . . . If something happens to both of us, our ma would want us together. If . . ." Benjy hesitated and then decided to just tell the colonel how he felt, even though he knew that he would be embarrassed. "You see, sir . . . I wouldn't want to live if my brother was dead."

Benjy had spoken what Kenny was also feeling deep inside. "Yes, sir, I feel the same way. You see, we're twins and we haven't been away from each other much. I don't think I'd be much good to anybody if you took Benjy." Kenny felt his face getting warm.

"That is exactly the reason why I want you separated!" The colonel crossed his arms over his chest and leaned forward. "You boys need to be apart so that you can develop your own personalities!"

Kenny frowned.

"I have twin daughters." The colonel looked into each of the twins' eyes and then out of the window. "Damn! It's against my better judgment!" He turned to face the door. "Sergeant!"

The S-1 NCO appeared instantly. He had been waiting just outside the door. "Yes, sir?"

"What kind of assignments are available where they can stay together?"

"One of the line units sir—all of them are short of men."

"No . . ." He placed his hand under his chin. "They could end up in separate platoons, and I don't think they would like that either."

Benjy smiled when the colonel glanced up at him.

"There's a vacancy in one of the tracker teams, sir. We lost three men on the Red Wing Team during Loc Ninh, and the handler won't accept anyone we've sent him so far."

"Perfect!" The colonel looked at Benjy. "Can you boys track?"

"Sir, we were raised tracking in the mountains of North Carolina."

"Send them over there and see if they can fit in." The colonel went back behind his desk, wearing a tight smile. He looked up and returned the twins' salutes. "You boys take care of yourselves, and after this war, I'd like for both of you to meet my daughters. I've got a feeling *they* aren't going to be happy unless they marry twins!"

Kenny's eyes widened as they left the colonel's office. He reached up and pulled back on Benjy's shoulder. "You know, Benjy, I haven't thought about that, but that might be a good idea."

"What's that?"

"Us marrying twin girls!"

The Labrador retriever lay just inside of her miniature sandbag-bunker doghouse and watched the three men approaching her master's bunker. It was too hot outside for her to get up and check them out. She had just returned from an exhausting fifteen-day patrol and her pads were cut and sore.

The administration NCO stuck his head inside the bunker entrance and called out, "Dixson!"

There was a pause, and then a voice from one of the cots answered, "He's over at the shitter!"

"I've brought over a couple replacements for your team." The sergeant didn't go into the bunker, but waited at the entrance.

"Fuck!" A tall skinny black soldier stepped over to the doorway, wearing only a pair of olive-drab undershorts. "Man, we just fucking got back here from patrol, and you come and wake us up in the middle of the fucking day!"

"Do you want these replacements or not?" the sergeant asked defensively. "I can always give them to someone else."

"Dixson makes those fucking decisions. Have them wait behind the bunker until he gets back!" The soldier ignored the twins and spoke to the sergeant. "I'm going back to sleep." He left the entrance and disappeared in the dark.

"Have a seat over there. Dixson should be back soon." The NCO pointed to the shady side of the bunker. "I've got to get back to my office. If you have any problems with Dixson, come on back. Normally an NCO has to accept whoever they get assigned, but because of the dog . . ." He paused in mid-sentence and looked over at the doghouse bunker. ". . . getting along with you, he gets to *pick* his men."

Benjy dropped his heavy duffel bag in the shade, and Kenny followed suit. "Shit! That was close!"

"It's not over yet. If this Dixson character doesn't like us, we're back on the fucking block again!"

The soft whine of a dog in pain reached the twins.

"Where did that come from?" Benjy cocked his head to listen better.

"The other side of the bunker." Benjy had already started walking around the structure. He stopped when he saw the dog's bunker with the small wooden name card above the entrance. "Molly?"

The dog whined again.

"Molly, come on out here so we can see you." Benjy sat down a couple of feet in front of the doghouse entrance.

She whined again and scooted out the doorway

just enough so that her front paws and head were exposed.

"Damn! Look at her paws, they're fucking raw!" Benjy's voice lowered. "What asshole is taking care of her?"

"We need some fat and ashes." Kenny looked around the immediate area for a mess hall and didn't see any.

"Open a can of lima beans." Benjy reached over and scratched the Labrador retriever behind the head. "You sure are a pretty dog."

She responded by shoving her head against his hand.

Kenny opened a can of C rations he had in his pack and scraped off the thin layer of fat that covered the ham and lima beans onto the can's cover. He saw a spot on the ground behind the bunker where someone had built a small wood fire, and used his knife blade to mix some of the ashes into the fat on the can's cover. "Here, Benjy."

"This ain't going to hurt a bit, girl." Benjy took hold of one of her sore front paws and gently rubbed a little of the fat and ashes into it. He repeated the procedure again and she started wagging her tail and came all the way out of her bunker so that Benjy could put some of the homemade ointment on her worn back paws. The mountain remedy wouldn't last long, but it did remove the stinging from the abrasions until something better could be applied.

* * *

Sergeant Dixson entered the bunker and threw the roll of toilet paper he was carrying on his cot.

"Did you talk to the replacements?" The black soldier spoke from his bunk in the dark bunker.

"What fucking replacements, Mason?"

"They were supposed to be waiting outside next to the bunker! If those motherfuckers have taken off on me. . . !" Mason leaned up on one elbow.

"What the fuck is going on?" Another man lifted himself up on a nearby bunk.

"Go back to sleep, Eagle."

The soldier obeyed and dropped back exhausted on the cot.

"You say they're outside?" Dixson started back toward the door.

"Yeah."

"Do you have Molly in here with you guys?"

"No, man . . . why?"

"She's not in her bunker!" Dixson started running for the exit. He would kill the bastard who had stolen his dog. He turned as soon as he left the fighting bunker and ran around to the shady side and slid to a halt. Mason, followed by Eagle, bumped into him. The three of them looked down at the sleeping replacements with Molly lying between the two of them. She lifted her head and gave a warning growl.

"Fuck me! My own dog's growling at me!" Dixson shook his head slowly from side to side in disbelief.

"Looks like we've found our replacements."

Eagle hiked up his fatigue pants and went back inside the bunker to get his cigarettes.

The twins had been exhausted from the trip over to Vietnam and the weeks of in-processing and training. Kenny had slipped into a deep sleep but Benjy had been awakened by Dixson's voice.

"So you're the new replacements?" Dixson twisted the end of his long handlebar mustache.

Benjy nodded.

"Do you know how to track?" Dixson lit a cigarette and inhaled deeply, not expecting a positive answer.

"We've done a bit in our time."

"What do you mean by *we*?"

Benjy nudged Kenny awake. "My brother and I."

Kenny pushed his cap back out of his face and sat up.

"Well, I'll be a fucking cunt!" Dixson scratched his head and called back into the bunker, "Eagle, get your ass out here!"

"What's up?" Eagle exited the bunker.

"Look at this shit! They sent us fucking *twins*!"

Benjy felt his temper rising again. "Look at it this way, Sergeant. *I'm* good, so double it with my brother!"

"Cocky little fucker, isn't he?" Dixson took the cigarette out of Mason's mouth and finished it in one long drag. "We'll see how good you are out there in the fucking jungle."

Benjy gave the sergeant a curt nod to confirm the statement he had made. He didn't know how good you had to be to survive out there in the jungle, but he did know that there hadn't been anyone during their training that even came close to Kenny and him in the woods, and the jungle couldn't be that much different. The principles must be basically the same.

Sergeant Dixson had remained behind with Molly while the rest of his team went over to the mess hall for supper. He always used the time alone to groom her and ensure that she was well-fed. The division veterinarian had flown out to their base and had treated Molly's cut paws and had left two sets of specially made soft rubber boots for her to wear in the field. The vet had also spent some time with the scout dogs assigned to the brigade, but he had always shown preference to Molly and had made the special trip because he had heard that she had been injured. All of the scout dogs were large German shepherds and had acquired bad reputations for mauling enemy soldiers and on occasion even American soldiers, but Molly was a tracker dog and worked off ground scent. Her mission was to follow ground scents over terrain where the soldier-trackers were unable to pick up visible sign, whereas the scout dogs were trained to respond to airborne scents and alert their handlers when they picked up a foreign presence. Both types of dogs were trained to locate trip wires, mines, fortifications, tunnels, and storage areas in the jungle or in hamlets.

Red Wing Team had the best reputation in the

First Infantry Division for detecting enemy activity and had been used during the Battle of Loc Ninh, where two of the five-man team had been killed in action. Dixson was proud of his dog and of the team and worked hard when they weren't in the field to train the team to function as a single unit in the jungle. He was very good and wouldn't tolerate anything but perfection from Molly and the men.

Dixson brushed Molly's coat and thought of the special qualifications of Mason and Adam Eagle-Catcher. Mason was a street kid from Chicago and Eagle was a Cherokee Indian from a reservation in North Carolina. As soon as Dixson had heard that the twins were from the mountains of North Carolina, he hoped that they were as good at tracking as Eagle was. Their first day of training had worked out better than Dixson had hoped for. The twins fitted in perfectly and could even read the dog.

Dixson looked up and saw his team walking toward the bunker from the direction of the mess hall. The only one he was worried about was Mason. The skinny black soldier had been hanging around a group of troublemakers who had refused to go out in the field, and once the division commander had given in to them and assigned them to rear-area jobs, they became almost unbearable to live with. Mason was starting to pick up a lot of prejudice from the black militants, and on a number of occasions Dixson had had to come down hard on the black soldier to keep him in line. There wasn't a better man in the field than Mason when it came to searching a village or hamlet—nothing missed his eye in any area with buildings and streets—but he couldn't find a ten-foot-wide trail in the jungle if he was standing in the center of it. Adam Eagle-Catcher was just the opposite; he functioned perfectly in the jungle. The major differences between the men were what had made Red Wing Team so effective. Dixson watched the four men approaching the bunker and wondered what the twins would be good at.

"Dogshit for chow!" Mason shook his head. "Sorry, Molly. I didn't mean to offend you." He looked at Dixson. "You'd be better off eating some C rats."

"I'll gut through it. I need to talk to a couple of my buddies anyway about running some ambushes for us tomorrow so we can work Molly." Dixson picked up his webgear and weapon. He put Molly on her six-foot leash and started to leave. "Eagle, you pull the first shift on guard, followed by Mason and then Benjy and Kenny. I'll take the last one."

"Roger that, Sarge."

"We're going to work out tomorrow around the base perimeter, so be ready to move out at first light."

Eagle nodded. He was the assistant team leader and was very proud of the corporal stripes he wore. "So you guys are from around Linville?" he said, addressing the twins.

"Yeah . . ." Kenny nodded.

"We operate a tourist shop near the Cherokee National Forest." Eagle smiled. "White man pay good wampum for authentic Indian souvenirs!"

* * *

Benjy felt someone kicking the bottom of his boot and opened his eyes. He reached automatically for his M-16, hanging on the wall above his cot.

"Guard duty, white boy." Mason kicked the sole of Benjy's boot again. "Don't fall back asleep because I don't plan on going back up on the roof to wait for you."

"I'm awake." Benjy unscrewed the top of his canteen and took a sip of water to clear his throat. "What time is it?"

Twenty-one-thirty hours." Mason sat down on his bunk and pulled his boots off.

Benjy grabbed his gear without saying anything to Mason. He realized that Mason was waking him up a half-hour early, but he didn't want to make any trouble. Mason had been on their cases. Benjy decided that he would let this one slide because he was a new man, but he wasn't going to take *too* much shit. . . .

The night was fairly quiet inside of the perimeter. Loud music could be heard coming from the troop hootches inside of the compound and the artillery would fire a harassment and interdiction round every once in a while. It was impossible to listen to the jungle on the other side of the barbed-wire barrier. Guard duty was a matter of waiting for a trip flare to go off or for the enemy to open fire on the base camp. Benjy had been on top of the bunker for less than a half-hour when he heard someone climbing up on the bunker from his rear. He turned and saw his brother's shadow.

"Mason's smoking pot in the bunker." Kenny laid his gear down near Benjy and curled up on the still-sun-warmed sandbags with his camouflaged poncho liner wrapped around him.

Benjy didn't answer and kept his eyes on the black tree line outside the perimeter. An AK-47 gunship opened fire in the distance near the city of Loc Ninh. The mini-guns sent streams of red tracers from the aircraft to the ground and it looked like the aircraft was hosing down the land. The tracers didn't fall in a straight line, but swayed back and forth in a fluid motion. The sound reached the bunker where Benjy was sitting quite a few seconds after the guns had started firing. It wasn't the sharp .cracking sound of an M-60 or the heavy, terrifying thudding sound of the .50-caliber machine gun, but a soft hum as the Gatling guns fired.

"It's sort of pretty." Kenny was sitting up next to him, watching.

"You'd better get some sleep or you'll be dragging ass in the morning."

"Can't sleep." Kenny pulled the poncho liner closed around his neck. "I hope Mason doesn't keep fucking with us."

"Me, too, because I'm going to kick his ass before I spend my whole tour over here being his scapegoat."

Benjy had whispered, but his voice still carried into the bunker through the firing ports. Mason shifted his homemade sandbag pillow up higher on the bunker wall and inhaled a long toke from his pipe. He smiled and exhaled before slipping over to the firing port and calling up to the twins. "What are you two doing up there? Beating each other off?"

Benjy felt his face getting red. "You'd better shut the fuck up or—"

"Or what?" Mason's voice rose and fell.

"*Or* I'll kick your ass!"

"Mason! Get your ass back in bed and shut up!" Dixson's sleep-filled voice ended the conversation.

Benjy spent the remainder of his shift fuming. He knew that he was going to have to fight Mason or they'd never have any peace. He looked over at his sleeping brother next to him and realized it was like looking in a mirror. They were too close to each other; he knew that. But when he was separated from Kenny, even for a few hours, he became very nervous.

Benjy looked up at the moon and sighed. Why didn't people understand that Kenny and he were *one* person living in two bodies?

Dixson woke up and saw the bright light shining through the bunker door. He cursed and woke up Eagle and Mason before leaving the bunker to chew out the twins for sleeping on guard duty and not waking him for his shift. He nearly ran into Benjy, who was making a canteen cup of hot cocoa on a heat-tablet fire. "Where's your brother?"

"Up top on guard." Benjy nodded.

"Why didn't you wake me for my guard?"

"You were snoring and Kenny thought you needed your sleep. Besides, he said that he wasn't tired and couldn't sleep."

Dixson cooled down when he saw Kenny stand up on the bunker. "Thanks, I was dog-tired last night. That last field trip kicked our asses."

"We've heard that the NVA gave the division a tough time last November." Benjy constantly stirred the cocoa so it wouldn't burn on the bottom.

"It wasn't NVA . . . Vietcong troops . . . *main* force Vietcong from their Ninth Division. They even got into the Special Forces camp at Loc Ninh, but got their asses kicked, leaving a hundred and forty-seven dead on the airfield."

Benjy's eyes snapped up from the cocoa. "There's a Special Forces camp near here?"

"Just a couple miles down the road." Dixson smiled. "Why do you ask?"

"I know a couple of Green Berets."

"Well, don't expect to get into their compound. They aren't that friendly, and treat line units like shit, even though we saved their asses!"

Benjy shrugged. He didn't want to get into an argument with his NCO.

"We're going over to the mess hall for breakfast and then we're going to sweep the area around the base for a training mission to shake out any loose ends we might have." Dixson was politely saying that he wanted to check out the twins' abilities.

"We'll be ready when you get back." Benjy returned his attention to the cocoa.

The twins had their gear ready and were waiting

outside the bunker when Dixson and the rest of the team returned from the mess hall.

"I've got to take a shit before we leave." Mason flashed a contemptuous look over at the twins. "Do you boys want to come with me?"

"That's enough, Mason!" Dixson was about fed up with Mason's attitude toward the new men. "There's only five of us and we've got to work together or *all* of us are going to suffer. Now, knock it off!"

Mason went into the bunker and came back out carrying a partially used roll of toilet paper. He flashed a look over at the twins to let them know that it wasn't over yet.

Dixson put Molly on a twenty-five-foot leash and led the way out of the compound to the tree line before he stopped to brief the team. There wasn't very much danger in patrolling the outside of the base camp's perimeter, but it was excellent practice for the team to work the tree line around the compound, and at the same time gave the infantrymen a break from the dull job.

"This is the way we work." Dixson was speaking to the twins. "Molly will alert me to any trails or devices near us and I'll alert you trackers by using the hand signals we've been practicing. I don't want *any* talking once we start patrolling. Normally we'll be working ahead of an infantry company's point element, or if things are getting real hairy, we'll travel with the point. In any case, talking will get us killed."

The twins nodded their agreement. Dixson didn't

know that they had a language all their own, comprising hand and body signals.

"Seeing that this is your first trip out in the jungle, I want one of you on each side of me up front. The best way to learn is to do it. Mason and Eagle, I want you guys to cover the rear flanks as we move." Dixson looked back over at the twins and added, "I was talking to a couple of scout-dog trainers last night and they swept this area yesterday, using five dog teams, so we shouldn't run into anything, but like I said, this is a good way to train. Mason!"

"Yo!"

"I don't want you getting bored on me. Even though this is a shakeout mission for the new guys, I want you to set a good example."

Mason nodded. He hated working the jungle, but loved it when they hit a village. He had an uncanny ability to detect camouflaged tunnel entrances and hidden caches in a village, and loved doing it, especially when he found a really good setup and could see the villagers' faces when their hiding places were discovered.

"Let's move!" Dixson reached down and patted Molly. "Go, girl!" He let out the full length of the leash and watched the dog work the area.

The team started out rough for the first couple of hours, but then the twins settled into the pattern and the search became extremely thorough. They stopped when they reached a small overgrown banana grove and took a break. Kenny could see from the empty C-ration cans and cigarette butts that the area had been used frequently by the infantry patrols and other scout-dog teams for a midway break area. He signaled Benjy that he was stopping near a stand of young bamboo, and his brother joined him. The twins shared water out of one canteen and watched the rest of the team light up cigarettes and stretch out in the shade of the banana trees. A large corner fighting bunker could be seen on the perimeter, where the team stopped for a break. The guard sitting on top of the bunker in a bright green plastic lawn chair waved that he saw them.

Benjy continuously scanned the area around him. He was still hunting. The twins had been taught from the first day that they went out in the woods with old Hillard Green that if you were hunting, that's what you did until you returned home with your game. They had been reminded numerous times by the old man that even when you were resting, you remained alert for game, because many a time a hunter missed a big buck who had sneaked up on him when he was resting in the woods.

Kenny looked over at Molly and saw that she kept lifting her head and looking over at a dense stand of jungle foliage. She was not giving an alert, but she would rest her head on her front paws and then lift her head and look back at the same spot, as if she were curious about something.

"Cover me," Kenny whispered to Benjy, and then casually got up with his rifle.

"Where are you going?" Dixson turned his head slowly on his laced fingers from his prone position.

"Gotta take a shit."

"Don't wander off too far. We'll be starting up again in an hour or so."

"I'm just going over in the bush a little ways." Kenny started angling off in the jungle, making it look like he just wanted a little privacy.

"Ain't you going with him?" Mason made the sarcastic remark to Benjy.

"I said, enough of that crap!" Dixson didn't open his eyes.

Molly watched Kenny disappear behind a large-leafed plant and whined.

"Hush up, girl!" Dixson gently slapped her shoulder. "He's only taking a shit."

Benjy had been watching his brother, but kept glancing at Molly. She had shifted her eyes from Kenny back to the same spot in the jungle that had interested Kenny. Benjy didn't know what was going on, but he sensed that his brother wasn't taking a crap.

As soon as Kenny was out of sight, he changed his direction and circled back to the spot that Molly had been looking at. He felt like a fool, but he used every bit of stealth he had ever learned to move through the jungle without making a detectable noise. Kenny figured that the worst that could happen was that he got some decent practice stalking. He could see Molly lying next to Dixson, and watched where she was looking. She would glance at the jungle where he was hiding and then look back over to the spot that had interested her. The dog's eyes guided Kenny to where he wanted to go.

When he figured he was within a couple of meters of the spot Molly had been interested in, he stopped crawling and listened. The jungle was quiet. He waited. Patience was something he had learned before he had turned six years old in the North Carolina mountains. Without patience he would never have caught his first trout or, for that matter, enough wild game to feed his family for one meal.

Kenny saw Dixson stir and sit up and look at his watch. He figured he had been lying there about twenty-five minutes. The jungle floor less than five feet in front of him moved slightly. At first Kenny thought it was his eyes playing tricks on him from the salty sweat that had dripped in them, but then a tiny black slit appeared on the jungle floor and the lid of a spider hole opened about five inches. Kenny could see the sleeve of an American jungle-fatigue uniform and became confused. What were Americans doing out here in a spider hole? He glanced over at Molly and saw that she had gotten up on her feet and was staring hard at the jungle in front of him.

Molly alerted.

Dixson was busy lighting a cigarette and Eagle and Mason were dozing against their packs in plain view of the perimeter fighting bunker. Benjy had been watching where his brother had gone. He saw Molly alert. He reached for his M-16.

Kenny reacted as if he had been in Vietnam for five years. He removed the pin from an M-26 hand grenade and let the pin pop. He counted to five before he rolled the live grenade into the dark slit that had appeared on the jungle floor and pressed his cheek down against the decomposing jungle floor.

The explosion brought an instant reaction from the team. Dixson's first reaction was to look at Molly. He saw that she had alerted.

"VC!" Dixson rolled over on his side and pointed his M-16 in the direction Molly was looking in.

"Don't shoot! Kenny's over there!" Benjy shouted.

Kenny called out, "Benjy, circle around and cover me. I think I've got him!"

Mason and Eagle looked confused after being awakened from their light naps.

"Sergeant Dixson! Over here!" Kenny's voice was excited.

Benjy was the first one to react, and ran across the open area of the old banana grove and joined his brother. Kenny had gone only fifty feet, but had taken a roundabout way of getting there. Benjy ran in a straight line, carrying his M-16 at the ready. He wanted to be the first one to his brother, but more important, he didn't want Mason to panic and open fire. Benjy stumbled over something and regained his balance. He looked down and saw that his foot had caught the edge of a number-ten-size can that had been painted and buried halfway in the loose dirt on the jungle floor. He paused just long enough to see and smell the urine in the can before running the last couple of meters to join Kenny.

"What's going on?" Benjy scanned the area in a half-circle as he talked.

"VC!" Kenny pointed with his rifle barrel at the open spider hole.

"Damn!" Dixson had joined them with the rest of the team. "The motherfucker is wearing American fatigues!"

"Hot shit!" Eagle saw the empty and full cans of C rations in the small sump hole in the bottom of the tiny pit. The VC had been eating American rations on a regular basis.

"Pull him out of there." Dixson pointed with his weapon. Molly whined and kept looking at a slight rise in the ground about twenty-five feet behind the spider hole. She still hadn't alerted again.

"Something's weird about this." Dixson was very nervous.

Eagle and Kenny pulled the dead VC out of the spider hole, and as soon as the torn-apart body was removed, they could see the crawl hole the body had been hiding. Dixson reacted instantly and started giving commands. The team broke up and searched the jungle for bunkers. Molly looked up at her handler with a confused expression, as if to ask what he wanted her to do.

"Find, girl . . . Find!" Dixson extended her leash.

Molly whined, confused, and halfheartedly alerted to the slight mound on the jungle floor.

Eagle skirted around to the left and searched for air holes on the ground. Once his eyes adjusted to the area, he detected three more of the cans filled with urine and human excrement, and then he saw the five-inch cut-off piece of bamboo sticking up out of the ground. Eagle dropped a live grenade down the hole and warned the team. The explosion was muffled and a small puff of smoke came back up out of the hole.

"Underground bunker." Dixson's head was moving constantly from side to side. "But there aren't any firing ports." He sounded confused.

"That's one *big* fucking bunker!" Mason was judging it based on the size of the mound.

"Let's go back to the spider hole." Dixson started backing up. "Keep your eyes open for any other exits!"

Molly whined again and looked confused. She didn't understand why her handler was attacking the American scent. The cans had contained urine and feces that had been taken from American latrines inside the compound and placed in the cans around the VC observation post to throw off the dogs. The ruse had worked perfectly, and the VC had even gone as far as having their men wear *dirty* American fatigues stolen from laundries in Loc Ninh that serviced American units. The VC smelled like Americans to the dogs.

"Who wants to crawl into the hole?" Dixson looked for a volunteer.

"Fuck that shit! Look how small that fucking hole is!" Mason didn't want anything to do with it. Eagle wasn't all that happy about the idea either.

"Come on! It can't be booby-trapped. You can see that he used it." Dixson nodded at the VC wearing the torn remains of the American fatigues. A captain's bars were still sewn on the collar, and the nametag read "Buckingham."

"I found the hole. I'll go down," Kenny volunteered. "I need my flashlight out of my pack."

"Benjy, go get it for him." Dixson gave a disgusted look at Mason. He had expected one of his more-experienced men to volunteer.

Benjy returned carrying two flashlights. He didn't ask the sergeant if he could go, but just followed his brother down into the spider hole. He had to wait until the Kenny was all the way in the narrow tunnel before he could follow. The tunnel was just wide enough for him to wiggle behind Kenny's jungle boots.

Kenny held his flashlight out in front of him and could see were the twenty-foot tunnel ended. He could feel the claustrophobia closing in on him and wiggled faster to reach the opening, even if it meant running into some VC. He had to get out of the tunnel quick.

The crawl was worse for Benjy because he couldn't see anything but Kenny's boots.

The twins fell into the large chamber and their flashlights swept the twenty-five-square-foot area. Five dead VC lay scattered around the room, and a wrecked radio-receiver sat twisted on a bamboo table in one corner of the underground bunker. An American Coleman lantern hung from the ceiling, but it had been turned off. The room had been lighted by three American PRC-25 batteries hooked up in a series that powered a single light bulb.

"Everything in here is American!" Kenny couldn't help whispering the discovery.

"Except the dead bodies." Benjy's statement was made matter-of-factly. "Let's get out of here and tell the sarge."

When they exited the tunnel, the twins saw that the area was being secured by the base camp's ready-reaction platoon. The guard on the bunker had heard the grenade's explosion and had alerted them.

"What's in there?" A lieutenant asked the question.

"Five dead VC and a lot of American equipment." Kenny nodded down at the tunnel.

"Motherfuckers were observing our camp!" Mason sounded offended that they would do such a thing.

"What bothers me is that we never detected them and we've patrolled this area a number of times." Dixson glanced at the twins but kept to himself what he was thinking. They would have gone past the observation post again if it hadn't been for Kenny.

"That's a smart idea for them to use American soldiers' feces and urine to throw off the dogs." Benjy was amused by the VC's cleverness.

"It also tells us that some of the shit burners on base are VC!" Dixson didn't like the idea of hiring Vietnamese nationals to work inside the base camps.

"We've got to report this to the colonel and to the division intelligence officer." The platoon leader smiled at Dixson. "Your tracking team did a damn good job!"

"Thanks, sir." Dixson glanced sheepishly at Kenny.

Then the lieutenant dismissed the tracker team. "You can take your men back inside the perimeter now. I'm sure my platoon can handle sweeping the area."

The Vietcong soldier watched the Americans from his hiding place up in the tree, and as soon as the handler and the dog were out of sight, he dropped from the tree and ran down the narrow path toward the city of Loc Ninh. He paused only once to look back over his shoulder, and his pale blue eyes flashed his hate. He would have been blown up inside the bunker with his uncle and his brother if he had been on time at the rendezvous site.

CHAPTER 7

CHRISTMAS COMES EARLY

February 1968

The twins were at the shower point washing off the mud when the black Special Forces jeep pulled up behind the bunker. Mason could see that a Chinese Nung was driving the vehicle and that there were two more fully armed Nungs riding in the back of it. A black command sergeant major was riding in the shotgun seat.

"Is there something I can do for you, Sergeant Major?" Mason called down from the top of the bunker.

"Yes, I'm looking for my sons."

"Who they assigned to?"

"A tracker team named Red Wing."

"This is Red Wing."

"There names are Benjy and Kenny Kingston."

Mason nearly fell off the bunker roof. "They're *your* sons?"

"I call them that. Have you seen them?"

"Yes, sir! Sergeant Major!" Mason was impressed and shocked at the same time. "They've gone over to the shower point to clean up. We just had a small encounter with six VC."

"Oh?"

"Yeah, those boys of yours sure are good!" Mason smiled.

"They should be . . . I trained them!" Yates winked up at the black soldier. "Do you mind if we wait here for them?"

"Help yourselves, Sergeant Major. You can wait inside the bunker if you like; it's cooler in there."

"Thanks, but we'll stay with the jeep." Yates got out of the vehicle and stretched his legs. He had read the after-action report the First Division had submitted to the Loc Ninh Special Forces camp and nearly dropped the paper when he read the name Kingston on the report as the tracker who had initially discovered the VC complex.

Benjy was the first one to see the black jeep parked behind their bunker, and nudged Kenny. "It looks like we've got visitors."

"Division intelligence?" Kenny squinted, trying to see who was standing next to the jeep. The man wasn't wearing Army-issue jungle fatigues.

"Could be . . ." Benjy increased his pace but he couldn't walk much faster because he hadn't laced his boots after taking a shower at the quartermaster shower facility. He had planned on changing his socks when he got back to the bunker. Clean clothes had a habit of *walking* away at the shower point, which was in constant use all day long by infantrymen coming out of the field.

"Shit! It's Sergeant Major Yates!" Kenny started running, even though his boots flopped on his bare feet.

Yates saw the boys coming and broke out in a wide grin. "Well, looky what we've got here!"

Kenny stopped a foot in front of the senior NCO. Yates ran his hand through the soldier's wet hair and then hugged him awkwardly. Kenny had his arms full of dirty gear. Yates looked at Benjy and repeated the warm greeting.

Mason watched the reunion from the top of the bunker, his eyes narrowed.

"Do we have a *lot* to tell you, Sergeant Major!" Kenny raised his eyebrows.

"We should kick your ass!" Benjy frowned and gave the sergeant major a threatening glare. "If we had known the shit we were going to have to put up with over being twins . . . !"

Yates chuckled. "It could be worse . . . you could be black."

"I don't know about that!" Kenny glanced up at Mason. "Sometimes it's the blacks who are harassing the whites."

"Really?" Yates looked where Kenny was looking and saw Mason staring at them.

"Come on! I want to introduce you to my team sergeant!" Benjy tugged Yates's sleeve.

"I'd like to, but we're pressed for time." Yates looked down at his military watch. "I've cleared it with your CO for the two of you to visit with me over at the A-Team this afternoon for a couple of hours." He winked. "Hurry up and get finished dressing so we won't lose any more time."

"Great!" The twins disappeared inside the bunker, and it seemed like no more than a minute passed before they emerged again dressed and wearing all of their gear.

"Going to war?" Yates teased the boys.

"We have to wear all this stuff when we leave the compound." Kenny shrugged and squeezed into the back of the jeep between the Nung guards. "There isn't much room left back here."

"Benjy, put your webgear on the floor in the back and we'll share the front seat." Yates adjusted the gear he had between the front seats and made a makeshift seat for Benjy to sit on with his legs straddling the floor gearbox. "It's only a couple of short miles over to the camp."

The twins didn't care how far it was; it was good seeing the sergeant major again.

The guards at the gates of the Special Forces camp waved the sergeant major through without stopping him because he was with men from their camp and using their jeep. The driver stopped in front of the American teamhouse and waited until the Americans unloaded before parking the jeep in the shade to keep the seats from getting hot.

"Come on inside and meet some friends of mine." The sergeant major led the way down the long hallway to the back corner, where the team bar and meeting area were located. All of the Special Forces teamhouses were built basically the same: individual rooms occupied most of the long house, but one end was usually divided between a community kitchen and a team meeting area.

A very tall redheaded sergeant stood up and held out his hand for the sergeant major to shake. "Good seeing you again, Sergeant Major! I was one of your trainees back in 1965."

"McKeon, isn't it?"

The man's face lit up. He hadn't expected the sergeant major to remember him. "Yes! I went through the engineer course."

"You might remember the Kingston twins." Yates pointed at the twins, who were standing in the dark hallway behind him.

"Shit, yes!" McKeon stepped over to where he could see them better. "Hot damn! You boys have grown some!"

Kenny remembered the tall redhead. Benjy's mind drew a blank, but he pretended he remembered. A lot of SF trainees had gone through the mountain training while they had been scouts.

"Let me get the captain over here. He'll be glad to see you, for sure!" McKeon cranked the ringer on the field telephone and waited for someone down in the Tactical Operations Center to answer. "Hello, TOC? Send the captain over to the team-house, Sergeant Major Yates is here on a visit." He hung up the field telephone and looked at Yates. "Do you want a cold beer?"

"No, thanks, but a cold soda would hit the spot just fine." Yates looked over at the twins.

"What kind?"

"Shasta orange if you've got it. If not, anything cold will do."

"You guys?" McKeon waited for the twins to order.

"Same is fine," Benjy answered.

"Joc?" McKeon spoke to a young Vietnamese who had been standing behind the bar, restocking the refrigerator.

"Yes, sir?" The young man turned around, and the first thing Yates noticed was his pale blue eyes, a physical trait that was extremely rare for a Vietnamese, even when one of the parents was European.

"Do we have any cold orange?"

"Yes, Sergeant. We have plenty." The accent was a mixture of Vietnamese, French, and a tinge of a Southern drawl from whoever had taught him English.

Yates watched the Vietnamese open the cans and set them on the wooden bar for Benjy. The physical rarity wasn't Yates's main interest, it was the fact that one of the dead VC in the bunker destroyed early that morning had also had blue eyes. The discovery had been unusual enough for the First Division to enter it in their intelligence report.

The captain stormed into the room laughing. "Yates! Damn good to see you again!" He shook the sergeant major's hand with exaggerated vigor, but the smile was honest enough. "What brings you out here? I thought you had the B-Team at Tay Ninh."

"I do, but my boys were assigned to the First

Division and shipped out here, so I had to find an excuse to fly out here and take care of them."

"Is there anything we can do to help?" The captain was sure the sergeant major already had something in mind.

"As a matter of fact . . . there is." He smiled and winked at the captain.

"Name it."

"Well, my boys have been assigned to a combat tracker team and I'm afraid they're going to need some special equipment." Yates saw that the twins were puzzled. "They've been given all the basic *leg* bullshit items, but nothing that will work if they have to go into a tunnel and *find* something in there." Yates saw the interest on the Vietnamese face and figured now was a good time to find out if his suspicions were correct. "They've been with the unit only a couple of days and already they've uncovered a VC observation post. Killed six Vietcong this morning." Yates saw the hate flash in the Vietnamese's blue eyes and would bet money that at least one of the dead VC had been related to him. The Vietnamese dropped down behind the bar and pretended to be arranging bottles behind the counter. Hate burned his eyelids.

"Well, let's go over to our supply bunker and see what we can dig up for them." The captain led the way out the back door and over to the underground supply room, through tunnels connecting the ammunition-storage and food-supply areas to the main facility.

The young Vietnamese left the teamhouse and

walked to one of the perimeter bunkers, where he could calm down. The bunker was occupied by three VC infiltrators who had been working inside the camp since it had been built.

"Do you have anything with a silencer on it?" Yates could see a row of submachine guns racked against the wall.

"Do we have silenced weapons, the man asks!" The captain handed Yates a 9mm Swedish-K submachine gun equipped with a silencer. "How's that?"

"Perfect." Yates handed the folding-stock weapon to Kenny. "What do you think?"

"Why do we need a silenced weapon?"

"If you're going to work the bunkers and tunnels, you're going to need this stuff or lose your hearing!" Yates looked back at the captain.

"I don't have another Swedish-K, but I have an old forty-five-caliber M-2 submachine gun that has an excellent silencer on it."

"Let's see it." Yates took the offered WWII weapon and handed it to Benjy. "I would have liked to have both weapons of the same caliber to facilitate ammunition resupply, but these will have to do. The M-2 won't be a problem getting ammo for, but the 9mm could cause some trouble."

"Naw . . ." The captain shook his head. "As long as they're in the III Corps area, there'll be SF people nearby where they can scrounge ammo." He reached into an ammo box and removed two pistols. "Now, these are hard to come by. We got them from some friends in SOG." He laid the two

9mm Browning pistols on top of the wooden crate. "I hate to part with these."

Yates hefted one of the silenced pistols. The long silencer at the end of the barrel threw the balance off, but the weapons had fourteen-round magazines that worked as a counterbalance of sorts.

"I'll need *quite a bit* for them." The captain watched Yates's reaction.

"You've got it. I can't let my boys leave here poorly equipped." Yates hooded his eyes at the captain as a warning not to get too greedy. The twins had missed the body language going on between the sergeant and the captain. There would be some heavy trading going on for the weapons after the twins left. "How about some decent flashlights . . . five-cell?"

"Better. I've got something better." The captain rummaged through a stack of crates and then called over to his team sergeant, who had been watching the whole thing from a seat on a case of tiger suits. "Top! Where in the hell are those hats?"

"I think back over there by the batteries." He stayed sitting on the box.

"Yeah!" The captain found what he was looking for and held one of them up for the sergeant major to see.

"A miner's hat?" Yates wasn't shocked at seeing a coal miner's hat. He had been in Special Forces too long for that. "Where did you find them?"

"My old team worked Nui Ba Den's caves, and I special-ordered a hundred of them from the States. I thought they might come in handy someday, and kept a dozen . . . or so." He handed one to each of the twins. "They've been slightly modified with airborne chin straps, so they'll stay on if you have to make any erratic moves."

Benjy slipped his black miner's hat on and flipped the switch. A bright beam lit up the far wall of the bunker. "Perfect for tunnels!" He could have used it for his crawl down the dark tunnel earlier that day.

"We'll take . . . four of them." Yates smiled at the captain. "Spares . . . and some batteries?"

"Sure, Sergeant Major." The captain smiled back. The B-Team sergeant major was going to have to pay off a mighty long tab.

"Throw in some ammo and we'll be finished for today." Yates handed the weapons and gear to the twins. "Oh, by the way, Captain . . . while we're down here alone, I've been wondering about something . . ."

"Shoot, Sergeant Major." The captain was expecting some sort of hook to the deal, but threw in a mention of what he wanted for the weapons and gear before the senior NCO could maneuver. "I want a 100KW generator for the stuff."

"You got it. I'll have it delivered before the end of the week." Yates saw the surprise on the captain's face; he knew the man would have settled for two 10KW's and would have picked them up. "That's not what I wanted to ask. It's about the young Vietnamese you have working for you."

"Joc?"

"Yes." Yates looked back at the entrance. "Is it safe to talk in here?"

The captain became all business. He nodded for the team sergeant to check the entrances and waited until the NCO returned and confirmed that everything was clear before answering the sergeant major. "Now it is."

"What do you know about him?"

"His father was a rich plantation owner—he had damn near ten square miles of working fields just west of Loc Ninh . . . a place called Xa Loi Thien." The captain stepped closer to Yates. "Why do you ask?"

"What happened to the plantation?"

"The way that I understand it, the Vietminh caused a lot of hell over there, making raids out of Cambodia, and the father had to pay huge taxes to them to be left alone. When the French lost the war, the Vietminh disappeared and the Vietcong took over. The plantation was raided and the French owner and his Vietnamese wife were . . . executed."

"Joc? What happened to him?" Yates listened intently to the captain.

"He and his brothers and sisters went to live with their mother's sister in Loc Ninh." The captain's voice lowered. "I assure you that he *hates* the Vietcong because they killed his parents!"

Yates nodded in agreement. "It would seem so."

"What do you mean, *seem* so?"

"One of the VC killed this morning in the bunker had blue eyes just like your man Joc's."

The captain flashed a look over at the team sergeant. "Is that possible?"

"I don't know, sir. I've never met Joc's brothers." The team sergeant seemed nervous.

"You've taken him home on the weekends before, and you've never met his brothers or his family?"

"He always makes excuses that they're not home." The team sergeant frowned. "Now that I think about it, I've never met his aunt or uncle . . . or, for that matter, he's never invited me into his house."

"We'd better check this shit out!" The captain looked worried, and he had a reason to be. Joc had the run of the A-Camp, including the TOC. There had been no reason to suspect him of being a VC agent, especially with the story that the VC had killed his family. "Thanks, Sergeant Major . . . I might have a real problem here!" The captain frowned as he tried recalling the team's operations and linking them with information that had been available to Joc.

"Well, we've got to be getting on back." Yates started toward the bunker entrance, followed by the loaded-down twins. "Thanks for your hospitality."

"Thank *you*, Sergeant Major—you just might have saved our asses." The captain was serious. The whole A-Team could have been overrun if the VC had a mole as well-placed inside the camp as Joc was. "Sergeant Major?"

"Yes, sir?"

"Forget about the generator . . . we owe you!"

Beads of sweat appeared on the captain's forehead. He had three companies due to patrol the Cambodian border, starting in the morning, and he remembered that Joc had asked for the week off, also starting tomorrow morning. The captain also remembered that Joc had arrived in the teamhouse only a few minutes before the sergeant major and the twins. He hadn't been in the A-Camp all morning—he said he had been sick.

Joc hurried out the main gate, carrying his indigenous rucksack over his shoulder that contained all of his personal items. He did not plan on returning to the Loc Ninh Special Forces camp. The guards at the main gate looked at him curiously, but they weren't alarmed. Joc was well-known in the camp and was favored by the Americans. They waved him by even though it was late in the afternoon to be leaving the camp. He walked normally until he was out of sight of the perimeter guards and then started running hard toward Highway 13. There was a good chance that he could catch a late ride into the city, and if not, he knew a number of places to spend the night in the jungle.

The Special Forces captain left the underground TOC with the South Vietnamese LLDB commander. Both of them were convinced that Joc had some type of affiliation with the Vietcong and therefore should be questioned. They searched the whole camp but couldn't find him. The last place they checked was the main gate, and the guards told them Joc had left the camp about two hours earlier.

Joc had managed to hitch a ride with a farmer who had sold three pigs to another farmer near Loc Ninh. Commerce continued during the war and operated around the military units from both sides. To the local villagers the war was a nuisance that occasionally took its toll in lives, but if they were careful and paid the Vietcong their taxes and cooperated with the South Vietnamese government, they were pretty much left alone. The only real threat to them was an American infantry or armored unit searching their villages. A weak officer would allow his men to steal and to rape the village's women, and if *anything* was discovered that could be associated with the Vietcong or North Vietnamese Army, the Americans would burn the village. Trying to be neutral in the ever-changing war was a dangerous tactic but a required survival skill. Most villages were controlled by the South Vietnamese government during the day and by the Vietcong at night.

Joc thanked the driver of the small three-wheeled vehicle and slipped away from the main street of the city. He decided to take the back streets to his aunt's house and not risk being detected by the ARVN military police. Joc's thoughts went to his older brother and his uncle as he walked down the alley. His brother had been four years older than Joc and had been a rising star in the Ninth Vietcong Division under his uncle, who had commanded the 273rd Regiment. If the Americans only knew *whom* they had killed in the bunker earlier that day, they would be thrilled. It wasn't every day they killed a Vietcong colonel and a senior intelligence major. The Vietcong Ninth Division had suffered severe losses during their ill-advised attack on the Loc Ninh city complex. Joc had told them that the Special Forces camp was too well-defended to attack in strength. He had recommended a skilled sapper attack first, to be followed by a battalion-size assault. The division commander had disapproved of his plan and had suffered hundreds of casualties. He secretly didn't trust the French half-breeds, as he called Joc and his brother, and had ordered the attack. Joc's uncle had obeyed, but he had also sent a message to the NVA commanding general that he felt the division commander was making a fatal error in underestimating the enemy's strength in Binh Long province. He would not have dared writing a personal note to the NVA general who commanded the communist forces in South Vietnam, except for the fact that they had been good friends and had fought the French together as lieutenants in the Vietminh Army. The division commander had learned of the message and as a punishment had sent Joc's uncle to reconnoiter and plan a sapper attack against the American compound.

Joc mumbled to himself as he walked in the shadows next to the buildings. War would be so much easier if there weren't any politics involved among the men who had to fight the war, but he knew that as long as there were stars to be won for men's collars and power to be gained, there would be politics in war. He smiled to himself. He wasn't very good at playing the political game, but his aunt was an expert with very few equals, men or women. She would tell him what to do. Joc could handle the battlefield as well as anyone his age, but his aunt was the political tactician. It was his aunt who had convinced the whole family to join the Vietcong after Diem's military bandits murdered his parents and burned their plantation. The President of South Vietnam had formed his own secret tax-collecting teams and would levy a special tax on all the wealthy landowners, especially the French who had stayed after the downfall of their colonial government. Paying taxes to the official South Vietnamese government and to the Vietcong was difficult enough, but when Diem's bandits demanded taxes at a rate double the federal tax rate, his father had refused to pay, and because he owned the largest plantation in the province, Diem had made an example of him. The secret tax team had dressed up to look like Vietcong and murdered Joc's parents after they had tortured them.

Joc stopped walking and closed his eyes tightly, trying to drive away the image etched on his eyelids. He had come home from school and found them spread-eagled in front of their villa. They had been stripped naked and his mother had been raped numerous times before they had murdered her by cutting open her stomach and pulling out her intestines. His father had been murdered by a one-inch-thick bamboo pole shoved down his throat.

Joc took a half-dozen steps before he opened his

eyes again and started running. He reached the gate to his aunt's house and opened it with his key. He could smell the incense burning from the prayer sticks in front of the shrine and knew where his aunt would be.

She didn't look up when Joc stepped into the room, but the men sitting cross-legged on each side of her turned to give him a courteous nod. Joc recognized both of the men. The older one, on his aunt's left, was a North Vietnamese brigadier general and the man on her right was a Vietcong colonel and his uncle's closest friend. Both of the men were dressed in the simple suits that South Vietnamese businessmen wore.

Joc took a seat near his aunt and waited until she was done praying for his uncle and his brother. She had not cried, and when she turned to face her nephew, her face was solemn. She waited for him to speak.

"I think they have detected me at the A-Camp."

"You must go then and hide in the secret zone until they stop searching for you." Her voice was calm. The tragedy of losing her husband had not affected her logic: his death as a soldier could have come at any time.

"Are you sure?" the brigadier general asked. Joc had been providing a tremendous amount of valuable information to the NVA in III Corps, and the general hated to think they had lost that source, especially after their defeat at Loc Ninh. The NVA needed Joc's intelligence.

"I am sure. There aren't very many South Vietnamese who have blue eyes. My brother and I are the only two I know of." Joc felt the grief in his chest but continued. "A black American sergeant major came out to the camp today and looked at me. I could almost read what he was thinking, but one of our men inside the camp caught part of a sentence from where he was hiding behind some crates in one of the ammunition bunkers. They were discussing my brother's blue eyes."

The brigadier general nodded. The Americans weren't very smart when it came to gathering intelligence, but even a fool could see something as obvious as blue eyes and tie it in with Joc's family. "Maybe you should go too." He spoke to Joc's aunt. "They will be suspicious with your husband and nephews missing, and it will only be a matter of time before they identify them."

"I am too old to leave my home." She reached out and touched her nephew's hand. "Go . . . quickly."

Joc bowed to his aunt and left the room. He would have to put as much distance between himself and Loc Ninh as he could before daylight. He wasn't afraid. The trip would be swift to the secret zone in Cambodia, less than fifteen kilometers away from Loc Ninh, and their only danger would be a stray artillery round or an air strike, and he had provided the VC with a list of all the air strikes and artillery action planned for the next three days.

CHAPTER 8

THE PREK CHHLONG SECRET ZONE

April Fool's Day 1968

Joc slept through the entire next day after his arrival in the Cambodian secret zone and was wakened by a Khmer Rouge soldier wearing the red-and-white-checked scarf that symbolized unity against the Cambodian government of Prince Sihanouk. The Cambodian communist spoke Vietnamese so poorly that Joc had to ask him to repeat himself a half-dozen times before he understood what the man was trying to tell him.

"Colonel . . . want you to come . . . now!" The Khmer Rouge soldier used his AK-47 to gesture in the direction of the command bunker.

Joc took his time getting dressed, and enjoyed watching the guerrilla becoming more nervous. There was something about the Khmer Rouge that bothered Joc. It seemed to be made up of criminals who had joined the communist movement not because they believed in the system but because they would have been executed for their crimes if the government ever captured them.

The sun was slipping behind the trees as Joc followed the irritated soldier to the bunker. He felt even more exhausted after the long rest than he had when he had arrived at the secret zone near the Prek Chhlong River.

The colonel smiled when Joc entered his office and saluted. "Joc! I am so sorry to hear about your brother and your uncle."

"They were soldiers and died soldiers' deaths in our struggle." Joc parroted the party line.

"Your uncle was a good friend of mine. It is a shame that he died after surviving so long in this war." The colonel was thinking that he too could end up rotting in some jungle bunker before it was all over with. "And your brother showed such promise!"

Joc remained standing at attention and only nodded in agreement. It was not good to show any emotion to one's superior because everyone had lost somebody in the war.

"At least your little brother is doing well in Moscow! I hear that he is the best cadet in his military school."

"When did you hear that, sir?"

"One of our Russian advisers mentioned how well our men were doing in their military academies and mentioned your brother by name. The PAVAN commander was very impressed! The rest of the evening was spent talking about our young people serving in Russia and China."

"When was this, sir?"

The colonel touched his lips with his finger and thought. "A week ago at dinner. We were meeting near the headquarters at Mimot." The colonel looked shyly away from Joc and added, "We were discussing our great victory at Loc Ninh!"

Joc managed to keep control of his tongue.

"We lost a thousand good soldiers, but the Americans have reported three thousand of their soldiers dead and their First Division unable to conduct operations!"

Joc believed in the communist cause, but he didn't like it when they exaggerated their victories over the Americans. He knew that the Ninth VC Division had been decimated, not the Americans. He also knew that the colonel was aware of his report *not* to attack Loc Ninh.

"You have gained quite a reputation as a spy." The colonel smiled again.

"I do my best, sir."

"I have been instructed to take care of you while you're here with us. The general thinks that within a couple of months we can sneak you back into Binh Long province."

"Binh Long?" Joc knew that he would always be on the South Vietnamese intelligence lists; returning to Binh Long would be signing a death warrant.

"Yes, you are much too valuable there. Who knows, maybe when this war is over you'll get your family plantation back as a reward for your service."

"That would be an honor, sir."

"So! What would you like to do while you're staying here with us?"

Joc shrugged. "Intelligence work? I can decode American radio transmissions for you. I am very good with their slang expressions after working in the Special Forces camp."

"Yes, you would be very good at that. . . ." The colonel smiled, revealing that he had already decided where he was going to assign the young lieutenant. "We had a couple of other ideas."

"Wherever I can be of the best service to you, sir!" Joc bowed slightly.

"Very good! Then it's settled!" The colonel left the authoritarian security of his desk and came around to rest his hand on Joc's shoulder. "We've been having a problem with some of our allies."

Joc's forehead wrinkled. "The Russians?"

"Oh, no!" The colonel's face became grim. "The Khmer Rouge."

"Everyone has problems with them, sir!" Joc looked disgusted.

"True, but they are our allies and they keep Prince Sihanouk's puppet soldiers away from our supply lines. The Sihanouk Trail is very important to us and cannot be cut!" The colonel's voice rose as if the trail had already been closed.

Joc had heard about the secret agreement Prince Sihanouk had signed with Ho Chi Minh. Officially, the Cambodian government would remain neutral, but secretly the port city of Sihanoukville would be open to North Vietnam and communist-bloc countries and a free access would be granted from the port to the border cities of Mimot and O'Rang. The Sihanouk Trail would go from the port city up to O'Rang; the Ho Chi Minh Trail would come down from the north through Laos, and the two would meet at O'Rang.

"I understand, sir." Joc waited for the colonel to continue.

"We must remain friendly with the Khmer Rouge, no matter how bad they are, until we can infiltrate Phnom Penh with our agents." The colonel went back behind his desk. "The problem is that the Khmer Rouge are in control of the prisoner-of-war camp outside of Mimot. They are barbarians!" The colonel's voice rose again.

Joc waited at attention.

"We want you to take the position of assistant camp commander under the Khmer Rouge captain."

Joc was shocked. A Vietcong officer had never been assigned under the operational control of a Khmer Rouge! He thought fast. The colonel had used the word "we." Someone very high up must have told the colonel to assign him to the POW camp, so there was no way he could refuse the position. "I would be honored, sir!"

The colonel smiled. He had been worried that the Vietcong officer would refuse the insult to serve under a Khmer Rouge guerrilla, in which case a major incident could occur. If they shot Joc for insubordination, the Vietcong high command would lodge a complaint in Hanoi, and if they allowed the Khmer Rouge to continue their inhumane treatment of the American prisoners, they would receive a complaint from Hanoi. The official policy was to treat all American POW's with a semblance of dignity.

"You don't know how much I appreciate your cooperation, Lieutenant. I will not forget this." The NVA colonel bowed slightly, telling Joc the interview was over.

"I am honored to serve the cause in any capacity that I can." Joc saluted and left the bunker.

The Khmer Rouge guard was waiting for him at the entrance. It was now obvious to Joc why a Khmer Rouge had come to get him for the colonel. The smelly man was his guide over to the POW compound, located on a tributary of the Prek Chhlong River. An old Mercedes-Benz was waiting for him outside the command compound on the dirt road that would take them out to Highway 7.

Joc smoked an American Salem cigarette after offering the Khmer Rouge escort one. The man took five cigarettes out of the pack and didn't thank him. Joc ignored the bad manners but wouldn't offer the man another one. The ride down the poorly maintained road was bumpy. The highway had intentionally been allowed to deteriorate by the NVA to throw off American satellite cameras, but not so badly as to interfere with the heavy trucks hauling supplies to NVA troops in the sanctuaries lining the Cambodian border.

The Mercedes pulled off the road on a deeply

rutted trail and slowed to a crawl. Joc reached up and grabbed the hand strap to keep from bouncing on the back seat. The driver negotiated the jungle trail for a couple of kilometers and stopped when he reached a barbed-wire-and-bamboo gate.

Joc didn't need to be told that they had arrived at his new assignment. He exited the vehicle carrying his rucksack full of personal items. The guard waved at the soldier standing near the gate and laughed a welcome. Joc assumed that his escort was also a guard at the camp who had been sent to bring him back. The first thing to register to Joc's senses was the horrible smell of something rotting. He looked around the area but couldn't see the source as he followed the Khmer Rouge guerrilla into the split-bamboo hut. The guard threw his shoulders back and hefted his AK-47. Joc saw a fat man sitting behind a makeshift desk, and a naked American standing behind him against the wall. Red welts crossed the American's stomach just above the line his pubic hair formed and near the base of his penis.

"Welcome to Camp Phum Khnang Krapcu, Lieutenant!" The grossly fat Khmer Rouge captain smiled, showing a mouthful of rotting teeth.

"Thank you . . . sir."

The captain's eyebrows rose slightly. It was the first time an NVA or Vietcong officer had addressed him as sir.

Joc saw the fear in the POW's eyes. He could tell, even though the soldier was filthy and his face was covered with grime, that he wasn't older than nineteen, and small for his age. "Don't the Khmer Rouge have clothes for their prisoners?"

The captain stuck his lower lip out and shook his head. "We don't put clothes on our pigs or water buffalo . . . why should we dress these animals?"

"Doesn't the North Vietnamse Army supply you with prisoner uniforms?"

"Yes . . . but I find it profitable to sell them to our people." The captain felt no shame about his greed.

"Where will I be staying?"

"We have a house for you near the stream. Would you like to see it now?"

"Yes."

The captain spoke in rapid Khmer to the guard and then looked at Joc. "He will show you where to go."

Joc looked in the American POW's eyes and saw the fear spread. He could guess what the captain was going to do to the young soldier when he left. "I'll take him with me, sir. I might as well start my interrogations now."

A slow smile spread over the captain's face. "Please . . . I am getting bored with him anyway."

Joc beckoned the POW to follow him out of the hut. The man stumbled and nearly fell on the floor. The captain lashed out with his whip and caught the soldier's left buttock. A sharp scream slipped out between the man's bruised lips.

"Americans!" The captain's voice was filled with contempt. He waved them out the door with his whip. "They are worthless soldiers!"

Joc paused in the doorway and looked back into the room. "Have you *fought* the Americans . . . sir?"

"No, but if this is what they're like, I would enjoy it!"

"Don't judge the enemy by their prisoners . . . or you might be surprised." Joc nearly gagged from the smell of the POW standing behind him. The camp was built next to a stream, but obviously the POW's had not been allowed to bathe or wash the excrement off their bodies.

"The Khmer Rouge can defeat those women in a week!" The captain lifted a bowl of partially eaten rice off the small table behind his desk.

"Yes, sir!" Joc left the hut and followed the guard over to the new bamboo-thatched hut that had been built for him. The American POW crowded up close behind him, and the smell was almost overbearing. "Stand back!" Joc spoke in English.

The POW's face reflected his surprise. "You speak English, sir!"

"Of course." Joc looked inside his new home and was satisfied with the spartan furnishings.

"Sir . . . please don't let him have me again . . . I don't think I could stand it!"

Joc looked at the soldier's filthy face and saw the fear. "Stand what?"

The POW didn't answer his question, but repeated his plea. "Please, sir! The Vietcong are supposed to be under the Geneva Convention."

"We are guerrillas, not regular North Vietnamese

soldiers. You would have us shot as spies if we were caught." Joc could think only of his dead brother and uncle, and wondered why he felt pity for this American. "What is your name?"

"Specialist James Buchanan, sir."

"What unit were you with?"

Buchanan didn't hestitate. He was long past the point of giving only his name, rank, and serial number. "I was a machine-gunner with the First Division, sir."

"Did you kill any Vietcong, Specialist Buchanan?" Joc slipped into a slight French accent.

Fear flashed over the young POW's face. "Sir . . . sir . . . I was a soldier."

"A good answer, Specialist." Joc lit a cigarette. "How did you get captured?"

"We were fighting near the border and I got separated from my platoon and wandered across the border. I thought that I was heading south, but I guess I wasn't."

"You could have been heading south and still crossed into Cambodia, if you were in the fishhook area of South Vietnam." Joc could see that the POW was relaxing as he talked to him. "How long have you been here?"

A confused look covered the man's dirty face. "I don't know. Six months?"

"Where are the rest of the POW's?"

"There are nine of us in this camp, including one officer, but he'll be leaving soon."

"Really?" Joc inhaled deeply from his cigarette.

"Yes, sir. They ship the officers out of here

within a couple of days to another camp. Only enlisted men stay here"—he glanced over at the commandant's hut and the fear returned to his eyes—"with the Khmer Rouge."

"Take me to the compound."

When the POW turned around, Joc could see the welts from the quirt across his buttocks and back. He could also see dried blood on the insides of the soldier's legs.

Buchanan struggled to walk the short distance to the small cage that housed the eight American POW's. All of the men were naked and filthy. Joc spoke in rapid Vietnamese that confused the guards and then slowed down and spoke slowly in simple words. He ordered the guards to open the cage and take all of the POW's down to the stream. The guards hesitated and looked over at the commandant's hut. Joc placed his hand on his holster and repeated the order. Slowly one of the guards unchained the door and screamed at the POW's to come out. The guards punched and bullied the men all the way down to the stream.

Joc waited until the prisoners were standing along the bank of the shallow, fast-running water and then spoke in English. "Wash yourselves."

One of the older POW's flashed a hate-filled look at Joc. "Are you going to shoot us?" None of the men moved toward the water.

"No."

"You're lying."

"Why should I lie?"

"Fats in there said that the only time we could wash ourselves was right before he shot us."

"I just arrived here. I am the new assistant commander and I said to wash!"

"Why are you being nice to us?"

"I am not being nice to *you*." Joc almost gagged again. "I am being nice to *me*! I cannot stand the smell!"

Buchanan looked at the water and decided it was worth the risk. He stepped into the knee-deep stream and sat down. The cold water felt good on his cuts. He slowly reached down and washed the blood and dried feces off his body.

The other POW's saw the look on Buchanan's face and joined him in the stream. If they were going to die, they might as well be clean.

Joc watched the men scrub themselves, using sand off the bottom of the stream and tiny pieces of gravel. A couple of the men pulled grass growing on the streambank and used it as makeshift washcloths.

A scream came from the commandant's hut and the fat captain waddled out into the sunlight. He tried running to the streambank where Joc stood but could only manage a pathetic fat-man's roll. "Stop! Stop!"

The POW's scrambled from the stream and stood dripping on the grass.

"Is there a problem, sir?" Joc lit a Salem and offered the captain one.

The fat Khmer Rouge officer came to a sudden halt and took the cigarette. "American? Very good!"

"I have a whole pack for you in my rucksack." Joc smiled.

The captain turned his attention to the prisoners. "No washing! Animals do not wash!"

"We even allow our water buffalo to wash themselves in Vietnam." Joc kept smiling.

"Not these animals!" The captain's voice rose an octave. "No washing!" he screamed in Khmer.

Joc watched the faces of the POW's and realized that all of them except the officer were terrified of the fat man. "I have been given orders from the commanding general of the Central Office for South Vietnam to interrogate all of these prisoners, and I cannot do that when I am puking because of their smell!"

"You will get used to it!" The captain started drooling from the corner of his mouth and his eyes lost their focus.

Joc realized that the man must be insane. "Sir, let's go back to my hut and I'll get you the cigarettes." Joc turned the captain around gently and shoved him down the trail.

The night sounds from the jungle were a soothing lullaby for Joc. When he was a little boy, his mother had opened the windows in his bedroom wide and tucked in his mosquito net around the bed so that he could listen to the night sounds of the plantation. Now Joc lay on the bamboo mat he used for a mattress and smoked a cigarette in the dark. His thoughts slipped to his dead brother and the war. He could not remember when there hadn't been a war going on around him. He wondered what it would feel like to have peace. To be able to travel around Vietnam without having to carry a weapon.

A piercing scream from the direction of the commandant's hut quieted the jungle creatures. Joc sat up on his bamboo cot and listened. There was no sound on earth more horrible than a man screaming from the pit of his soul.

The man screamed again, and Joc strapped on his pistol as he walked in the dark toward the commandant's quarters. He could hear someone sobbing inside the structure as he drew near. The soft light coming from a kerosene lantern flickered through the cracks in the walls of the hut. Joc knocked on the side of the door panel and waited.

"Come in!"

Joc stepped through the cloth-covered entrance and saw the newly captured American Air Force captain spread-eagled on his stomach over the captain's desk. He could see streaks of fresh blood running down the man's legs. "What are you doing so late at night?"

The fat Khymer Rouge captain smiled. "Interrogating our new prisoner before we ship him out in the morning."

"I see, and has he told you anything yet?" Joc lit a cigarette. The guard who had escorted him to the camp reached out for one and Joc put the pack back in his pocket. The guard glared at him without trying to hide what he was thinking.

"Oh, yes, he has tried telling us everything he

knows, but I don't speak English very well!" The captain laughed so hard that the fat around his waist shook. The half-dozen guards inside the hut started laughing too. The American captain had been selected for their nightly entertainment, and they had placed bets on how fast he would break down. The guard who was torturing him at the time would win all the money.

Joc could see a bloody bamboo shaft and guessed what they had done with it. The pilot had burn marks covering most of the tender parts of his body. "I think you've had enough fun with him for one night. I need him alive."

The captain waved his hand for Joc to take him, and smacked his lips to signal that he was hungry. A guard stirred a bucket of some kind of stew and served the officer.

Joc used his hand to signal the guards nearest the American to carry him back to the prisoner compound. They looked at Joc and ignored his command.

"My men are too tired. They have worked hard all day. If you want to take him, then *you* carry him back to their cage, or you can leave him here." The captain burped.

Joc tried finding a place that wasn't bloody on the pilot to pick him up by, but gave up and grabbed the nearly unconscious man under the arms and carried him out of the hut.

The American groaned and opened his eyes. "The Geneva Convention . . . you must respect it!"

Joc shook his head. "You fool . . . you stupid

fool! You are a prisoner of the Khmer Rouge and they respect nothing but power and no one's laws but their own."

The guard at the cage looked at Joc in the moonlight in disbelief. He couldn't believe that an officer would touch one of the prisoners.

"Open the gate!" Joc's voice left no room for doubt who was in charge. The guard obeyed and Joc dropped the POW on the floor by the door. "Take care of him!" He could see in the moonlight that the other POW's were all awake and squatting together in the far corner, trying to keep warm by condensing their body heat.

The young specialist Joc had met earlier scooted over to the Air Force captain and turned him over on his back. There wasn't much more that he could do for him.

Joc watched the POW's shaking from the cold mist that was filling the valley. The temperature had fallen twenty degrees from the daytime high, and when you were naked, that was a major drop.

"Where is the supply hut?" Joc barked the question at the guard.

The Khmer Rouge soldier nodded down a narrow trail.

Joc had to use his flashlight to find the camouflaged building, and saw that a cheap lock and chain were used to secure the thick door. The chain was more for visual warning than for security, since the door was bamboo poles tied together by bamboo strips. Joc used his knife to hack through the bindings and within minutes was inside the small hut.

He selected a dozen sets of black peasant pants and shirts and another dozen NVA field blankets.

The guard at the cage nearly fell over with fright when he saw Joc return carrying the load of clothes and blankets that belonged to the commandant. The Khmer Rouge guards weren't even allowed to use the blankets for themselves!

Joc dropped his load in front of the gate. "Open it!"

The guard stood there in fear. "I cannot, Lieutenant! My captain will shoot me if I let you give his belongings to those animals!"

"Give me the keys! I will assume full responsibility!" Joc pointed his pistol at the guard's head.

The soldier obeyed Joc, but as soon as the Vietcong officer turned to open the cage, he ran off toward the commandant's hut.

Joc unlocked the cage door and threw the clothes and blankets inside. He didn't say a word, but stood there and watched the men scramble into their new clothes and wrap the blankets around their shoulders. He also noticed that the young American soldier he had met in the commandant's office wrapped a blanket around the naked captain before he covered himself.

Joc could hear the commandant huffing before he could see him on the path. He removed his pistol and held it at his side where it couldn't be seen.

"What are you doing with my supplies?" The captain's voice was as high-pitched as a young girl's.

"I have issued some of them to the POW's.

There is still plenty left in your storage area." Joc struggled to keep his voice level.

"I want them back now!"

"Captain! The Vietnamese Army issued those items to you for use on your prisoners! If you take back what I gave them, I will report this incident to my superior, and I guarantee that you will not receive any more supplies at all!" Joc waited a couple of seconds for the threat to sink in, then added, "If you allow them to keep what I've given them, I'll help you to recoup your losses."

"What if I just have you shot?" The captain's eyes gleamed red in the moonlight.

"That would cause my superior to send *two* officers to replace me, and one of them will be a major."

The fat man frowned. "You will help me to increase my supplies?"

"Yes."

"Fine."

The fat captain glared at the American specialist Buchanan, and as fear rose in the young soldier's eyes, Joc reacted quickly. "You! Come with me!" He beckoned the American to follow him. "I need you to wash my shirt before the blood ruins it!"

Buchanan followed Joc to the cold stream. When they were out of hearing range of the cage, he said, "Thank you, sir. Captain Strickland wouldn't have lasted the night in there."

Joc stopped at the streambank and removed his shirt. "The Vietnamese Army are soldiers, not barbarians!"

Buchanan waded into the water and started rinsing the blood out of the khaki shirt. He looked downstream, and the thought of escaping entered his mind.

"If you try it, I will have to shoot you."

Buchanan returned his attention to the shirt and began rubbing the cloth between his hands. Joc took a seat on the bank and listened to the night sounds returning. He hated being where he was; it was much better to fight in combat than to torture helpless men.

"Sir?" Buchanan had left the water and was holding out the shirt.

Joc snapped out of his deep thought and took the shirt. He pointed down the path to the POW cage.

"Sir, if you take me back there tonight, he'll send for me and—"

"What does he do that makes you so afraid of him?" The captain was insanely cruel, but this soldier was almost beyond terror.

"Please . . . shoot me." Buchanan started crying. "Just shoot me."

"Go back to the cage!" Joc's rough voice hid the confusion he felt. A Vietcong officer he could not show pity for the enemy or the Khmer Rouge would consider him weak. Buchanan obeyed and walked ahead of him down the path. The Khmer Rouge captain's snores could be heard even at the POW cage, and Joc could see the relief on Buchanan's face.

The young American paused at the gate and

looked back at Joc. "We all thank you, sir . . . for the clothes."

Joc gave a curt nod and walked away. He was glad the guards couldn't understand what the American had said to him.

Joc had not slept all night. He was trying to figure out a way to tell the colonel he would like another assignment. He could not torture people, and knew that he would end up killing the fat Khmer Rouge officer himself if he had to stay much longer. One day was too long to spend with that human pig. He had had very little respect for the Khmer Rouge before coming to the POW camp, and now everything he had heard about them had been confirmed. They were brave enough to kill women and children but were cowards when it came to fighting armed men.

Joc ground out his cigarette and placed the butt in the pile next to his bed on the floor. He had made his decision: he would go to the colonel and tell him exactly what was going on at the camp and ask that he be given command of the POW camp or be relieved of duty there. He felt better the minute he had made his decision.

The very first gray rays of sunlight were filtering through the jungle canopy as he stepped outside, feeling tired but relieved. He could smell rice cooking somewhere near the commandant's hut and started in that direction as he tucked in his shirt.

The sound of an automatic weapon firing dropped Joc on the ground in practiced reflex. The machine gun was joined by a heavy volley of automatic small-arms fire. Joc was confused; this was a well-defended NVA sanctuary only five kilometers from the Central Office for South Vietnam and a four-star NVA general, yet the weapons he heard were clearly American.

Joc's training took over. He removed his pistol and started running at a low crouch toward the POW cage. A Chinese Nung wearing a tiger suit and camouflage paint sprang out on the trail in front of him, facing in the same direction Joc was going. Joc shot him in the back and jumped over his body. As he ran on, he came to the conclusion that the Americans had launched a raid to free the POW's. When he reached the cage, he saw that the door was open. He heard screaming and stepped into the cage. The pilot was stretched out on the floor where Joc had left him earlier, except that now his throat had been cut. The commandant and two of his Khmer Rouge guards were cutting the throats of three more prisoners who were too weak to resist them.

"What are you doing?" Joc shouted.

The captain paused in his bloody task. "Orders! I am following orders! No POW's will be rescued!"

"You swine!" Joc reacted without thinking. He shot one of the Khmer Rouge soldiers in the back of the head and pointed his pistol at the second guard, who was starting to slash at Buchanan, who was trapped in a corner of the cage. Joc pulled the trigger and the bullet hit the Cambodian between the shoulder blades. The man spun around wearing a shocked look and Joc shot him again in the mouth. "Vietnamese are warriors! We do not butcher!" Joc glared at the fat captain, who had drawn his pistol and was starting to raise it. Buchanan dived for the fat captain's arm.

Joc hesitated for only a second before shooting the Khmer Rouge officer between the eyes. He felt an exhilarating sense of accomplishment, and then it sank in on him: the Khmer Rouge were his allies.

The sound of automatic weapons drew closer to the POW cage. Joc stepped back to the doorway, holding his pistol out in front of him. He could see the eyes of the remaining Americans and knew they were waiting for him to open fire.

Joc's eyes locked with Buchanan's for a second, and then Joc went out the door and started running down the trail away from the sound of the weapons until he met a platoon of North Vietnamese soldiers coming to reinforce the camp. Joc had heard them coming down the trail and had stopped to fire a couple of rounds behind him: they would think he was fighting a rear action.

"Am I glad to see you!" he told the NVA lieutenant in charge of the platoon. "Our POW camp was raided! Let's go!" He turned and led the NVA counterattack on the camp.

Joc approached the POW cage cautiously and found that it was empty except for the dead Khmer Rouge guerrillas. The NVA platoon swept the area and found two dead Americans and seven dead Chinese Nungs.

The platoon leader and Joc searched the dead

American bodies. "They are American Special Forces," Joc told the platoon leader. "We will not find anything of importance."

The platoon leader removed a Rolex watch and a twenty-*bot* gold necklace from one of the dead Americans. Joc knew from working with the Special Forces at Loc Ninh that the purpose of the gold chain was to bribe local tribesmen and villagers if the soldier was captured or wounded. The platoon leader looked questioningly at Joc.

"It's yours. I won't say anything," Joc said as he lit a cigarette and watched the platoon leader stuff the watch and chain—the equivalent of three years' pay—into his pockets.

CHAPTER 9

∞∞∞∞∞∞∞∞∞∞∞∞

DARK HOLES

MAY 1968

Mason watched the twins disassemble their new weapons on the poncho liner behind their bunker and wondered why a black command sergeant major would go out of his way to help a couple of white North Carolina mountain kids.

"Both of these weapons are blow-back-operated." Kenny shoved the thick spring back in behind the bolt of his Swedish-K.

"Yeah, I was surprised how easy they were to fire. The barrel hardly moved off target." Benjy used a cloth to wipe a light coat of oil over the parts as he reassembled his M-2 and screwed the silencer back on the barrel. "They're a little awkward and heavy, but they should work fine in the tunnels."

"We'll have our chance pretty soon. Sergeant Dixson said he would probably come back from brigade headquarters with some orders."

"Did he say where?" Mason had overheard their conversation. He was still a little aloof with the twins, but nowhere near as hostile as he had been before seeing them with Yates.

"He didn't say where, but there's talk up at Brigade that a couple tracker teams are going to be sent to work the tunnels and bunkers around Bu Dop."

"Shit! That's a Special Forces camp right on the fucking Cambodian border!" Mason dropped back down on the bunker and rested his head against two sandbags he had stacked up for a pillow.

"The colonel has worked out some kind of an agreement with the Special Forces C-Team commander that they would provide an early-warning screen with their commandos along the border for the American units, and we would provide artillery and other support for their A-Camps. We're part of the *other* support." Kenny looked at Mason. "It could be a lot worse . . . we could be humping the fucking jungle."

"You like those fucking Green Berets, don't you?" Mason was looking up at the sky with his hands folded behind his head. He was supposed to be on guard, but no one took base-camp-perimeter guard seriously during the daytime.

"We know quite a few of them." Benjy returned his attention to his submachine gun. "They're all-right guys."

Mason twisted his mouth before speaking. "Do you think the captain is going to let you keep those weapons?"

"Why not?" Kenny removed the empty magazines from the NVA chest pouches designed to hold AK-47 magazines and started reloading them from the boxes of 9mm ammunition he had scrounged from the A-Team at Loc Ninh.

"There's a division regulation about using unauthorized weapons." Mason was jealous because Yates had gone out of his way to get the twins the special gear.

"Who's going to tell him?" Kenny sensed Mason's jealousy.

"He probably already knows."

"Knows what?" Dixson joined the conversation as he approached his team's bunker.

"Mason thinks the captain is going to make us turn in our weapons and carry M-16's again." Benjy flashed a look at Mason.

"Forget about it. He's already mentioned it to me, and I convinced him we won't be able to get anyone to work the tunnels if we don't modify the equipment we carry. He's agreed to give it a chance, but the brigade commander isn't at all crazy about the idea."

Benjy shrugged. "Then we should take the brigade commander down in a hole with us sometime. That would change his mind quick!"

Dixson sat down in the shade. "We've got a mission!"

The twins stopped working on their weapons and looked at the sergeant. Eagle came out of the bunker, and Mason sat up.

"So?" Eagle took a seat next to Dixson. "Where

the fuck are they sending us? Are we going to work with a unit out of the First Division?"

"Bu Dop."

"I told you so!" Kenny pointed his finger at Mason.

"When?" Eagle leaned back against the cool sandbags. From the rumors that were floating around the division recon company, he knew that the area around Bu Dop was extremely hostile.

"As soon as we can load up." Dixson smiled sheepishly at his men.

"To-*fucking*-day!" Mason's head appeared over the edge of the bunker.

"As soon as we can load up," Dixson repeated, his voice becoming authoritative. "Molly is healed and ready for field duty."

"Oh! Our lives are run by a fucking dog now!" Mason's voice changed to a wail.

"You know as well as I do, Mason, that duty on a tracking team depends on the dog, and when she's ready . . . we go! If you don't like working with this team, you can go back to a line unit, or do like some of your buddies have done and *bitch* so fucking much that the general reassigns you to a *safe* job in the rear area!"

"Fuck you, Dixson!" Mason jumped down from the bunker and landed a couple of feet in front of the sergeant.

The twins watched to see what would happen next. They picked up their weapons just in case the sergeant was going to fight Mason.

Dixson stood up. "I'm tired of the bitching, man!

Tired of it!" Dixson was showing the strain he was under as team leader. "Either join this team or get your ass over to where you're happy . . . but the bitching has got to stop."

Mason looked slowly from face to face and stopped when he reached Eagle. "What do you say, *red* brother?"

"I agree with Dixson—there ain't no room for racial crap on this team." Eagle grinned. "We can start that shit when we get back to the States."

Mason nodded and smiled. "I've got to get my stuff ready."

The team realized they were going into a hot area when their Huey was escorted out to Bu Dop by four Cobra gunships. Two of the fighting helicopters flew behind them, down low, just over the treetops, and the other pair took turns weaving and dodging to the sides and out in front of the team's transport helicopter. Benjy sat next to his brother in the open side door and watched the dark green jungle slip by underneath their feet. The side-door gunner had motioned them to get their legs back inside, but the twins ignored him. They were enjoying the cool breeze created by the slipstream rushing over the helicopter's airframe.

One of the gunships veered off to the right and opened fire with its mini-gun while its sister ship maneuvered for a follow-up pass. A stream of green tracers attacked the air around the lead gunship but stopped instantly when a pair of rockets kissed the NVA gunner's camouflaged position.

Benjy nudged Kenny in the ribs and pointed down at the action as their helicopter banked away from the antiaircraft position in the jungle. The Cobras that had been hanging back in the rear shot forward and took over the duty of escorting the Huey the remainder of the way to Bu Dop.

The transport Huey dropped down on the marked helipad inside the camp's perimeter just long enough to unload the combat tracker team while the Cobra gunships buzzed around the surrounding jungle. The empty Huey's rotor blade changed pitch and the helicopter rose straight up from the pad and then turned slightly in midair to a new compass heading before taking off.

Three minutes after the tracker team touched the ground, the dust in the air was the only sign that a helicopter had landed. Dixson dropped down on one knee and brushed the dirt off Molly's back. She nuzzled up against him and he could feel her trembling. Molly didn't like helicopter rides, but she would obey Dixson and sit quietly next to him inside the shaking machine.

"Hot shit!" Two men left the A-Team's tactical-operations center and walked toward the tracker team. The shorter of the two hurried forward, wearing his short-brim field cap pulled down over his eyes. "Sergeant Major Yates told me you kids were in-country!"

Benjy tried identifying the familiar voice. "Rickman?"

"You can bet your skinny ass!" Rickman hugged

Kenny. "You little shit! You've grown a foot and gained ten pounds!"

Mason leaned over and whispered in Eagle's ear, "Do those fucking twins know *everybody* in Vietnam?"

Eagle shrugged. "Hey, it makes it easier for us."

"What are you doing out here at Bu Dop?" Benjy scanned the camp quickly and then looked back at Rickman.

"*Boy*! I built this camp . . . remember?"

"That's right! Sergeant Major Yates mentioned that you had built an A-Camp and then extended over here." Kenny adjusted his silenced Swedish-K on his shoulder.

Rickman's eyes caught the movement and commented, "So what are you kids doing out here with equipment like that?"

"We're a tracker team . . ." Benjy smiled and introduced Dixson to Rickman. "We lucked out and got to stay together." He looked over at his teammates. "That's Mason, the best tracker in a village, and that's Adam Eagle-Catcher. He's *almost* as good as Kenny and me."

"Shit!" Eagle shook hands with Rickman and the A-Team captain, who had simply stood by during the reunion.

"Well, let me show you where you can spend the night, and the captain will brief you on what's going on out here." Rickman led the way to the American teamhouse and showed the tracker team where they could put their gear. He put Dixson in a room with the operations sergeant and Mason and Eagle in an empty room. "He's in the field with one of our companies and won't be back until late tomorrow." Rickman saw the look on Eagle's face. "You're not intruding—we're used to sharing our billets with visitors." He returned his attention to the twins. "You kids can bunk in my room. I've got duty tonight."

"What kind of duty?" Kenny followed Rickman down the hall of the teamhouse and dropped his rucksack on the floor inside the room.

"Night watch. We've got a fairly decent night program going on out here, and we've got to monitor it constantly. It's proving to be better than night patrols."

"We'd like to see it in operation." Benjy spoke for both of them.

"Good! After you're fed, we'll go look at it." Rickman turned his attention to Dixson, who was starting to feel neglected. "The dog can stay with you if you like."

"Thanks."

"Come on over to the TOC and I'll show you what's going on and then you can decide just how much you want to get involved." Rickman qualified his statement. "We don't know the capabilities of your team."

Dixson nodded. He liked the attitude of the Special Forces men. They didn't try bluffing when they didn't know about a subject.

Mason waited until the NCO's left and then addressed Kenny. "How the fuck do you know so many of these Green Beret types?"

Kenny glanced at Benjy before answering. Yates had told them to low-key their involvement with Special Forces because a lot of people were jealous of the Green Berets and would take it out on the twins if they knew how involved they were with them. "My brother and I worked as scouts for the Special Forces training group back in North Carolina, and we've met just about every one of them who's taken training there in the past two years."

"So that's how you got so good at tracking!" Eagle thought he'd found the answer to a question that had been bothering him.

"Sorta." Benjy didn't want to tell Eagle that the twins were the ones teaching the Green Berets about tracking.

"Let's walk around the camp and see how it's set up." Benjy nudged his brother. "You guys want to come along?"

Mason shook his head. "I'm going to get some sleep."

"Me too." Eagle adjusted his rucksack on the cot for a headrest and stretched out. "Until it's time to eat."

"If Sergeant Dixson comes back soon, tell him we're walking around the camp." The twins left their rucksacks in Rickman's room but carried their weapons with them.

Dixson spent three hours being briefed in the TOC by the captain and Rickman. The area surrounding Bu Dop had been very hot a couple of weeks ago, and then suddenly there was nothing.

"That doesn't make sense." Dixson reached down

and scratched Molly behind the ears. "I know that the NVA will sometimes withdraw from an area, but your camp definitely is a thorn in their side."

The captain rubbed his upper lip, where he was trying to grow a mustache. "We agree. They're up to something, but we don't know what."

"That's why we requested your tracker team." Rickman tapped the map with his grease pencil. "We wonder if they've gone underground on us."

"Why would they do that so close to the border?" Rickman kept his eyes on the battle map. "They could just slip back to one of their Cambodian sanctuaries. That's easier than building an underground complex."

"We have a lot of activity around the camp at night, but during the daytime we can't find anything."

"Do you have patrols out at night?" Dixson didn't understand; if they had contact at night, then they should have some NVA kills.

"We've got a new system set up for detection. Starlight scopes and a new AN/PPS-4 radar that can detect personnel up to fifteen hundred meters." The captain rubbed his chin. "Like I said, we detect a lot of activity at night and mortar the shit out of them, but come daylight, we can't find a fucking thing! I know that we're not missing all of the time!"

"So that's the reason for your dog." Rickman reached over and patted her. "What's her name?"

"Molly." Dixson watched to see if Molly would growl, but she just leaned a little over to the side so that Rickman could scratch another place. "She's an *attack* dog." Dixson was getting a bit jealous because she was letting *everyone* pat her. First it was the twins, and now this Special Forces type was just taking over.

"Really?" Rickman continued scratching the dog. "My dad's a veterinarian and I've been raised around animals all my life. She sure fooled me."

Dixson tugged gently on the short leash and got Molly up on her feet. "We've got to get some rest before morning."

"I hope you're going to grab some chow with us." The captain stood and arched his back to get the stiffness out.

"We've brought plenty of C's."

"You're more than welcome. It's not stateside food, but it fills you up."

"Let me check with my team first. They might have already eaten."

"I'll walk you back. It's probably already dark outside by now." Rickman left the underground TOC with Dixson.

The twins sat next to Rickman in the tower and watched the sergeant scan the area, using the large tripod-mounted starlight scope. The scopes came in different sizes, from small hand-held units to those that could be mounted on rifles—and then the largest model, like the one Rickman was using.

The land-line telephone rang once and Rickman picked it up and listened for a minute before answering with a single whispered word. "Roger."

He moved the scope to an open area at the southwest corner of the camp and adjusted the focus before tapping Benjy and pointing for him to take a look.

The air in Benjy's throat stopped halfway out when he looked into the green light and saw the five-man column of NVA walking along the far tree line. The starlight scope brought in every detail with its eerie green light. Benjy could make out their facial expressions as they leaned forward to counter the weight in their packs.

Kenny tapped his shoulder and Benjy moved over so that his brother could see.

Rickman squeezed Kenny's shoulder and whispered, "Quiet."

The sound of mortar rounds leaving their tubes down in the camp drew Benjy's attention away from the scope. The 81's inside of the compound were opening fire on the NVA patrol. Kenny watched as the rounds impacted near the NVA and two of them fell over dead. The remainder of the patrol disappeared back into the jungle without a sound after they had located their dead comrades and removed their packs.

Kenny whispered in Rickman's ear, "How do they find them in the dark?"

"They use tiny pieces of reflector tape." Rickman sat down below the level of the sandbags and lit a cigarette behind his hat as he held it up to his face. "This goes on just about every night. We don't think they've detected the radar yet because we hide the dish during the day." Rickman took a long drag off his cigarette while Benjy kept watch with the starlight scope. "You kids better go get some rest. Tomorrow is going to be a long, hard day out there in the jungle."

Sergeant Rickman swallowed the two small white amphetamine tablets with his vitamins. It was asking for trouble, taking the strong stimulants, but there was no other way to maintain the rigorous demands on his body without collapsing from exhaustion. He took amphetamines to wake up in the morning and barbiturates to fall asleep. He smiled at his reflection in the small mirror on the wall of his room and spoke to his own image. "You fooled yourself during your last tour, old boy, but you're smarter now, aren't you?" Rickman winked at his reflection. "You're fucking addicted again, aren't you?"

The door opened and Kenny stuck his head in. "Are you talking to someone?"

"Only to myself."

"We're about ready to leave. Is the security platoon ready?"

"They should be. I woke them before first light when I got off duty." Rickman slipped his webgear harness over his shoulders and latched the pistol belt around his waist. He could feel the false energy from the pills reaching his limbs. "Let's go!"

"The tracking team is waiting by the main gate." Kenny glanced over at Rickman; he thought the sergeant was acting a bit strange.

"This should be a short patrol, so I'll take my

Thompson." Rickman removed the WWII forty-five-caliber machine gun from the pegs on his wall and got a bag of magazines. He had tried finding a drum for the weapon, but there weren't any available in Vietnam, only the classic magazines.

"It looks heavy." Kenny paused in the hallway and adjusted his Swedish-K's carrying strap over his shoulder. He carried the weapon with the silencer pointed down at the ground. None of the men were carrying their rucksacks, only combat gear and ammunition. The patrol was going to sweep the jungle in a two-kilometer circle around the camp and return before dark.

Dixson saw Rickman and Kenny coming toward him and got to his feet from his seat in the shade of the bunker. "Saddle up!" he commanded the rest of his team. The CIDG commando platoon had assembled and was waiting for the patrol to start.

The tracker team took the point for the small combat patrol. Dixson had Molly on a twenty-five-foot leash, with the twins working his flanks looking for visual sign. Molly became alert as they approached the area where the NVA had been mortared the night before.

Benjy signaled Kenny to join him and pointed to the fresh earth scattered over the decomposing vegetation under the jungle tree at the edge of the tree line. Kenny saw the blood on the ground and went over to check the location where the second NVA had fallen and found the same thing—blood and fresh dirt. The twins were sure of the sign and beckoned for Rickman and Dixson to join them for a verbal meeting. The twins had used hand signals that only the two of them understood.

Kenny leaned over so he wouldn't have to speak above a soft whisper. "The NVA last night were carrying dirt in their rucksacks." He looked for a reaction in Rickman's eyes.

"Dirt?" Dixson wrinkled his nose.

"They're digging a tunnel and they don't want it discovered." Benjy joined the conversation. "That's why they're backpacking the dirt out."

Rickman frowned. Benjy's comment explained all of the activity around the camp and the lack of contact with the NVA. "See if the dog can back-track their trail."

Dixson flashed a dirty look at Rickman but didn't say anything. He had taken Rickman's comment as an insult; there was no doubt that Molly could backtrack the enemy's trail.

The trail wove in and out of the trees in an intentional serpentine pattern so that any patrol from the camp would not be able to see the trail that circled the A-Camp in the jungle. Molly followed the NVA scent with ease to a position exactly 180 degrees from the camp's main gate. She stopped and alerted at a thick stand of young bamboo.

Dixson warned Rickman, and the commando platoon spread out and took up prone positions while the tracker team checked the area. The entrance to the bamboo thicket was so well camouflaged that they would have missed it completely if it hadn't been for Kenny looking up into a nearby giant mahogany tree. One of the huge limbs of the tree reached out and ran parallel to the edge of the bamboo thicket. Kenny signaled with his eyes for Benjy to look up. He saw the worn marks in the bark on the limb and smiled. The NVA were extremely cagy. They had used a rope to lift the rucksacks filled with dirt over the bamboo so that a patrol from the camp wouldn't see a trail leading into the stand of thick undergrowth.

Kenny signaled for Dixson to bring Molly over to where he was standing and pointed up at the thick branch. Dixson missed the clue and Kenny used one of the team hand signals that represented extreme caution—the opening and closing of his left hand. Eagle dropped down in a low combat crouch and searched the jungle for the clue the twins had found, along with Mason, who was all business.

Kenny entered the bamboo stand, using the silencer on his Swedish-K to part it. Benjy was close behind, followed by Molly. Ten feet into the thicket they came to the center of a perfectly cut-out circle.

Molly alerted and Kenny fired. The silenced 9mm weapon made barely any noise beyond the bolt sliding back and forth. The NVA guard slumped over and fell into the clearing from his hiding place. He had been given strict orders not to fire and give away his position unless the actual entrance to the tunnel had been discovered, and then it would be only to alert the men digging inside to escape through one of the other entrances or vents.

Molly went over to what looked like a wall of bamboo and alerted again. Once the dog had shown them where to look, the twins could see the camouflage mat and pulled it aside to reveal a four-foot hole that was the tunnel's entrance. The unusual entrance told the twins that they were dealing with a major engineering project. Normally the entrances to NVA tunnel systems were very small so that the chance of detection was lessened. The large entrance told the twins that the tunnel down below was huge, designed for a large number of men to move swiftly through to their objective.

Rickman joined the twins and whistled softly through the gap in his front teeth. "Shit! They're digging under our berm into the A-Camp!"

Kenny glanced over at his brother and smiled. He had been about ready to say the same thing. "You ready, Benjy?" Kenny removed his miner's cap from the small field pack on Benjy's lower back and hooked the battery onto his pistol belt.

'Where the fuck do you kids think you're going?" Rickman grabbed Kenny's shoulder.

"There's only one way to know for sure if they're digging toward your camp or just building an underground bunker system, and that's to shoot an azimuth aboveground in the direction of the camp and repeat the process underground." Kenny watched Benjy shoot the azimuth with his compass as he talked to Rickman.

"The odds are that at least a couple NVA are down there!" Rickman didn't like the idea of the twins going underground. "I'll call back and have our engineers bring out some CS tear gas and we'll blast the tunnel."

"That's a good idea, but first we've got to check

it out." Benjy unbuckled Kenny's small field pack and removed his miner's cap. "Don't worry, Sarge . . . we'll be careful."

It was Benjy's turn to take the lead, and he left his M-2 submachine gun aboveground and used his silenced 9mm pistol. Kenny followed with his Swedish-K for backup firepower. For Rickman's sake, both of the twins were acting with a lot more bravado than they were actually feeling as they slipped down through the dark entrance of the tunnel.

The beam of Kenny's headlamp illuminated the sides of the damp earth. The twins waited for a couple of minutes until their eyes adjusted to the different light and they recovered from the initial fear of entering the claustrophobic tunnel. Benjy had tried hiding his fear of being underground, but Kenny almost instinctively felt it. It had been much easier for Kenny working the tunnels than it had been for Benjy, and that was one of the very few differences between the twins.

Benjy signaled that he was ready to move down the entranceway to the main shaft, which they both knew wasn't very far away. They moved slowly and relied on their hearing much more than their eyes for information. Benjy saw the wall in front of him and knew the tunnel was making a sharp turn. He inhaled a deep lungful of the earthy air and slipped forward with his pistol making the turn ahead of him. The main shaft appeared and was almost a welcome sight because it was so wide. Benjy made the turn, followed closely by his brother with the submachine gun ready. There were a dozen NVA rucksacks lining the far wall and a neat arrangement of digging tools. The main shaft was wide enough for three men to walk abreast, but the twins had to bend over to keep their heads from hitting the top. Benjy signaled Kenny that he was going to shoot an azimuth and tucked his pistol in his belt while Kenny covered him. The light from Kenny's headlamp couldn't reach the end of the tunnel. It had to go at least two hundred meters, and there still might be more after that if there was a bend in it.

Benjy signaled that they should move out, and maintained the lead position even though they could have walked abreast. NVA tunnels were filled with pits and booby traps, and it would have been foolish to enter unknown ground side by side.

Kenny waited until his brother was ten meters ahead of him before he started following him against the right side of the wide tunnel, while Benjy hugged the left side to give Kenny as much room as he could for the submachine gun, just in case they ran into something. NVA tunnels usually had subtunnels running from them, which were used for storage or medical and sleeping quarters. You couldn't see the branches until you were right on top of them.

Benjy stopped and turned off his headlamp. Kenny did likewise. They waited in total darkness for their eyes to adjust to the lack of light, and slowly a faint yellow glow appeared ahead of them. Neither of the twins could judge the distance in the odd setting, but they knew the light had to be less than fifty meters away.

Kenny heard the soft snap coming from Benjy's fingers and knew his brother was moving forward slowly. He followed with his shoulder rubbing against the wall to keep him oriented. Kenny felt the fear in his stomach and knew that Benjy had to be terrified.

The glow became brighter as they drew closer to the opening in the side of the tunnel. Kenny could see a faint outline of his brother in the dim light when he reached the side cave, and felt his breath leave his lungs. He hadn't realized how long he had been holding his breath. Benjy knew that Kenny could see him, and signaled with his hand for him to hurry forward. Kenny reached the opening and looked in at the dozen sleeping NVA soldiers. A tin kerosene lantern had been turned down to its lowest possible level and was burning with a faint yellow-blue glow.

Kenny stepped forward and pushed the safety off with his thumb just as one of the NVA sat up and squinted at the dark opening. He was about to say something when Kenny pulled the trigger. Benjy used his silenced pistol to back up his brother. Most of the sleeping NVA soldiers didn't even wake up from their exhausted sleep. Only one of them groaned during the silent execution.

Benjy entered the small cave and made sure all of the NVA were dead. He saw a portable radio leaning against the side of the cave and tilted it toward him so that he could read the frequency setting on the dial before backing out of the cave to join his brother. Kenny had turned his headlamp back on and was searching for any more side caves to the main shaft. The face of the digging appeared as a rough earthen wall compared to the smoothed sides where the NVA had taken their time to square and level. Benjy had to give them credit for doing good work.

Kenny went over to the face of the tunnel and started pacing off the distance back to where they had entered. Benjy followed. The side entrance appeared, catching both of them off-guard. The way in had seemed much longer than the way back.

Benjy frowned and looked at the entrance. A muffled noise was coming from up above. Kenny in the lead, stuck his head out of the hole. The roar of automatic weapons firing and the bright sunlight forced him to duck back down inside. "Shit! There's a firefight going on topside!"

"Fuck! Just what we need!" Benjy had crawled next to Kenny and was touching cheeks with him when he spoke. The words sounded like explosions in his ears. "What are we going to do?"

Rickman had been watching the entrance and saw Kenny peek out and then slip back down. He scurried over to the opening and yelled down inside, "Come on! Move your asses!"

The twins obeyed and crawled out into the light, blinking and desperately trying to adjust their eyes to the painful searing rays of sunlight filtering through the layers of dense bamboo. To Rickman and the rest of the patrol, the light was dim.

"Damn! Where were you guys?" Dixson was

holding Molly by her collar and was curled up next to a large anthill.

Benjy could barely make out Dixson's outline. "What kind of fucking question is that!"

An AK-47 opened fire less than ten meters away and was answered by a volley from the commandos.

"You guys have been underground for over an hour!" Dixson sounded pissed. "The NVA hit us only a couple of minutes after you guys entered the tunnel. We've been waiting for you!"

"Let's get the fuck out of here!" Rickman started moving backward. "They're pissed off!" The NVA had taken heavy casualties trying to assault the platoon. The camp was firing directly from its western berm and had been dumping hundreds of mortar rounds on the NVA positions and had stayed in contact with the platoon. Rickman had been forced to wait for the twins to come back aboveground. He couldn't call in heavy artillery or air strikes because he didn't know where the twins were underground.

At the same time the platoon started withdrawing, the NVA had decided that they had enough, and the two combat units separated their contact.

The platoon and combat tracker team waited at the edge of the jungle while the camp commander laid down a heavy volley of artillery and mortar fire around them. Rickman divided his platoon in two and took the first two squads across the open ground to the front gate, which remained closed until the very last second. The tracker team and the last two squads rushed the gate at a full run. Kenny could almost feel the NVA bullets striking his back as he ran as fast as he could toward the gate and relative safety.

"Fuck!" Rickman was lying against the berm inside the camp, breathing hard. "Never fucking again!"

"Never again what?" Dixson was leaning over trying to get his breath. The only member of the patrol who wasn't winded from the hard run was Molly. She sat on her haunches waiting for the humans to get their acts together.

Rickman took a couple dozen deep breaths before he could answer. "Let anybody go underground without a radio."

"I second that shit for sure!" Dixson agreed.

"What the fuck were you guys doing under there?" Mason queried the twins.

"It sure didn't seem an hour to us." Benjy looked at Kenny for confirmation.

"More like twenty minutes." Kenny got back up on his feet. "We had a little run-in with some NVA down there. They were sleeping and we zapped them." He looked at his brother. "I counted eleven."

"I counted twelve." Benjy shrugged.

"What in hell are all of you talking about?" The A-Team captain stood in front of them with his hands on his hips.

"We discovered a tunnel, Captain." Rickman had regained his breath but not his strength, and he remained sitting. "It looks like all of that movement at night was the NVA hauling dirt out of a tunnel."

"We shot a couple of azimuths . . ." Kenny removed the almost empty magazine from his weapon and replaced it with a full one as he talked. "Eighty-five degrees was the main tunnel. It ran almost due east from the tree line."

"And it was a hundred and seventy-three meters long from where we entered it."

The captain took a couple of seconds to orient himself in the camp, and then shock flashed across his face. "Those motherfuckers are almost directly under our western berm! They were digging their way inside our camp!"

"No shit, sir!" Rickman couldn't help making the comment. The tunnel explained a lot to the Special Forces men. "I bet if we do a little research on all of our contacts in the past couple of months, we'll see that the NVA have been keeping us away from the tunnel site." He looked at Molly. "If it wasn't for her, they would have gotten away with it."

"Can you give a dog a valor award?" The captain grinned. "She damn sure deserves it!"

"Sir, we'd better blow that tunnel before they can use it." The team's senior engineer had joined them at the gate.

"Yes! Come and show us where the tunnel runs." The captain started walking to the west wall of his camp, followed by the twins and the rest of the tracker team. They all climbed the earth berm and cautiously looked out over the open ground. The mortar teams were still dropping an occasional round in the jungle where the firefight had taken place to prevent the NVA from sweeping the area.

The team's executive officer was assembling two CIDG companies to sweep the perimeter of the camp before dark.

"You can see the edge of the bamboo thicket." Rickman pointed out the area to the captain, who was using his compass to shoot a back-azimuth.

"It should intersect our berm about here . . ." He was walking along the top of the berm as he spoke, ignoring the possibility of an NVA sniper watching him from the tree line. The captain stopped walking and stomped his foot down in the loose soil. "Here!"

The twins sat inside the berm bunker eating C rations and watching the team engineers placing shape charges along the azimuth the captain had taken. The executive officer had secured the western side of the camp with the CIDG companies and had swept the area where the firefight had taken place. They had found twenty-two dead NVA soldiers and a number of blood trails leading back into the jungle.

"Fire in the hole!"

The twins could hear the engineer call out the warning that he was about to detonate the series of shape charges. The whole bunker shook and a cloud of dust was sucked up off the ground from the tremendous explosion that was directed down into the earth.

"Come on, let's get up on top where we can see." Benjy led the way out of the bunker to the roof and waited with his brother until the dust cleared.

"Un-fucking-believable!" The captain was standing next to the bunker with his mouth hanging open. A depression in the ground ten feet wide and four feet deep went from the edge of the jungle to the berm surrounding the camp. A section of the earth wall between two of the fighting bunkers had collapsed where the very front edge of the NVA tunnel had stopped. "Another week and they would have been inside the camp!"

CHAPTER 10

RED STAR EXPRESS

July 4, 1968

Command Sergeant Major Yates stood in front of the large Plexiglas window in his B-Team office and watched the different-colored hand flares burst in the night sky. He smiled and shook his head. The troops were celebrating the Fourth of July by firing tracer rounds in their weapons and popping multicolored hand flares. The combat fireworks display was pretty, but would make the supply officers pull out their hair trying to replace the huge amounts of wasted munitions.

Yates went back to his desk and picked up the top sheet of yellow telex paper to read again the information the POW's had given on the Cambodian POW camp in Mimot. There was little doubt in his mind that the Vietcong lieutenant who had saved the five POW's lives was the same Joc that had worked for them at the Loc Ninh Special

Forces camp. The description was just too close for coincidence. Yates wished he could have debriefed Specialist Buchanan personally, but the soldier had been medevacked back to Japan and would be in the States before the end of the week. Buchanan had been the one who had talked the most to the VC lieutenant and would be able to provide the most information. Yates decided that he would wait until Buchanan reached the States and would try to link up with him on a MARS radio hookup.

The telexed intelligence summary lying on his desk under the POW report was very disturbing to Yates. It had been compiled by the First Division's special security unit and had a high rating for accuracy. The report could also be supported by the Bu Dop camp commander's report. What bothered Yates was that a member of the combat tracker team who had been down in the tunnel had reported seeing an NVA radio with the Special Forces command frequency set on the dial. The frequency was one of the top-secret command nets that were used only when an A-Camp was under attack and communication was extremely important. Yates needed to know how the NVA knew the frequency.

"Sergeant Major?" Bradshaw stuck his head in the office doorway.

"Yes, Bob." Yates turned away from the window.

"It was the twins who were in the tunnel." Bradshaw had just gotten off the radio with the Bu Dop operations sergeant. "They've done a good job out there."

Yates nodded. "Thanks for making the call for me, Bradshaw. I needed to know for sure."

"It wasn't much of a problem getting through to the camp this late at night." Bradshaw changed the topic. "It's a pity we didn't get those twins in Special Forces. Do you know what they could do in one of the Greek Projects or with SOG?"

"It's not over yet." Yates slid the yellow telex message back down on his desk. "At the rate they're going, they'll be buck sergeants before they leave Vietnam, and then we can probably get them into training group."

"I can see it now!"

"See what?"

"Those twins going through the Pisgah training!" Bradshaw started laughing. "Shit, they'll end up teaching the cadre!"

"Yes, we'll have to make some modifications for them if we send them through Phase III." Yates's mind was still on the messages. "This VC that was working out at Loc Ninh is starting to bother me."

"How's that, Top?" Bradshaw took a seat in one of the rattan chairs near the sergeant major's desk.

"I've run a number of checks on him, and even the South Vietnamese secret-police reports have nothing on him."

"So? Why worry, then? He probably just got scared when they started investigating him and he's hiding with a relative in Loc Ninh." Bradshaw had heard about the blue-eyed VC.

"The Provisional Reconnaissance Unit has targeted his aunt for termination." Yates glanced over his desk at Bradshaw.

"Shit! If he's not a VC, he'll be one when those fucking butchers are finished with his aunt!" Bradshaw sat up straight in his chair. "Who turned them on to her?"

"You know the rules." Yates looked down on his desk and fingered through the yellow copies of the intelligence summaries until he found the one he was looking for. "She's appeared on three confirmed lists as an enemy agent and her name has gone on the elimination sheet. In fact, she's number three for all of South Vietnam."

"That means she won't last very long!" Bradshaw lit a cigarette and softly blew out the match. "I think they're making a really big mistake, especially when the POW's reported that her nephew saved their lives during the prisoner snatch at Mimot."

Yates knew that once the PRU had you on their assassination list, your chances of living for very long were slim, unless you had a way of quickly getting out of the country. Yates took a seat behind his desk and turned to look back out the window. His thoughts returned to his last tour of duty in Vietnam and the meeting he had had with the intelligence community at the Special Forces headquarters in Nha Trang. He had been the only person disagreeing with formation of the PRU organization. All of the Vietnamese in the PRU's were recruited out of South Vietnamese prisons and all of them were known murderers and psychopathic butchers. They had been promised their freedom if they served *honorably* for three years with a PRU assassination squad. The Americans commanding the squads weren't very much higher on the human-development ladder than the South Vietnamese they led. Headquarters had overruled Yates's hostile objection to the formation of the PRU's and had relieved him of duty as the senior operations NCO at the headquarters because of his stand. It wasn't that Yates didn't believe in eliminating double and triple agents. That wasn't the point. It was *how* the PRU was going to be used that had bothered him, and the first six months the PRU teams were in operation had proved extremely embarrassing and had required a series of major operational modifications. The PRU squad that went into operation up in Da Nang had used their newfound freedom and special equipment to assassinate all of the lawyers, prosecutors, judges, and witnesses who had testified against them during their trials. A bloodbath of loyal South Vietnamese went on for two weeks until the CIA and the South Vietnamese secret police identified one of the PRU men and solved the problem. The members of that team were sent back to prison, where they mysteriously all died of a fever within a month, and the two Americans in charge of the team had an unfortunate boating accident and drowned off an island in Da Nang harbor. The Da Nang incident hadn't prevented the organization from operating, only added the requirement that suspects had to appear on three separate intelligence lists before they could be recommended for elimination.

"Bradshaw, call Nha Trang and see if we can get her name removed from the PRU list, at least until we find out the status of Joc Rochambeau, alias Lieutenant Joc Vo Nguyen."

"Now?"

"Please. You know how fast the PRU work, especially when they're assigned women and children."

The Buddhist monks walked with their hands hidden in the cuffs of their long orange-yellow robes. Both of the men had their heads shaved, and if a trained observer had looked closely, he would have seen that the skin on top of their heads was several shades lighter than the skin on their faces.

The older monk pulled down on the tiny cord at the gate and a pleasant bell tinkled their arrival. The gardener hurried over to the wrought-iron gate and opened it quickly without questioning why the brightly clothed monks were visiting his mistress. She had been very depressed lately since the death of her husband. The first month had been fine, but she seemed to get more depressed as time went by.

"Is your mistress home?" The voice of the middle-aged monk was extremely soft.

"Yes, she is in the shrine." The gardener pointed in the direction of the small concrete building in the center of the garden.

The monks bowed and smiled their thanks before leaving the old man to prune his mistress's favorite Chinese apple tree. He had spent only a few minutes working around the tree when the monks left the shrine and slowly walked back up the path.

They nodded as they passed and let themselves out of the gate.

The gardener frowned. The monks hadn't been inside the shrine long enough to have said a single prayer. He looked worried and started walking over to the red-framed doorway. Perhaps she had been feeling ill and sent the monks away. If that were the case, he would make her go inside and rest.

The old man shoved the silk curtain aside and stepped into the cool air of the shrine. He saw his mistress lying on her back with her arms crossed on her chest. His old eyes saw that there was blood covering the front of her *cao-die*. He knew she was dead. The single bullet from the silenced pistol had entered the back of her head and blown away the front of her forehead and face. What made the old man gasp was the wrinkled old breasts that had been placed on the altar of the shrine in front of the gold-plated Buddha. The gardener was a retired Vietcong soldier and had done many evil things during his tour of duty, but he had never seen anything so sacrilegious. He left the shrine and started walking as fast as he could toward the gate. Pain racked his old body, but he ignored it. The monks couldn't have gotten far away on foot. He left the garden gate unlocked and hurried down the street and turned toward the main business and market district of Loc Ninh. The streets were filled with farmers bringing their produce to market and women shopping. He could see the bright robes of the monks in the distance and increased his pace, closing the gap between them. The monks were walking casually, showing no concern that they might be followed.

A taxi driver parked next to one of the stores saw the old man struggling to hurry somewhere and looked in the direction he was going in. "Old man! Do you need a ride home?"

The old gardener stopped and looked into the young man's eyes. He gave a secret sign and the taxi driver smiled and gave the correct countersign. "May I be of assistance to you in your old age?"

"Please. I need a ride for only a couple of blocks." He looked down the street and saw the orange-yellow robes growing smaller.

The taxi driver wove his three-wheeled cycle cab through the crowd and caught up to the monks in a matter of minutes.

"Thank you . . . comrade." The old man whispered the last word under his breath and added, "I can make it the rest of the way on my own. You had better leave very quickly when you let me out."

The old man shuffled as fast as he could until he was directly behind the two monks. He reached under his shirt and removed the forty-five caliber pistol he always carried from its shoulder holster and shot both of the monks in the back of the head.

The crowd parted around him and stood watching as he tore open their robes to reveal their hidden weapons. He paused to look at the faces surrounding him and then slowly started shuffling back up the street toward his mistress's villa.

* * *

Bradshaw tore the message off the telex machine and sighed deeply. The PRU list of successful missions had come over the machine, and the code was simple: each person on their hit list had a number, and when a person had been terminated, his number appeared on the daily report as a successful mission. If the hit failed or the intended victim just disappeared, then the number would appear as a pending operation. Lieutenant Joc Rochambeau's aunt's number was the first number on the successful list.

Bradshaw handed the message to Sergeant Major Yates. "Bad news, Top."

Yates read the first couple of lines and shook his head. "They fucked up! We might have had a chance of turning him to our side, but not after this!"

The NVA captain stood at rigid attention next to the entrance to the underground concrete bunker complex. He wore an immaculate uniform, and even the leather on his brown holster had been highly shined.

Joc paused in front of the officer and saluted. "Lieutenant Joc Vo Nguyen reporting, sir!"

"Wait here, Lieutenant, and I will see if he is ready for you." The captain nodded for the sergeant standing across from him to take over and disappeared into the bunker.

The general stood in front of the battle map and listened to the staff brief him on the proposed invasion plans. He glanced at the captain when he saw movement in his peripheral vision. "Yes, Captain?"

"Please excuse me, General, this will take only a moment." He conferred briefly with the general and then the two men walked out of the briefing room.

Joc came to attention when the general entered the small room he was waiting in. He couldn't believe his eyes. He was looking at the North Vietnamese Napoleon, General Vo Nguyen Giap.

"I am so sorry to hear about your aunt's death." General Giap was well aware of the effect his presence had on people and waited patiently for the young lieutenant to get control of himself before continuing. "I hear that she was assassinated by a PRU squad dressed as Buddhist monks."

"Yes, sir." Joc fought to gain control of his voice. He sounded like a schoolboy.

"You have suffered a number of losses recently, with your brother and uncle also being killed. I heard too, that the POW camp you were assigned to was raided and you lost your commander during that fight." The general allowed sarcasm to seep into his voice when he mentioned the Khmer Rouge officer. He tolerated the Khmer Rouge only because Ho Chi Minh had signed an alliance with their leader, but he had asked Ho Chi Minh a number of times for permission to wipe out the whole Khmer Rouge organization and had been denied.

"It is an honor to serve as a soldier for our fight for freedom from the colonial lackeys!"

General Giap allowed the trace of a smile to

appear at the corners of his mouth. "You are a loyal patriot and that's why I want you to take command of the 133rd Signal Company."

Joc's eyebrows rose but he regained control of his expression and waited for the general to continue.

"The position requires the rank of major, but that has already been taken care of." Giap smiled and waited for his comment to sink in. Joc had been promoted, skipping over the rank of captain.

"Thank you, sir!"

"You will earn it. We need your services down in Cu Chi."

"Cu Chi, sir?" Joc almost bit his tongue for interrupting the senior general.

"Yes, Major. The 133rd Signal Company is responsible for monitoring all the radio traffic out of General Westmoreland's headquarters. Do you know who General Westmoreland is?"

"Yes, General! He's the American commander for all the invading troops in South Vietnam." Joc was impressed by the assignment and the trust General Giap was showing in him. There were hundreds of full-blooded Vietnamese who would give anything for the chance to work for General Giap. Joc was being honored by the most powerful person in North Vietnam, with the exception of Ho Chi Minh.

"He isn't important . . . nothing more than one of their West Point pawns with a very poor history for military planning." The smile left Giap's face. "But there are excellent officers serving on his staff who have been causing our forces a great deal of trouble." Giap's tone became gloomy. "We just suffered a disastrous defeat at Loc Ninh, as you well know."

Joc was shocked that a senior NVA officer would speak openly to him about the loss of the Ninth VC Division and a regiment of NVA.

Giap saw the look on the young officer's face and added, "You will hear much more about what is going on in South Vietnam when you take command of the 133rd Signal Company. We have our best intelligence teams there, and every single person in the company speaks fluent English."

"Thank you for the honor, sir!" Joc said, and kowtowed in front of the general.

"I expect you to work hard and provide the intelligence we need for our upcoming operations."

"You have my loyalty, General!"

Giap left the room and returned to the briefing room. It wasn't often that he would personally assign a major to a mission, but the 133rd Signal Company would be playing a key role in the major operation they were planning for the very near future. That operation would change the whole course of the war and, with just a little luck, win it for his forces.

"Are you pleased with my choice, sir?" This question came from the commanding general of the Vietcong Ninth Division, who was sitting at the far end of the briefing room's conference table.

"He is part French, and that bothers me," General Giap answered reflectively.

The man took his cue and answered, "His family

was butchered by Diem's henchmen. I am sure that he is a loyal communist."

"Of that there is no question, but how loyal is he to *us*?"

Joc arrived at the supply command center and reported to the lieutenant colonel who commanded the operation. He would be assigned a supply unit to travel with until he reached Tay Ninh City, where he would link up with an underground VC intelligence-gathering unit that would take him to the 133rd Signal Company in the tunnels of Cu Chi. Joc had heard stories that a VC soldier could travel from Cambodia to Cu Chi without ever having to come aboveground from the elaborate tunnel network dug during the war with the French. Cu Chi supposedly had underground hospitals that were as good as the ones aboveground, and complex airlock systems that prevented the Americans from gassing the whole network. Joc was looking forward to his new command.

He squeezed the front tire on the bicycle the quartermaster lieutenant had issued to him. He was not required to carry supplies now that he was a major, but even his uncle had volunteered to haul supplies when he was making an administrative trip between South Vietnam and the NVA sanctuaries in Cambodia. The bicycle had been modified to carry a heavy load of supplies instead of a passenger. The seat had been removed and a wooden platform installed in its place. A long rod had been welded across the handlebars so that a person walking next to the bike could push the load uphill by holding on to the seat grip and handlebar rod. Each bike could hold about three hundred pounds of supplies.

The short blast from the quartermaster's whistle signaled that it was time to move south. The wide path became a one-way highway filled with hundreds of NVA soldiers and bicycles. The men had been resting along the side of the trail at intervals of about twenty-five meters so that a single artillery round couldn't catch more than two bikes at once.

The walk into South Vietnam was almost enjoyable for Joc. There was a surrounding network of patrols to warn them of any enemy night ambushes as they moved swiftly down the road-and-path network toward Nui Ba Den.

The trail curved slightly and started a gradual uphill climb. Joc leaned forward into his load and let his mind turn to the Americans. He had never understood why they allowed themselves to get sucked into a land war in Asia, especially in Vietnam. Before the war, he had respected the intellect of the Americans and had actually wanted to go to college in California. His father had become livid and told him that at least one of his sons would attend Saint Cyr in France, the elite military academy. Joc wondered what his father would have thought if he knew that one of his sons was attending a military academy in Moscow and the other two had served with the Vietcong. Joc shrugged his shoulders and pushed harder. The Americans had been suckered by the French government into supporting their colonialist ideas after World War II and had refused to help Ho Chi Minh establish a free democratic government. Joc wondered how many Americans knew that Ho Chi Minh had gone to the Americans *first* for help and had been turned down. American politicians had decided to support their allies even though they were wrong in their colonial conquests. Any man with a little vision in the 1950's could have seen that all of the Asian and African governments that had been suppressed by the European powers were not going to accept further foreign rule after World War II. France's pathetic defense of her homeland had shown the Vietminh freedom fighters that the French were paper tigers who could be overthrown.

Joc shook his head as he walked next to the bike. He could not understand the Americans; of all the people on earth, they should have been the first ones to understand how the Vietnamese people felt about a colonial government thousands of miles away telling them how they must live their lives. Joc knew the price his father had paid when he openly took a Vietnamese wife. It was accepted for a Frenchman to have a Vietnamese mistress, but highly unacceptable to marry one and then demand that the offspring be treated as French and allowed to go to private French schools and clubs. His father had won most of his fights for acceptance with the local French authorities, and his children had been allowed to attend private schools, but he himself had never been able to penetrate the exclusive all-French Polo Club in Saigon with his Vietnamese wife.

The great American soldier-stateman Marshall had been able to see the future for Europe, and MacArthur had proved a better statesman than general when it came to rebuilding Japan, but none of them could see the struggle for freedom that was going on in Vietnam—a struggle that paralleled America's own.

The NVA soldier pushing the bicycle ahead of Joc pulled over to the side of the trail. The quartermaster officer in charge of the bicycle convoy had called for a short break. Joc unscrewed the cap on his American canteen and took a long drink of water and continued thinking about the American involvement in Vietnam. He could understand both sides of the issue. America had just finished a major world war and wanted peace. She had been sucked into a ground battle in Korea and had always been uncomfortable fighting a battle next to China. He could understand America's reluctance in getting involved in Vietnam—another country that touched borders with China. He could understand why the United States refused to help Ho Chi Minh throw off the French yoke, but what he couldn't understand was why, after the Americans had turned down the just cause of Ho Chi Minh's government for a united democratic Vietnam, they supported the criminal regime of the South Vietnamese Ngo Dinh Diem.

The quartermaster officer signaled them to start down the moonlit path again. Joc pulled his bicycle up off the ground and started along the trail, keeping his distance from the man in front of him. He could see the shape of Nui Ba Den, the Black Virgin Mountain, looming up in front of him. They were getting close to Tay Ninh City and would reach it easily before daylight. Joc's thoughts slipped back to the American POW's and then to the Special Forces men he had worked for in Loc Ninh. He couldn't help thinking that he *liked* them. They had treated him as an equal in the camp, even though he was a hated half-breed in Vietnamese society. The Americans had accepted him and had treated him extremely well.

Joc bit his lower lip. It would be easier to fight the Americans if he could hate them.

The supply convoy split up and Joc's section took a trail that led to a storage area in the caves under Nui Ba Den. The Americans and South Vietnamese controlled the top of the mountain, but the complete cave network was Vietcong. Occasionally the Americans would launch a major offensive against the caves and suffer numerous casualties. When that happened, the VC forces would fight a staged underground battle that would allow the commandos to capture certain storerooms of weapons and ammunition. Most of the weapons were old and worn and had been replaced in the field with new AK-47's, but the Americans accepted them as a major find and would withdraw from the caves to count their booty. Joc couldn't remember when a

South Vietnamese or an American unit had actually captured a critical supply depot from them.

Joc turned in his load of supplies and his bicycle and waited until he was picked up by one of the Tay Ninh underground. He was escorted to a safe house in the city and allowed to shower and sleep for five hours before he was awoken and fed a late breakfast.

"Major, we have a ride for you to Cu Chi today." The agent sat across the table from Joc and stared into his blue eyes.

"By truck?" Joc sipped from the painted china cup of hot green tea.

"No . . . we were able to get you on a bus all the way to Trang Bang. From there you will be escorted to your unit." The man's expression was hidden behind a pair of dark sunglasses. He had not introduced himself to Joc.

"I would like to ask a favor of you."

"Please, ask it."

"Could you find me a pair of sunglasses before I go outside?" Joc smiled. "I have a problem that needs to be camouflaged."

The Vietcong agent removed his sunglasses and handed them to Joc. "Please . . . be my guest. I understand how it is to have a distinguishing physical irregularity."

Joc took the offered gift but his eyes were locked on the hole in the man's head where his left eye had been gouged out crudely by some blunt instrument.

"I was a guest of the Saigon secret police for a couple of days of questioning." He tried smiling, but the gesture made the empty socket look even more ghastly.

"Thank you!"

"I can get another pair quickly enough." The man stood. "Are you about ready to leave?"

Joc nodded and thanked the woman whose house he had been a guest in before slipping on his leisure-suit jacket. He was going to travel to Trang Bang dressed as a middle-class gold dealer for a large Saigon banking firm.

The old bus was parked on a side street and the driver was changing the front tire with the help of a dozen street urchins he had hired. Joc stood back near the wall of a building and watched. The intersection was busy and a large number of military vehicles passed the bus. Joc watched a South Vietnamese policeman direct traffic and tried to note how many military vehicles passed his location and what they were carrying.

A jeep stopped nearby and waited for the policeman to change the flow of traffic. Joc was counting the soldiers riding in the back of the convoy of two-and-a-half-ton trucks speeding through the intersection and ignored the idling vehicle.

"Do you know where Tay Pho Rum Street is?"

Joc almost answered the American's question without thinking, but at the last second looked over at who had spoken to him and saw the black sergeant major who had come out to Loc Ninh the day he had left.

Command Sergeant Major Yates stared at the hidden eyes behind the sunglasses. He sensed that he had seen the small Vietnamese before, but he couldn't place exactly where.

The Vietnamese shook his head and replied in rapid Vietnamese that he didn't understand what the American wanted. A man standing near Joc answered the sergeant's question in broken English. "Two blocks . . . down road . . . turn right."

"Thank you." Yates kept his eyes on Joc and rested his hand on his pistol. He was just about ready to reach up and remove the Vietnamese's sunglasses when the policeman blew his whistle and signaled for the jeep to move through the intersection. Yates turned around on his seat and continued staring at the Vietnamese wearing the dark glasses.

Joc smiled and waved good-bye.

CHAPTER 11

∞∞∞∞∞∞∞∞∞∞∞∞∞∞

BILATERAL CU CHI

August 1968

"Fuck!"

"What did you say?"

"Fuck it!" Mason shook his head as he walked toward the rest of his teammates sitting along the edge of the perforated-steel-planking taxiway.

"Fuck what, Mason?" Eagle kept his eyes closed and his face directed at the hot tropical sun. He resembled a lizard sunning itself.

"We're on alert again!"

"Where to this time?" Kenny pushed his green beret back out of his eyes and blinked rapidly.

"Someone's going to kick your ass for wearing that unauthorized beret." Mason's voice betrayed a slight tinge of jealousy. The twins were wearing the authentic green berets given to them when they worked for the Special Forces training group.

"Where have we been alerted for?" Eagle sat up

and faced Mason. He wasn't particularly keen on going back along the Cambodian border again.

"Cu Chi, man! The fucking tunnels of Cu Chi!" Mason spit out the Vietnamese words. "You know what that means?"

"What?" Benjy chewed on a bamboo toothpick.

"We are going to get our asses kicked!"

"Sounds like you're too chickenshit to go," Benjy taunted Mason. He was tired of the man's constant carping.

"Get up on your feet, motherfucker!"

Benjy saw Mason coming and rolled over on one side. Most of the force from Mason's kick landed against the rucksack.

Benjy was up on his feet in a crouch waiting for Mason's next attack. The black soldier feinted another kick and threw a roundhouse punch that caught Benjy's right ear, sending a sharp pain through his head.

Mason stepped back and wound up for another overhand swing and was stopped by a right hook to his solar plexus. The blow jarred his rib cage. Mason took another step backward and struggled to catch his breath before continuing the attack.

Eagle and Kenny sat with their backs against their rucksacks watching the long-overdue fight. Mason had been picking on Benjy off and on for weeks.

Mason dropped down on one knee, pretending that he couldn't breathe, and picked up a handful of dirt. He coughed and then staggered to his feet. "You're one fucked-up dude!"

Benjy had seen Mason pick up the dirt and was waiting for him to throw it at him. When the dirt came, it still caught Benjy a little off-guard, but he stepped back out of the way. "Save that shit for the movies, asshole!"

Mason came at Benjy, swinging wildly with both arms. Kenny smiled as he watched. He had fought that way once, and Benjy had worked out an effective defense a long time ago. Benjy sidestepped and threw a hook that caught Mason square on the jaw.

"What in hell is going on here?" The commanding voice stopped the fighting.

Benjy saw the eagle on the officer's collar and the MP's standing behind him with billy clubs drawn.

"Nothing, sir. We were just practicing some hand-to-hand combat moves before we left for the field," Mason answered.

"Hand-to-hand?" The colonel scoffed at the explanation. "Who are you with?" He spoke to Eagle.

"The four of us are a combat tracker team assigned to your headquarters, sir." Eagle mumbled the last part.

"Sergeant!" The colonel spoke to his MP platoon sergeant. "Take these men with you and check out their story."

The team grabbed their gear and hurried off the taxiway over to the brigade headquarters.

Sergeant Dixson entered the office after making sure Molly was resting in the shade next to the plywood office complex. He saw his team sitting in a row outside the colonel's office and ignored them as he went directly into the room. Dixson wasn't with the commander more than a couple of minutes before he came back out and spoke to his men on his way out of the building. "Let's go!"

Kenny was the first one out, followed by Benjy. Eagle and Mason brought up the rear. Mason caught up to Benjy and grabbed his sleeve. "I'm sorry."

Benjy swallowed and answered, "Me too."

"Let's get loaded up!" Dixson was so mad at the team that he couldn't look any of them in the eye. The colonel had stood him at attention like a damn recruit and chewed his ass about having control over his men. "We're riding the last CV-7 Caribou in line. Now, move it!"

Eagle threw his gear on the tail ramp and hopped inside the fixed-wing aircraft and turned around to help Dixson with Molly. The sergeant flashed Eagle a look that summarized what he was thinking.

"Hey, don't take it out on me, Sarge!" Eagle pointed at Mason and Benjy. "They're the ones who started the damn fight." Eagle yelled so he could be heard above the roar of the engines.

Dixson shook his head and braced himself against the red nylon netting for the takeoff. He was thinking what the colonel had told him about the recent race riots up in Quang-Tri that nearly caused the whole brigade from the Fifth Division to be deactivated. The riots had been kept secret, but they had been serious. White officers and NCO's had been shot by black soldiers. The war was taking a bad turn; hippies and gutless college professors were causing problems back in the States, and drugs were beginning to cause morale and discipline problems in the troop units in Vietnam. Now the racial crap! His team better have it out of its system this time. Or else!

Major Joc Vo Nguyen's guide took him to the well in the center of the village and slid a ladder down the five-foot-wide opening. He led the way down the dark hole. Joc had been hiding in the jungle until dark before his infiltration into the tunnels his detachment occupied near Ap Cho, south of Cu Chi. The ladder's bottom rungs rested in the water, but a little more than halfway down the well a large hole appeared in the stones. Joc stepped off the ladder into the dark hole that was the entrance from the village to the tunnels. His guide was standing next to the entrance, holding back a heavy piece of canvas. Once Joc was inside, he let the canvas drop back into place and felt his way in the dark over to another piece of canvas and pulled it back. Bright electric light flooded the chamber, and the guide signaled with his free hand for Joc to enter the main tunnel, illuminated by a light bulb every hundred feet.

Joc hurried down the busy underground thoroughfare, stopping often to let VC and NVA soldiers going the other way pass him. Secondary tunnels intersected the main one every two hundred meters. The guide turned down one of the secondary routes, and the tunnel narrowed only slightly.

Whoever had designed the air-filtration system had been a genius. Air circulated constantly from aboveground, and the whole system was designed with airlocks that would close down sections of the tunnels if the Americans used tear gas or smoke.

The guide stopped outside a wooden door that had been set perfectly in the clay walls. The word "KIN" painted in bold red letters indicated that the area beyond the door was secret.

A female Vietcong lieutenant was waiting for Joc when he passed through the door. "Major Vo Nguyen?"

"Yes." Joc smiled.

"I have been assigned to show you around your command. All of our people are dedicated, and we are very proud of the work we do here." She stood at attention.

"Thank you, Lieutenant . . ."

"Tong Le, sir."

"Please show me where to put my gear, and then we can tour the company area." Joc followed her down a narrow tunnel to the officers' sleeping quarters, where she stopped in front of a small opening draped with a bright red cloth.

"This is your room, sir." She waited outside while Joc put his belongings on the cot. The furnishings in the tiny room were Spartan but adequate. He had been given a room all of his own because he was the detachment commander; everyone else shared cots because there was always someone on duty.

Joc left the room and tried orienting himself as

they wove their way down the tunnels. They passed a mess hall that was cooking fish and rice. The smoke from the cooking fires went through an elaborate chimney system that connected with a cooking fire in the village above them so that it could not be detected. All of the mess halls were directly under the village, along with the hospital and operating rooms. The sleeping quarters were located in a circle beneath the village, and tunnels went like spokes in a wheel out from there to the storage and work areas. The 133rd Signal Company was located by itself away from the rest of the tunnels because of the sensitive work it did. The fewer people who knew its workings, the better.

The lieutenant stopped in front of a wide opening and let Joe enter first. The huge chamber was about fifty meters long and four meters wide. One side was lined with radios of all types: French shortwave sets, captured American field radios, large Russian command sets and even a couple of civilian radios that were monitoring the large public stations. All of the operators wore headsets and sat behind desks covered with stacks of paper containing intercepted messages from American combat units and from the American bases surrounding Saigon. Joe watched as the radio operators wrote down the coded messages and handed them to intelligence officers who tried to break the codes. Most of the American troops used homemade codes to talk to each other, and the agents broke them as fast as a normal person could translate something from one language to another. The process slowed down only when someone used a code book correctly, and then the decoders would have to consult the American SOI's and SSI's—standing-operating-instruction and the classified standard-signal-instruction books. Joc could see that someone was furnishing the signal company with the American code sheets, which changed every day.

"Sir, we have one more area to show you besides the aboveground antenna system. Please follow me." Tong Le walked down the long chamber to the tunnel entrance and knocked on the wooden door of the first room on the left. A gruff command to enter came from the other side. She opened the door and Joc was caught by surprise. A single NVA soldier sat behind two Americans who were monitoring four American PRC-25 field radios. Neither of the American soldiers looked up at Joc or the lieutenant. They seemed to be in a stupor.

Tong Le explained when he looked at her, "We found them hiding in a whorehouse in Saigon. As you can see, they are willing volunteers."

Her voice prompted one of the American soldiers to turn around, and Joc could see the despair in the hollow blue eyes that were almost exactly the same shade as his own. The American stared vacantly for a couple of seconds and then turned back around to write down something he was hearing in his headset.

Lieutenant Tong Le continued her briefing. "They deserted their units and have been listed as missing in action." She smiled. "We can do almost everything they do, but now and then some slang is used for a field code and they come in handy."

"Do we have any more American traitors working for us?"

"We have some in Laos that I've heard about, but these are the only two in our area. They work for heroin." Her last statement explained a lot to Joc. The American soldiers had become addicted to the drug and were working as male prostitutes in Saigon when the VC had kidnapped them.

The lieutenant led the way out of the room and waited until they were out in the tunnel before adding with a smirk, "We will be getting rid of those two very soon. The heroin is turning their brains into mush and they're no longer much use to us."

"Sir, we've just received word that the Americans are assembling scout and tracking-dog teams from all over III Corps to search the Cu Chi area for tunnels." Tong Le handed Joc the message.

"Interesting. Pass it on to the central office and ask for instructions. They might want us to shut down for a while until this passes." The dogs the Americans used were very good, and a concentrated effort in their area might jeopardize this whole operation. Shutting down for a couple of days would also give the men and women in the signal company a chance to visit their families.

"Yes, sir." Her voice was formal. A number of rumors were spreading among the VC officers about Joc's rapid promotion to major, and she wasn't going to risk being too friendly and then find out that he was a flash in the pan.

"Lieutenant Tong Le?" Joc's voice was soft.

"Yes, sir?"

"I am a loyal Vietcong, in spite of my French blood and my concern for the Americans we have working for us." Joc smiled with his mouth, but no lines formed around his eyes. He was giving clear warning that he would tolerate no disloyalty. "I care about everyone who works for our case and for victory."

"Yes, sir!"

"Good! I'm glad that we understand each other. Now you may see why I will not allow the American drug addicts to be executed." Joc noticed a slight tic at the corner of her eye. "Why do you hate the Americans so much?"

"They killed my father and opened his skull with what they called a tomahawk and shoved a playing card in the crack—what they called the ace of spades, which signifies death."

"Was this before or after you became a communist?" Joc leaned back in his chair.

She tried evading a direct answer to his question. "I was thinking about joining the party."

"Before or after?"

"Before."

"I see . . . so then the atrocity was your reason for becoming a Vietcong."

"Partially."

She was holding something else back, but Joc decided against pressing the issue. "So you already know what atrocities do: mostly they backfire, and instead of causing fear in an enemy, only create a more determined enemy." Joc appeared to study the stack of papers on his desk. "That is why we do not execute people who have helped us."

"Yes, sir!"

"Please let me know the central office's decision concerning our operation as soon as possible." Joc was aware that Lieutenant Tong Le was the central office commanding general's spy in the 133rd Signal Company. She had been fairly easy to spot. All the captains had accepted Joc's leadership, and the lieutenants, except for her, had obeyed him without question. She constantly questioned his decisions, even though tactfully and in private. But Joc had never confronted her with his suspicions. Sometimes it was best to let spies think they were operating in secret so you could keep an eye on them.

CHAPTER 12

❖❖❖❖❖❖❖❖❖❖❖❖❖❖❖❖❖❖

COOKING FIRES

August 1968

Mason always took the lead when they were sweeping through a village. The cavalry troop had cordoned off the small hamlet, and the infantry company, along with the dog teams, started through the streets.

Dixson dropped down on one knee and whispered in Molly's ear, "We can't let those dumb-ass scout dogs show us up, girl!" He looked over at the other tracker team and appraised the dog. "They've been rumored to be pretty good, Molly, but I know that you're better." Dixson patted her side and rubbed her hair.

"Come on, Sarge!" Mason called from behind the thatched house he wanted Molly to check out for him.

"Let's go, girl!" Dixson let Molly's leash extend and she started working immediately. "Good girl!"

The twins worked near Molly but were checking out the thatched huts ahead of the infantry troops. The armor major in charge of the combined operation had briefed all of them that the village had been peaceful for years and they were conducting a security sweep to make sure there was no stolen military equipment in the huts. The troops were not to take or break anything, and if anything looked suspicious, they were to call an NCO or an officer to check it out. The first two hamlets would be mostly boring inspections of the Vietnamese homes and animal pens to ready the combined American team for the more difficult targets later on in the week. The villages surrounding Cu Chi were the homes of the maids and laundry women who worked for the Americans on the base.

Benjy looked into a thatched hut and saw a young Vietnamese woman breast-feeding her baby. He stepped out again, embarrassed, and went over to the nearby pigsty and checked through the bean pods stacked in a corner of the pen. The pigs didn't like someone poking through their food and squealed their displeasure.

"Come on, Benjy." Kenny used the barrel of his weapon to point with. "Let's check out that rice bin."

Benjy hesitated. He was watching Molly, and she seemed to be interested in a large cooking fire, but every time she drew near it, she sneezed and turned away. It was either the heat coming off the charcoal or something had been sprinkled in the dirt around the fire. "Let's go see what's bothering Molly first."

Dixson held Molly's head in his hands and looked into her eyes. "Something bothering you, girl?"

"What's wrong, Sarge?" Benjy squatted next to Dixson.

"I don't know. Molly seems to want to alert, but then she changes her mind for some reason." Dixson used his thumbs to push back the dog's eyelids to see what was irritating her eyes.

Kenny scooped up a handful of the dry dirt near the fire and held it up to his nose. He coughed and shook his head. "Pepper!"

"The old woman must have spilled it while she was cooking." Dixson smiled back at the old woman who stood next to the five-foot wok set in the hot coals. She was stir-frying some kind of meat.

"Maybe . . ." Benjy thought something seemed wrong about the cooking fire. The fire had been built inside a large box filled with sand. At first glance it looked normal, except the fire was outside, which also made sense, because the wok was so large that it wouldn't have been practical to have it inside the small house.

"Something wrong, Benjy?" Eagle didn't like the way the old woman smiled constantly at them.

"Look at the way the fire pit has been constructed in that box. Have you ever seen that before?"

"Naw . . ." Eagle squatted and ran his index finger next to the edge of the box and the ground. The twins watched the loose sand and dirt filter down along the edge, forming what looked like tiny ant holes.

Benjy understood what Molly had been trying to tell them and pushed the safety off his weapon. "Tunnel!"

"Where?" Kenny still hadn't pieced together that the dirt disappearing under the fire pit meant there had to be a hole underneath the fire.

"Push the fire box over." Benjy kept his M-2 pointed at the old woman.

"What?" Kenny looked at his brother as if he were crazy. "That damn thing is too hot!"

"I mean push the *whole* fire box over. I'm sure there's a tunnel entrance hidden under the fire."

Eagle sat down so he could use his boot to push against the side of the fire box without burning his hands. The old woman started screaming something in Vietnamese at Eagle and tried hitting him with her cooking ladle.

"We seem to have found something." Dixson helped Mason hold the old woman back so that Eagle could push the fire box over. At first the large container refused to budge, but when Kenny sat down next to Eagle and put his weight into it also, the whole fire pit slid to one side and the corner of a dark hole appeared. "Damn!"

"Cover us!" Kenny spoke from his position on the ground. "I don't want to eat some AK rounds!"

Benjy pointed his weapon at the hole and watched as the tunnel entrance appeared. A long ladder could be seen once the entrance was all the way open. Kenny leaned forward and looked down at the bottom, where the opening of a large underground tunnel could be seen.

The old woman continued screaming at the Americans. She had performed the same trick with pepper every time the village had been searched before, and no one had ever suspected that she was guarding the main entrance to a major tunnel complex under her cooking fire.

"The bitch sprinkled the area with red pepper when she saw the dogs coming!" Dixson felt the rage bubbling up in his chest. Mason grabbed him by the arm to keep him from hitting the old woman, who had turned into a screaming banshee the instant the tunnel entrance had been discovered.

The twins dropped their rucksacks and removed the silencers from the packs and started screwing them on the barrels of the submachine guns.

"While you're doing that and getting the rest of your gear ready, I'm going to check out the entrance for booby traps." Eagle went over to the edge of the hole and started searching for trip wires or pressure devices around the hole.

"Let's get somebody over here to question this old bitch!" Dixson instructed Mason to go to the command track and bring back one of the ex-Vietcong soldiers who worked for the American units. He saw Eagle start down the ladder. "Be careful! You don't know what they've rigged up down there to surprise unwanted guests!"

"You ain't exactly talking to a fucking rookie, Sarge!" Eagle held out his hand. "Benjy, let me use your flashlight until you guys get your tunnel gear ready."

Benjy handed over his five-cell flashlight. "Don't go in the main tunnel where we can't see you."

Eagle flashed an angry look at Benjy. He had been the main tunnel rat for the team before the twins joined them. It wasn't that he missed working the tunnels, but he hated being talked down to by the new guys. "I'll clear it for you so we don't waste any time screwing around."

"I'm going to have the cav guys bring up a Mighty Mite system and blow some tear gas in there, so take your masks with you." Dixson picked up his radio.

"Shit, Sarge! Wait until we come back before you pump that shit in there!" Kenny hated it when they had to work a tunnel that had been gassed. The heat and sweat of their bodies made the gas burn their skin.

"Well, hurry the fuck up before whoever's down there gets away." Dixson was still pissed about the pepper and its effect on his dog.

Eagle went slowly down the ladder. He had heard Dixson mention the Mighty Mite system and wanted to be out of there before the engineers arrived. He hated tear gas, and the M106 riot-control-agent dispenser, dubbed Mighty Mite, pumped huge amounts of it into a tunnel network in minutes. He paused on the ladder and called back up, "Sarge! Have them bring a couple of BURB's instead!"

Dixson keyed his handset and spoke to the major

commanding the operation. He told him about finding the entrance to a large tunnel complex and asked for the portable CS gas blower to be brought forward, and added that he would like a couple of BURB's brought along too, with a combat engineer team to set the charges. The BURB—bunker-use restriction bomb—had been developed by men in the First Cavalry Division and worked perfectly for sealing major tunnels with tear gas. A BURB was a cardboard container for a 2.75-inch rocket warhead, two nonelectric blasting caps, approximately twenty-five seconds of time fuse and a fuse igniter. The device was filled with powder CS and then taped shut. The blasting caps provided sufficient explosive force to rupture the container and spread the tear gas through a long stretch of tunnel, which would remain there for a very long time, thus rendering that area unusable by the Vietcong.

Eagle continued down the ladder slowly, pointing the barrel of his M-16 ahead of him and holding on to the rungs with one hand. He paused frequently to inspect the wall around him for hidden devices and trip wires.

"How's it going down there?" Benjy leaned over the edge of the hole and cast a shadow over Eagle.

"It looks like the opening turns within a couple of feet . . . probably in case someone drops a hand grenade down here, so the blast won't go down the whole tunnel." Eagle shifted his weight on the ladder and tried squatting to see deeper into the man-size opening. "I'll be able to see better once I reach the bottom and turn on the flashlight."

"We're ready to come down." Benjy slipped his M-2 grease gun over his shoulder by its carrying strap and grabbed hold of the ladder.

Eagle turned his head to look up and felt the slight give in the ladder's second rung from the bottom when he stepped on it. The roar of the Claymore filled the hole and sent a blood-spattered dust cloud billowing up out of the Vietcong tunnel entrance. The ladder rung had been booby-trapped with a pressure device and Eagle's weight had set off the Claymore which had cut his legs off just above the knees.

"Eagle!" Benjy screamed down into the hole.

The old Vietnamese woman cackled something and then started laughing.

Kenny rushed over to pull his brother back away from the edge of the hole. "Wait!"

Dixson rushed over to the twins and tried looking down, but the rising dust blocked his view of the bottom. One of the nearby infantry squad rushed over and secured the area until the dust settled. Benjy was the first one to risk looking down again, and saw Eagle's torn body crumpled at the bottom of the well.

"Eagle's hit!" Benjy pulled his webgear off. "I'm going down after him!" He spoke with such force that no one tried stopping him.

Eagle moaned when Benjy grabbed him and lifted his incomplete body up over his shoulder. Benjy was surprised at how little Eagle was bleeding from the stumps where his legs had been. He struggled back up the ladder and laid Eagle down on a poncho Kenny had already laid out. "He needs a couple of tourniquets . . . fast!"

"*Medic!*" Dixson called over to the infantrymen, and two of them ran over with their aid kits.

The old woman pointed at Eagle's amputated legs and started laughing harder. Dixson removed his pistol and shot her between the eyes. She looked surprised for a second and then dropped down in a pile. No one said anything.

Eagle opened his eyes and blinked. "They're gone . . . aren't they?"

"What?" Benjy tried blocking the stubs with his body so Eagle couldn't see that his legs were missing.

"My legs . . . they're gone." Eagle's voice was calm. "I can't feel any pain . . . nothing."

"Don't worry about it, man, these medics will have you patched up and shipped on an early flight back to the States in a minute!"

"Benjy . . . stop them." Eagle's eyes were pleading.

"Stop who?"

"Let me die."

"Bullshit, man! You're not going to die!"

"Benjy!" Eagle tore at Benjy's sleeve. "I'm an Indian! You're from Carolina. You know how it is for us . . . hunting in the woods. . . . Let me die . . . peacefully. Dope me up and loosen the tourniquets."

"I can't do that, Eagle . . . you're my *friend!*"

"If you *are* my friend, you'll let me die . . . now!"

Benjy started crying. "I can't do that."

Eagle turned his head to one side and mumbled under his breath, "Mayapple . . . trout lilies . . . toothwort, I like them because they're simple and you can only find them in the deep forest where it's damp . . ."

One of the infantry medics asked Benjy, "What's he talking about?"

Eagle's eyes lost their focus. "Spring beauty . . . did you know that my people still gather the underground tubers? Yeah, they taste like sweet chestnuts . . ." Eagle's eyes focused on Benjy's face. "When you're hunting during the spring and you see a patch of spring beauties . . . think of me?"

"Sure, man . . . sure." Benjy could barely see Eagle through the tears washing his eyes.

"What's he talking about?" the medic asked again.

Kenny swallowed to clear the lump in his throat. "Flowers . . . wildflowers."

Eagle turned his head to one side and whispered to Benjy, "I got my first piece of ass next to a wild honeysuckle bush. The bees flew around my bare ass, but I didn't miss a stroke."

Benjy smiled and held Eagle's hand. He looked up in the pale blue sky, and the two of them traveled back to the cool mountain forests of North Carolina. Benjy felt the pressure leave Eagle's fingers and he didn't need to look down to know what had happened.

"Medic?" Benjy's voice was clear and cold.

"Yeah?"

"Where are you from?"

"Los Angeles."

"When you get back to the States, take a little time to check out the wildflowers." Benjy kept looking up at the sky. He didn't trust himself to look directly at another human.

"You turning hippie on me, man?" The medic saw the look Kenny was giving him and added, "Sure . . . I can do that."

Benjy released Eagle's hand without looking down.

Lieutenant Tong Le rushed into Joc's sleeping quarters and shook him awake. "Americans! They've gassed the northern tunnels!"

Joc's eyes popped open from his deep sleep and his mind began functioning instantly. "Seal the main operations chamber and post guards at all of the intersections." Joc pulled on his khaki pants over his shorts as he talked. "Get the classified message file packed in case we have to evacuate."

"Yes, sir!" The lieutenant gave the major a curt nod. "The reaction battalion had been alerted and is moving into position for a diversionary maneuver. The Americans have found the fire-pit entrance at Ap Cho." She sounded unsure. The fire-pit entrance had been in existence since the war with the French, and the old woman who guarded it was a living legend among the Vietcong soldiers.

"Make sure the courier pouch from the central office is removed from the code room." Joc strapped his pistol belt on and adjusted the red star on his belt buckle so that it lined up perfectly with the edge of his fly. "Take care of the pouch first. We cannot afford to have it fall into the hands of the Americans."

"Yes, sir." Tong Le's voice lowered. "What about the Americans in the code room?"

"Have their guard give them a larger-than-normal amount of heroin and let them sleep through this." Joc tried smiling but the gesture was lost when his thoughts went back to the problems at hand. "How far away are the Americans in the tunnel?"

"They haven't reached the new tunnel intersection yet." Lieutenant Tong Le was impressed at how calmly Joc was handling himself under pressure.

Joc nodded and left his sleeping quarters ahead of the lieutenant. There were a lot of things for him to do and very little time to do them. It was good that the Americans had found the old tunnel entrance that had been built during the French-Indochina War, instead of one of the new entrances that led directly to the 133rd Signal Company's chambers. The camouflaged entry to the new sector off the old tunnel was excellent, and unless the American tunnel rats were very good, they would pass it by and follow the hare.

At each of the critical junctions in the tunnel a decoy had been designed into the defenses to draw the invaders away from the most sensitive areas. The hare could be a booby trap, but in the most critical cases the hare was always a couple of troops left behind to keep the Americans from inspecting the camouflaged portion of the tunnel walls by drawing them away either by being intentionally seen and running or by opening fire on the intruders. The first option was the preferred method because it drew the Americans away from the critical area.

Lieutenant Tong Le passed Joc in the tunnel carrying the dark brown leather courier pouch over her shoulder. She was headed in the direction of the code room. Joc wanted to personally inspect the camouflage around the extremely critical new tunnel entrance. If the Americans passed by that single underground entrance to his complex, the only other way to find his operation would be for them to discover the well entrance in the village.

Kenny tried comforting Benjy, but Eagle's death had affected his brother deeply. "Here's some gum."

"Thanks." Benjy took the offered hunk of Bazooka bubble gum that they both chewed when they were underground. The gum served two purposes: it calmed them and it also kept their eustachian tubes open and helped improve their hearing. Benjy looked at his twin. "I didn't know he cared about wildflowers."

"He was an Indian. I guess they care about a lot of things we didn't think they care about."

"What's your favorite wildflower, Kenny?"

"I don't know, I guess chicory . . . I like the shade of blue the flowers are, plus I like the idea that each flower lasts for only a single day." Kenny looked down in the hole with the ladder and saw what remained of Eagle's legs at the bottom. "That sort of makes each flower special."

Dixson saw where Kenny's eyes were directed and figured he needed a distraction. "Kenny! Come here!"

Kenny obeyed his sergeant.

"You!" Dixson pointed at the infantry medic who was rolling Eagle into a rubberized body bag. "There are parts of his body still down below. Go and get them now so that we can continue our mission."

The medic gave Dixson a funny look as if to say going down into pits wasn't his job.

"Now!" Dixson started getting to his feet and the medic decided to obey the NCO. "Benjy! Come over here too! I want to brief both of you before you go underground." Dixson shifted his seat so that the twins would have their backs to the fire pit and couldn't see the medic bringing back Eagle's torn-off legs. "Check your URC-10's to make sure they're on the right frequency."

The twins removed the hand-held radios from their side trouser pockets and checked the frequencies and then made sure the batteries were working by keying the sets.

Dixson saw the bloody boot come up over the edge of the fire pit that held the bottom half of Eagle's left leg. He frowned, annoyed at himself because he had identified the dismembered part of his friend's body as the *left* leg. Kenny started to turn in the direction Dixson was staring.

"Kenny!" Dixson drew the young soldier's attention back to himself. "You don't have to go underground if you don't want to . . ." He looked at Benjy, who was the person he was really talking to. "You don't either."

"Who'll go if we don't?" Kenny tried again to see where Dixson kept looking.

Dixson grabbed the front of Kenny's jacket and pulled hard. "You look at *me* when I'm talking to you!"

The medic laid Eagle's right leg with the boot still attached to it on the edge of the fire pit. The second medic had joined him and was wrapping the gruesome remains in an extra body bag before carrying them back over to where the rest of Eagle's body lay.

Kenny was pissed off. "What's your problem, Sarge?"

"I don't want you seeing something back there . . . that's all!"

Benjy turned around. The medic crawling out of the hole leaned out to vomit. Benjy turned back slowly to face his sergeant. "*We* are going under and we're not coming back up until all of those motherfucking commie cocksuckers are dead!"

CHAPTER 13

DIRTY TRICKS

August 1968

Kenny tied the heavy nylon cord around the stake Sergeant Dixson had pounded in the ground a couple of feet away from the edge of the fire pit and asked Benjy, "Do you have the extra cord?"

"I've another one in my field pack." Benjy looked at the hole and swallowed. There was something about this particular tunnel that bothered him, and to make it even worse, he couldn't pin it down. Eagle's death had shaken him up, but there was something else. He glanced at the crumpled body of the old woman and wondered if she was a witch. She looked like the kind of person who would put a curse on someone.

"The infantry have sealed off the village and have been given orders to be on the alert for any extra villagers appearing out of nowhere." Dixson scratched behind Molly's ears as he briefed the twins. "If you guys run into *anything* that looks suspicious, I want you out of there!" He involuntarily glanced at Eagle's body bag. "It ain't worth it . . . Do you guys hear me?"

Kenny nodded. "We ain't gonna do anything stupid, Sarge. If it doesn't look right down there, you won't have to ask us to get our asses back topside! Right, Benjy!"

Benjy nodded his agreement. He had been looking at Eagle. "When are they going to fly him out of here?"

"Soon . . . a chopper is on its way." Dixson poked Benjy's side trouser pocket. "Did you check your URC-10?"

"Yeah, it's working fine."

"I want someone monitoring all of the time."

"Fine! But don't fucking play battalion commander on our asses!" Benjy's eyes flashed anger. "I don't need anyone riding my ass while I'm down there. We'll call *you* if we find something worth reporting."

"I'm just concerned—"

"Right! But we aren't exactly going on a stroll through the fucking woods when we're underground."

Dixson had taken enough of the sarcasm. "What's your fucking problem, Benjy? Have you grown a cunt?" He stood up. "You on the fucking rag?"

"He's just nervous is all, Sarge." Kenny nudged his brother and started to walk toward the fire pit, unraveling the cord as he walked. "This is going to be a pain in the ass."

"It'll keep you from getting lost underground. I've got a feeling this tunnel entrance leads into something big." Dixson kept Molly close to his side. She sniffed the air coming up out of the tunnel and growled a warning.

"Thanks, Molly . . . we needed that!" Benjy patted her shoulder and reached for the ladder.

"I'll take the point first!" Kenny cut him off.

"It's my turn—"

"Yeah, I know . . . but I feel good today." Kenny didn't want Benjy on the point because he would have to check out the entrance carefully for any more booby traps, and it was almost certain that there would be some pieces of Eagle still down there. It would be tough enough for him, but after Eagle had died in Benjy's arms he knew that it would be too much for his brother to handle.

Kenny felt his heartbeat increase when he reached the bottom of the ladder where Eagle had set off the Claymore mine. He scanned every single inch of the entranceway before risking a step inside. The miner's lamp on his head illuminated the cave walls perfectly where he was looking. If there were going to be any more booby traps, they would be before he reached the main tunnel. It took Kenny fifteen minutes to search the initial eight feet of the entrance before it made a sharp turn to his left. He went back to the entrance and waved Benjy down.

Dixson felt a lump in the pit of his stomach when he saw Benjy disappear down the hole. Molly growled again as if she could read her master's mind, and took a step toward the ladder as if to say she wanted to go with the twins. Dixson had tried using Molly before underground, but it was too difficult because she didn't like the cramped quarters of the normal tunnels.

Kenny walked forward, holding his flashlight in his left hand and his silenced 9mm pistol cocked with the safety off in his right hand. He had turned off his miner's lamp because he wanted to have instant control over the light in case they ran into a VC security unit. Kenny paused and inspected the tunnel shaft. It was considerably wider and higher than the entrance, and the sides had been smoothed out to almost a plaster finish. The strong beam from his five-cell flashlight reflected off a piece of olive-drab canvas that blocked the tunnel about fifty feet ahead of them.

Benjy signaled his brother by flicking his light on and then off. Kenny stopped and waited for Benjy to reach him. "My turn." Benjy took the lead.

The canvas flap was secured tightly and a stake had been driven into the floor to hold the rope loops at the bottom. Benjy could see that the canvas had come off the back of an American-made two-and-one-half-ton truck. He inspected the canvas before slowly unhooking the rope loop on the floor and lifting the flap to see what was behind it.

Bright light filled the tunnel the twins were in. Benjy blinked and dropped the flap. "Hot shit!" The words slipped out of his mouth before he could stop them. "Fucking electric lights!"

Kenny held his URC-10 to his ear and pressed the transmission switch. The six-inch rubber-coated antenna rubbed against the side of the tunnel and left a mark in the damp earth. "Dog Leader Six . . . Four, over."

Dixson had been holding his radio, and answered instantly, "Six, over."

"We've just found another tunnel that has electric lights!" Kenny's voice carried the excitement he was feeling. He had never heard of a team finding a tunnel with electric lights before. "It's fucking huge!"

"Be careful!" Dixson looked at the infantry captain sitting next to him. The officer had set up his command post with Dixson so that he could monitor what was going on underground. "How far have you gone?"

Kenny looked at the ball of cord Benjy had handed him when he took over the point. "Fifty feet . . . maybe a little more."

Dixson spoke to the captain without pressing the talk switch on his radio. "This is big. I think we've hit on a major underground complex."

The captain shook his head in mild shock. "I've personally swept this damn village a dozen times and never even suspected that the VC were here!"

"That's probably why they are. Who would ever suspect that they would have a major underground complex within sight of the Cu Chi base area?"

"I wonder if they have tunnels going *under* the perimeter?" The captain's expression changed from surprise to worry.

"They might." Dixson remembered the tunnel at Bu Dop.

"Have your men try to find another exit for us. I think I want to send another team down there to back them up." The captain was starting to worry about the security of the huge base area.

"Let's give them a chance first." Dixson nodded at the radio he was holding in his hand.

"Fine."

"Dog Leader Four . . . Six, over."

"Yeah?"

"Proceed . . . with extreme caution, over."

"You don't have to tell us twice!" Kenny slipped his radio back in his pocket.

Benjy had put his pistol back in its holster and had replaced it with his submachine gun. He didn't need to carry a flashlight as long as the VC were going to cooperate and light the tunnel for them. Benjy stepped out into the light after holding the flap back for a minute so that his eyes could adjust to the glare coming from the light bulbs. The long tunnel was empty and very quiet. He could hear the slight fizz and snap coming from a bulb near his head that was about ready to burn out. Benjy moved down the tunnel in a combat crouch. If he had wanted to, he could have stood straight up without touching his head on the roof, and the tunnel was wide enough for two people to pass each other without having to turn sideways.

Kenny made a soft noise to draw Benjy's attention and pointed to a small cage that had been left in front of what looked like a sealed bamboo door. The cage contained three fat rats.

Benjy frowned. Why would the VC keep rats in

a cage? He signaled with the barrel of his M-2 that he was going to check out what was behind the door, but Kenny rushed over to where he was standing and pointed at an eight-inch-square door cut high up in the sealed door. The small door was too high to be used as a peephole.

Kenny signaled for Benjy to cover him and he turned on his five-cell flashlight before unlatching the tiny door within a door. The other side was pitch black. Kenny cautiously held his flashlight so he could see what was in the room. At first it looked empty, and then the light caught movement on the floor. "Shit!" Kenny slammed the small door.

"What the fuck is wrong?" Benjy sounded scared.

"The rats!"

"What about the rats?" Benjy whispered.

"Snakes!" Kenny eased away from the door. "That room is full of *big* fucking snakes!"

Benjy studied the door again. Now the height of the small door made sense. The VC could just drop the rats in through the small door to feed the snakes on the other side. The question was, why were the snakes in the room? Benjy took Kenny's flashlight and opened the little door again. He held the beam so that he could see the floor, and was instantly met by the smiling face of a hooded cobra ready to strike. Benjy moved the beam of his flashlight quickly around the small room and saw that the cobra was the largest snake on the floor. A couple dozen small kraits and a bright green bamboo viper started moving on the floor just outside of the light that had awoken them. Benjy shifted the light to the walls and ceiling and saw the large hole in the roof. He understood why the snake were there.

"False tunnel entrance." Benjy closed the door. "Tell Dixson. This is some heavy shit!"

Major Joc Vo Nguyen hurried to clear the secondary tunnel so the infantry guards could arm the booby traps. He had sent all of his people back into the secure personnel bunkers underground and had stayed behind to lead the VC who would fight a rearguard action to protect the tunnel system. The idea was to surrender only the portions of the tunnels that had been discovered by the Americans, either by making the Americans think they had found everything or by making the price too high for them to continue underground and force them to tear-gas the tunnels. The sooner they could get the Americans to use the tear gas, the less danger they faced of a serious loss in soldiers and equipment. Joc watched the guards seal off and camouflage the secret entrance to the critical radio room. The antennas and radio hookups were too complicated to move to another portion of the tunnel network, so the best solution was to seal off the chamber and detour the tunnels around it. When the guards had finished spreading the clay over the bamboo frame the entrance to the radio room blended perfected with the rest of the tunnel wall.

Benjy saw the four bamboo doors with small wooden nameplates attached above them. he nodded for Kenny to open the first one, and he covered him. The room was full of old AK-47's and SKS rifles. The second room contained steel cans filled with ammunition, and the third and fourth rooms contained rice.

"Should we call this up?" Kenny asked. It was one of the biggest caches of weapons discovered by a tracker dog team since they had been in Vietnam.

Benjy nodded, but continued frowning; it was too easy. There weren't any guards, and the tunnel continued on past until it made a sharp ninety-degree turn.

Dixson was getting excited. "How far have you guys gone?"

"A hundred and fifty feet." Kenny kept his set keyed. "If you're going to send infantry types down here, warn them about the door with the *little* door on top built in. It's full of snakes!"

"Roger." Dixson looked over at the captain, who just nodded. "They want to come on down and bring that stuff up."

"I recommend that you all wait until we've finished checking this place out. There're a lot of weird booby traps."

Dixson didn't hesitate. "Agreed. Tell me when you're ready."

Benjy led the way to where the tunnel made the sharp turn. He inspected every inch of the floor and walls for trip wires or camouflaged pits and found none. Slowly he peeked around the corner and saw the chamber.

Kenny waited until Benjy had signaled before he

moved forward to join him. "Sleeping quarters. It looks like we missed everyone."

Six double bunk beds with bamboo frames and split-bamboo mats on them filled the small unlit room. The light bulbs stopped a couple of feet away from the chamber. Benjy entered the room after flipping up a corner of the large mat that covered the earth floor. He found nothing underneath it.

"They've gone." Kenny's voice reflected the relief he was feeling.

"It doesn't make sense." Benjy kept looking around the room.

"What?" Kenny wanted to call down the infantry-men to haul out the booty and get the hell back up in the sunlight again. The cool air in the tunnels was about all he liked underground.

"Why are the lights burning and why has it been so easy?"

"What are you talking about?"

"Look . . . six cots . . . this place is big enough for sixty men—and electric lights for six men?" Benjy kept scanning the walls. "It doesn't make sense."

Kenny was impatient. "What do you want to do?"

"Let's look around a bit longer." Benjy turned on his five-cell flashlight and his miner's lamp and started searching the walls of the sleeping chamber. "I think they *wanted* us to find this place."

"That doesn't make sense!"

"There's more to these tunnels than what we've

seen." Benjy looked back the way they had come. "Maybe they're hiding something *behind* the snakes."

Kenny had reached his limit. "Bullshit! I'm not opening that fucking door!"

Benjy stopped scanning the room. He went over and knelt in front of one of the bunk beds, which had been placed tightly against the dirt wall, and touched the ground with his fingertips.

Kenny joined him. "What did you find?"

"Four of them . . ." Benjy pointed at the four round marks on the floor in front of the bunk, then at the bunk bed next to the wall. "That moves." He slowly eased the barrel of his weapon over to point at the mat that hung down from the wall behind the bunks. It looked like a way to keep dirt from falling on the men sleeping on the cots, but Benjy suspected that it might be the entrance to another room.

Kenny moved slightly so that he was in line with the back wall and opened fire with his silenced Swedish-K. Small holes appeared in the matting. A soft grunt filtered back into the room, followed by a thud. Kenny changed magazines and fired again into the bamboo mat.

Benjy pulled the bunk bed away from the hanging mat, and Kenny nodded for him to pull the mat down. The body of a VC lay spread out on the tunnel floor. His surviving partner opened fire: the roar of an AK-47 filled the tiny chamber. Only the bright beam of Kenny's flashlight saved his life. The VC soldier was momentarily blinded and swept the area rather than aiming his weapon. Kenny pulled the trigger on his Swedish-K and the VC dropped down dead next to his comrade.

"Fuck! That was close!" Kenny changed magazines again and moved aside so he couldn't be seen by anyone else hiding in the dark tunnel. "You were right—all of this was bait designed to keep us from looking any further. That's why the guards wouldn't open fire until we had actually discovered them in the tunnel."

Benjy turned on his URC-10. "Dog Leader Six, this is Three, over."

"Six, send your traffic over."

"We ran into a couple of VC hiding in a camouflaged tunnel entrance. It looks like this complex goes on forever. We've found rice and weapons and a small sleeping area. We could use some backup down here. The place is loaded with booby traps. Bring Molly if she'll come. The tunnels are large enough to stand up in, over."

"Will do, out." Dixson grabbed his gear. "Mason! Let's go!" He handed his URC-10 to the infantry captain. "Would you have someone monitor our frequency?"

"No problem there, Sergeant." The captain smiled for the first time since the operation had started. "Whenever you're ready, call and I'll send down some people to help haul up the booty."

Dixson saw the truck arriving in the village with the Mighty Mite tear-gas dispenser. "You might as well put those guys on hold for a while. From what the twins say, it's too big down there for that thing."

Dixson was just about to go down the ladder when one of the infantrymen along the tree line jumped up and yelled back to his NCO, "Tunnel entrance!" He used the barrel of his weapon to lift the poorly camouflaged lid on the spider hole.

Dixson stopped long enough to shout, "Don't let anyone go down any holes within a hundred meters of us! At least one of the entrances is a trap and has a chamber filled with snakes!"

The soldier dropped the lid on the spider hole and backed away from it.

Dixson could feel Molly trembling as he walked backward down the ladder with her in his arms. Mason was waiting at the bottom, wearing an expression that told his sergeant that he didn't like tunnels. "Use your radio and let the twins know we're coming," Dixson ordered.

Lieutenant Tong Le buckled the straps around the bulging leather pouch and slipped it over her shoulder. The messenger from the central office wasn't due until late that night and she would have to carry the courier pouch until then. A low moan caught her attention. The sound had come from the room where the two Americans were being kept. Tong Le opened the door and saw the two men stretched out on sleeping mats in a heroin stupor. The guard assigned to them looked up at the lieutenant when she entered. She knew that he hated Americans as much as she did. As she turned slowly to leave, she whispered loud enough for the guard to hear her, "Kill them."

* * *

The single AK-47 firing nearby forced the guards to rush their final touches on the camouflaged entrance to the radio chamber. Joc signaled them to get their gear and move out quickly so he could cut the electric power throughout this sector. He wasn't going to light the way for the Americans.

Sergeant Dixson had just linked up with the twins when the string of lights blinked out. "It looks like our friends want us to operate in the dark."

Instantly the twins switched on their miner's lamps. "I'm glad you brought Molly with you. We need her nose to look for bobby traps."

Mason fumbled nervously with his miner's lamp and found the switch. He didn't like tunnels and wasn't ashamed to tell anyone who would listen.

"Let's put Molly up front where she can work the tunnel for traps and you twins can follow us." Dixson turned to Mason. "You pull tail gunner."

Mason nodded. There weren't any easy jobs underground. The VC would let a pair of tunnel rats pass by them and then ambush them from the rear so that their victims would have a hard time turning around in the narrow passageway to return fire.

Molly walked as if the tunnel floor burned her feet. She didn't like tunnels at the best of times, and the confusing odors of Vietcong, snakes, and bombs made her even more nervous. The smells were coming from everywhere. She stopped and looked back at her master.

"It's okay, girl . . . just do the best you can." Dixson's soothing voice started her off again down the tunnel.

She alerted when they reached a sharp turn in the passage. Kenny used his Swedish-K to cover Dixson, who moved forward holding Molly's leash in one hand and Kenny's 9mm silenced pistol in the other. Benjy had lent Mason his pistol so that the whole team would have silenced weapons.

Dixson pointed at the dark green wire stretched across the tunnel at ankle level. In the dim artificial light, it was almost invisible. Dixson lifted Molly over the booby-trap wire and waited until all of his men had cleared it. He looked around for something to mark the wire with but couldn't find anything in the tunnel, so he shoved his bayonet blade into the packed floor in front of it so that any infantry men who followed them later would have to see it.

Benjy's lamp reflected off the four-inch bamboo poles spaced out across the tunnel and then expertly tied together with smaller poles running in the opposite direction to make a perfect dungeon gate. The gate's purpose wasn't apparent to the Americans, but to the Vietcong it symbolized the entrance to the secret area of the tunnel system. During normal operations a guard was posted there to keep out unauthorized people.

Molly didn't hesitate going through the open gate, and started to move faster along the passageway. Then she reached a spot in the mud wall stopped to look back at Dixson.

"What's the problem, Molly?" Dixson searched the wall for a booby trap but found none. The twins were inspecting the wall ten feet in both directions, and except for its being a little damper than the rest of the tunnel, there was nothing to be found.

Dixson tugged on Molly's leash, but she only whined and refused to leave. She sat on her haunches facing the wall.

"There's got to be something hidden in the wall." Kenny laid his cheek against the damp earth and closed one eye so that he could look along the surface for any variation or bulge. "Benjy, shove your knife in the wall right in front of Molly."

Benjy looked incredulous but removed his prized Randall from its sheath and stuck the blade into the mud. It went in less than an inch and stopped. Benjy smiled at his brother. "There's something here."

The team watched as Benjy removed the layer of mud that covered a woven bamboo mat, then cut a hole in the matting and shone his flashlight through. "Hot damn! I'll be a fucking Yankee!"

"What is it?" Kenny pushed Benjy aside to have a look. "Damn!"

Dixson repeated the procedure. "Holy shit! We've got to secure this whole fucking area, above and below ground!" He fumbled to remove his URC-10 and had pressed the talk switch before he had the radio up to his ear.

The captain was already on the line.

"We've just uncovered a fucking radio room that must have a hundred fucking radios in it!"

"A storage bin of radios . . . is that what you said?"

"Fuck no! A radio room where you send messages . . . like in a division TOC."

Major Joc Vo Nguyen hung up the field telephone and addressed his officers and NCO's. "They have found the chamber." His voice was tense. "Alert the reaction battalion." He turned to Lieutenant Tong Le. "You must leave immediately with the secret documents . . . and you understand that they *cannot* be captured by the Americans."

"Yes, sir!" If the documents fell into American hands it would be almost impossible to prevent a major disaster to the Vietcong and the NVA forces already in position to attack the American Eleventh Armored Cavalry Regiment operating in the Parrot's Beak area. The 133rd Signal Company had discovered the secret codes the Eleventh ACR was using and had intercepted the American unit's battle plans.

Joc told his officers, "We must return and destroy everything in the chamber. The Americans must not capture the equipment, but even more important, they must not be allowed to study how we operate."

Dixson helped Benjy tear through the fake wall. The chamber was huge. The VC operators had left notepads and pens next to their radios, which meant they were planning to return.

Kenny had gone halfway across the chamber, followed by Benjy. The twins had been extremely cautious since running into the two VC tunnel guards. Their submachine guns were at the ready. Kenny stopped at the end of the chamber and whispered, "Did you hear something?"

Benjy shook his head but concentrated on listening for the sound that had alerted his brother.

"Again . . ." Kenny pointed at a small door in the side of the exit tunnel. "From there."

The door was open a crack, and Kenny paused to listen. It sounded like a man struggling to breathe. Slowly Kenny shoved the door open with the barrel of his weapon and prepared to open fire. Two men were lying on sleeping mats, and the only thing that prevented Kenny from firing was the blond hair of one of the men. The blond soldier gasped for air through a hole in his throat. Kenny's lamp picked up the bright red bubbles surrounding the hole.

Benjy stepped quickly into the room and checked the walls on either side of the door. He was so high-strung that anything moving would have caused him to open fire.

Kenny approached the wounded soldier and saw that a hole had been punched in the side of his neck. The other soldier was lying with his eyes open and his mouth parted. Saliva was still shining wetly on his cheek and his blood was just beginning to coagulate on the sleeping mat. Clearly the men hadn't been lying there very long; the assassin had left only a couple of minutes before the twins arrived, which meant he was still nearby.

"These guys POW's?" Benjy went over to the radios on the bench and shuffled through the stack of papers.

"This one's still alive." Kenny removed a bandage from his webgear and covered the hole in the soldier's throat. "He was lucky that whoever did this was in a hurry, because he missed his jugular."

The American voice caused the wounded soldier to open his eyes. He couldn't talk; only a gurgle came forth. Fear entered the man's eyes, and Kenny misinterpreted the cause. "Don't worry, buddy . . . you're safe now."

"Motherfuckme!" Benjy hissed. "These motherfuckers were VC!" He held up a message pad written in English.

"VC?" Kenny looked down at the panicked soldier.

"Yeah! Look at this shit! They were working with the communists!" Benjy tucked the pad into his fatigue jacket. "I'm saving this for his fucking court-martial!"

"What's going on in here?" Dixson stuck his head through the door. "I can hear you halfway to hell!"

"American VC!" Benjy pointed at the wounded soldier.

Dixson couldn't believe his eyes. He had heard about white cong but had never believed the rumors. "Look at his arm."

Kenny turned the man's arm over so he could see the inside. "Shit, he's a fucking heroin addict."

"Shoot the motherfucker!" Benjy pointed his

weapon at the wounded soldier. "The fucker will get off by pleading he was captured and turned into an addict by the VC!"

"No . . . we can't do that," Dixson objected.

"What are we going to do with him?" Benjy demanded. "We can't leave him here so he can warn the VC, and I damn sure won't leave him here to grease *our* asses from behind!"

"Mason!" Dixson called back into the radio chamber. "You stay with this guy until we return. We're going to search a little more of the tunnel leading out of here and then come back."

The exit tunnel went another twenty feet past the large radio chamber and then made a sharp turn to the right before disappearing.

Dixson looped Molly's leash in his hand and kept her close by his side. "I want the two of you to stay here and keep us from being surprised. I'm going back to the radio chamber and get some infantry down here. If we can locate this chamber from up above, we can open it up like an anthill. Can you guys handle it?"

"Sure," Benjy whispered, and turned off his miner's lamp. Kenny followed suit and they sat down against the tunnel wall to wait in the dark.

Joc led his sapper recovery squad down the narrow tunnel in total darkness. He was crawling on his stomach and stopped often to listen to the sounds coming through the air vents from up above. The reaction battalion had started mortaring the

American cavalry unit surrounding the village. Joc reached a ninety-degree angle and had to roll over on his side to make the turn. He had been down the passage only one time before during a training mission, and the cramped quarters had nearly paralyzed him with claustrophobia.

Mason sat with his back to the radios, facing the small doorway, so he didn't see the floor mat shift slightly under the radio bench. Joc closed his eyes and opened them again slowly; the beam from Mason's flashlight was like a tropical sun searing his vision. He waited in the tunnel until he could see clearly before pushing the hidden trapdoor to one side and slipping far enough out of the tight passageway to use his pistol.

Mason looked down at the sleeping heroin addict and wished he could escape from the reality of the war.

Joc made that wish come true. Mason didn't even hear the bullet that penetrated the back of his head, but the twins and Dixson did. Kenny spun around to stare in the direction Dixson and Molly had gone, while Benjy continued to watch the other way along the dark tunnel. Dixson turned off his miner's lamp and waited silently to see what would happen. It would be foolish to run into the room after hearing a shot. Mason's pistol was silenced, so Dixson was afraid that a VC had been hiding somewhere in the room and killed Mason. Whatever had happened inside that room, Dixson was staying put.

Joc waited until his sapper squad was out of the

tunnel and checked their weapons before signaling them to go out into the hall. After the tiny passageway the small room felt like wide, open space to Joc. He made sure the black American soldier was dead and saw that the two heroin addicts had had their throats cut and their VC guard was missing. Someone had bandaged one of the American's throats, and he was still alive but in no condition to escape. Joc signaled with his pistol and the highly trained sappers exited the room in the dark. They were the best night fighters the NVA and VC had.

Kenny heard movement and risked switching on his flashlight for a split second to make sure that it wasn't Dixson and Molly before pulling the trigger on his Swedish-K. He had kept one eye closed to maintain his night vision, more from a training response than from a practical point of view.

Benjy had taken advantage of the dim light in the opposite direction and saw that at least a dozen VC were creeping up on them. They were trapped in both directions. Benjy opened fire and backed around the corner when his silenced weapon was answered by a roar of AK-47 rounds. The dirt behind him danced and hunks of mud from the walls fell down and hit him.

Joc used the diversion to get his sapper team into the chamber and out of the passageway. All the VC who had worked in the 133rd Signal Company had practiced moving through the tunnels and chambers in total darkness, and now it was paying off for Joc. He moved swiftly down the chamber, using the rows of radios as a guide.

Dixson had ordered Molly to lie down under one of the radio benches out of the way. He waited until soft footfalls drew near and then fired blindly in the dark. His long silencer eliminated most of the muzzle flash, but in the total darkness Joc could see the slight yellow-orange glow and fire back. Dixson groaned and slumped forward on the damp earth. One of Joc's rounds had penetrated his heart.

Kenny backed up until his feet touched his brother. He spun around on his stomach in the dark and felt for Benjy's head. "Too fucking many of them! Let's get back in the room with Mason."

Benjy slapped Kenny's shoulder and held on to his sleeve as they moved toward the closed door. Fear was starting to play with Benjy's mind. He felt the door and pushed it open. Kenny shoved it shut behind him and both of them turned on their miner's lamps. Mason lay slumped over the wounded white cong, dead. Kenny saw the opening under the bench and pieced together what had happened. The roar of AK-47's filled the tunnel outside the door. The twins had only one option to avoid being trapped in the room when the VC returned. Kenny pointed at the tunnel the VC had sneaked in through. "It's our only chance."

"Let's go!" Benjy slipped the M-2 off his shoulder and tightened the strap so that when he crawled, he could keep it pointed in front of him. He left his miner's lamp burning. There was no way he was going to crawl into that tiny hole without light.

Kenny followed Benjy down into the narrow passage and pulled the floor mat back over the hole.

Benjy cursed and started crawling, using only his legs to push himself down the musty-smelling earth tube. He had to pause to figure out how to negotiate the ninety-degree turn, and ended up doing exactly what Joc had done. He could barely make out his brother's shoulder when he looked back. Kenny didn't have his headlamp on and was using the little light that filtered past Benjy to crawl by. The short tunnel ended abruptly and Benjy nearly tumbled out into the room that the VC had left only a few minutes earlier.

Benjy's light swept the room and found it empty of VC, but filled with equipment and the personal items of the VC who lived there.

Kenny looked around. "Where in the fuck are we?"

"You got my ass, but I'm glad to get the fuck out of here if I've got to dig my way out straight up!"

"They've stopped firing." Kenny listened. "We'd better warn the captain." He removed his URC-10 and whispered, "This is Dog Leader Three, over."

No answer.

"This is Dog Leader Three, over!"

There was a long pause and then an excited voice came over the small radio. "Dog Leader, this is Blue Fang Six. We are in contact with the enemy, at least a battalion-size force. Hold your own for a while until I can get some control up here, over."

"*We're* in deep shit down here, Captain . . . fucking VC all over the place!"

"Roger. Do the best you can." The transmission ended abruptly.

Benjy shook his head. "What do you think of that shit?"

"We've just got to do what the captain said— make do!" Kenny checked his weapon. "I don't like it, but we can't expect them to help us if they're under attack."

Benjy pointed to the doorway. "Let's go over there by the entrance and listen for a while to see what in the fuck is going on."

"Good idea." Kenny sat down on the right side of the entrance and Benjy took up a position next to him before they turned off their lights. "Fuck, it's dark."

A half-hour passed before Kenny nudged Benjy and whispered into his ear, "Sounds like they're not coming back for a while. Let's try finding a way out of here." He stood up and could feel Benjy holding on to his arm in the dark. Kenny had memorized the layout of the room and the tunnel and started walking forward slowly. They had gone about fifteen feet down the damp passageway when Kenny stopped short. "Oh, fuck!"

Benjy was reaching for his light switch when Kenny added, "It's only Molly. Oh, shit, girl, you scared me fucking silly!"

Molly had approached the twins in the dark by smell and had shoved her nose into Kenny's hand.

"What's Molly doing here?" Benjy's voice almost

broke. Molly would never leave Dixson if he were alive.

"What should we do?"

"We have to go back and check things out."

"Shit! I just want out of this fucking place!" Benjy knew the VC would be waiting, but he took the lead. He wrapped Molly's leash around his left wrist and kept her close to his side so he could feel her with his leg in the dark.

They hadn't gone ten feet in the tunnel when the lights came on. The glaring light bulbs made their eyes close automatically, but the twins knew they had to open them quickly or risk being caught by the VC. Kenny blinked rapidly and lowered himself into a combat crouch, ready to fire at anything moving. He kept his eyes on Molly, knowing she would alert them before the VC got close to them in the tunnel.

Joc had risked turning on the lights because he knew that American tunnel-rat teams traveled in pairs and they had killed two men. He needed the lights so his team could rig the chamber with high explosives and destroy the radios before the Americans captured it. It was a last-ditch effort, in case the reaction battlion couldn't drive the Americans away up above them.

Benjy started to turn the corner and Molly alerted him that there were VC ahead. Kenny stopped his brother and signaled that they should change magazines so they could lay down a lot of firepower before having to reload. Then they stepped around the corner together and engaged the surprised VC sappers.

Joc felt the bullets hitting him and thought that it was a weird way to die, so quietly. He dropped onto the dirt floor and could see under the benches. He couldn't move, but he could see the American boots as they moved toward where he lay, surrounded by his dead soldiers.

Kenny saw where the sapper squad had started to rig the tunnel with explosives and backed away. "New booby traps in the tunnel!"

"Shit!" Benjy turned around to make sure none of the VC were faking death. "What should we do?"

"Let's go back to the sleeping area. There has to be another way out of here."

"We know this way out." Benjy pointed to the tunnel. All he wanted was to get back to the surface.

"Yeah, but so do they, and if they're waiting for us, it'll be in that tunnel." Kenny indicated the direction from which they had entered. His eyes swept the chamber and came to rest on Sergeant Dixson's body slumped in the far corner. "Sarge . . ." Kenny ran to Dixson and rolled him over. He could see from the blood spots that the NCO had been shot three times, once in the heart.

Benjy turned away from the scene. "Let's get *out* of here!"

"C'mon!" Kenny felt the same way. If he didn't get some fresh air in his lungs, he would die.

The twins moved down the tunnel quickly, relying

on Molly to warn them of any traps or approaching VC. They were near the edge of panic, with just enough control that they could fight if they had to. The electric lights made movement a lot easier. The tunnel they were in ended abruptly and split into a pair of smaller branches.

"Which way?" Benjy looked back the way they had come.

"Molly . . . take us out of here, girl." Kenny loosened his hold on the dog's leash.

Molly whined and looked back toward the chamber Dixson was lying in, and then took a step to the right—toward the smell of fresh air.

"This way!" Benjy took the lead. The tunnel went fifty feet and dead-ended in a small chamber with a long bamboo ladder.

"We're out of here!" Benjy started forward, but Kenny grabbed his shoulder.

"Eagle." The name was enough to tell Benjy the ladder was probably booby-trapped. "Molly . . . seek." Kenny freed the dog so she could work the chamber. She alerted to the wooden ammunition-box lid the ladder had been set on to prevent its sinking into the soft clay. Two of the lids were placed side by side on the floor, but only one showed signs of wear from the base of the ladder. The ladder was now resting on the unworn box top. Kenny dropped down and used the tip of his knife to remove some of the dirt from the edge of the wood until he could lay his head against the floor and see under it. He dug away more dirt while Benjy kept guard. There had to be a simple way to disarm the booby trap because the VC needed to use the exit themselves in a hurry. Kenny pushed a little more of the dirt away and saw the side of an antitank mine. The VC had rigged the mine with a sensitive pressure device so that it would go off with only a few hundred pounds of weight on the pressure pad. The booby trap was simple. The VC would move the ladder over to the other box lid when they used the exit and would step over the lid that hid the mine. When they were finished with the ladder, they would shift it back to rest on the booby trap. Simple and effective. Kenny checked the other lid to make sure it wasn't rigged also and then moved the ladder.

"I'll go first." Benjy could see the sweat covering Kenny's forehead. Disarming booby traps was nerve-racking work, and exiting this tunnel was going to be dangerous anyway, because they had no idea where they were going to end up. It could be in the jungle or in someone's hut.

Benjy started up the ladder after testing his weight on the first rung. He felt a tingling sensation in his scrotum as the image of Eagle's torn-apart body flashed in front of his eyes. He swallowed hard and went on without looking down again. All his concentration was on the lid that covered the hole. When Benjy reached the top he cocked his head and listened for any sign that the VC were on the other side. He heard muffled gunfire and explosions. He glanced down and saw Kenny staring up at him with a worried look. Benjy winked and pushed gently against the heavy woven bamboo cover. It moved slightly, and he pushed harder, but the cover gave only a little more. Benjy frowned. Something had been placed on top of the exit cover. He felt panic flash through him and decided he would risk putting his back into it. He slipped his M-2 over his shoulder and signaled for Kenny to cover him as much as he could from the floor level and then put his back into it. At first there was a lot of resistance, and then the cover popped open, almost causing Benjy to lose his balance on the ladder. Fresh air, dim sunlight, and the sounds of a firefight reached him at the same time. A burned VC body had been lying on the cover to the tunnel entrance in a bunker that had taken a direct hit from a napalm canister. Portions of the VC's flesh were still smoldering, and what Benjy had at first thought was fresh air was actually tinged with burned bodies and gunpowder.

Benjy scurried out and swept the immediate area for any VC whom might have survived the air strike. Then he returned to help Kenny, who was trying to lift Molly through the opening.

"We're in a bunker somewhere near the village." Benjy checked the RPD machine gun, which was still in good operating order. The napalm had scorched the wooden stock, but it hadn't burned long enough to set off the ammunition or melt any of the working parts. The steel was warm to the touch. "Kenny, give the infantry captain a call."

Kenny had completely forgotten about their radios during the underground battle. He turned the set on. "Blue Fang Six . . . this is Dog Leader Four, over."

There was a short pause and the captain answered in a voice that was a lot calmer than before. "Leader Four . . . this is Six, over."

"We're aboveground, but we don't know where we are. Some kind of VC bunker that has an RPD in it and a couple of dead VC, over."

The captain shook his head in wonder. He knew exactly where the twins were. "You guys are in a VC bunker line that we've been blowing the shit out of for the past hour!"

"That's nice to hear!"

The captain wondered how he was going to get the trackers out of there without abandoning the fight. The initial half-hour of the battle had been in the Vietcong's favor. They had caught the American troops by surprise, but once the cavalry troop and the infantry got on their weapons, the tide of battle had turned. "How many of you are there?"

"Two . . . Sarge and Mason are dead."

"Can you work your way down to us?" The captain knew that wasn't going to work as soon as he asked, and added, "Or can you go back down through the tunnels?"

Kenny wouldn't ask Benjy to go back down there. "It's full of VC." A Cobra gunship made a pass, and hundreds of bullets tore into the cover on the bunker and into the earth all around the twins. "Shit!" Kenny ducked lower behind the bunker wall.

"What's going on?" The captain sounded worried.

"A Cobra just made a pass on us!" Kenny looked out of the firing slit and could barely make out a helicopter flashing above the treetops.

"I can see it from here!" The captain looked up at the banking chopper. "You're about three hundred meters due west of us and the village."

"Three hundred meters?" Kenny spoke into the radio but he was looking at Benjy. It seemed more like three hundred miles of tunnel they had crawled through.

"See if you can make it back to us, or hold out there until we can reach you." The captain couldn't guarantee their safety and couldn't stop the assault on the VC positions for just two men.

"Roger, sir, out." Kenny shook his head. "We're on our own, brother."

"I figured that shit!" Benjy was sitting with his back to Kenny, watching the trench leading away from the bunker. "Well, what do you want to do? We're fairly safe in here."

"You think so?" Kenny looked at the burned bodies only a couple of feet away from where he was sitting with Molly. "Lightning doesn't strike the same place twice; I wonder about napalm."

"If we go out there, we can get killed by our own guys *and* the VC."

"Like they used to say back in the training group: it's a target-rich environment out there."

"Right! At least our own guys won't shoot us on purpose!" Benjy shook his head and wrinkled his nose. "Let's go . . . I don't like the smell in here anyway."

Molly saved the twins' lives three times in ten minutes. She warned them of approaching VC in the trenches, so the twins were waiting for them. Kenny had taken the RPD light machine gun with them and as much ammunition in drums as they could carry. They had to watch both directions in the trench at the same time as they tried moving down the hill toward the village. The trenches seemed to run in a north-south direction, which made the task difficult.

Molly alerted just as they reached a deep spot in the trench that was over their heads. Benjy crouched and waited for the first VC to appear and opened fire with his silenced M-2 submachine gun, taking the first half-dozen VC by surprise. Kenny had been covering the opposite direction and spun around to give Benjy some covering fire. He watched as Benjy was smashed against the dirt wall from the AK-47 rounds hitting him and crumpled on top of a dead VC.

Kenny's breath caught in his throat and he lost all concern for his own life. Fear, pain, exhaustion, hate—every feeling and emotion left him and he started killing with the machine gun. Kenny's violent and unexpected assault down the trench caught the VC platoon by surprise. He stepped over dying men and ran on down the trench firing. It was more a slaughter than a battle. The VC soldiers could engage Kenny only one at a time in the narrow trench that zigzagged back to their company's command bunker, and the sound of an RPD firing confused them even more.

Kenny stopped when he reached the bunker and changed drums on the RPD. He was thankful that he had learned about Soviet and Chinese weapons when he had worked for the Special Forces training group. A VC sergeant stepped out of the bunker to see why the RPD was firing so close by, and died for his curiosity. Kenny showed no emotion; he would simply kill until someone killed him.

Lieutenant Tong Le heard the RPD, grabbed the courier pouch, and ran out the other exit of the bunker. At all costs, the contents of the pouch must not be captured by the Americans. The mistake she made was thinking that the RPD firing outside the bunker was manned by one of the VC. Kenny swung the barrel of the weapon around and tore her back open. He removed one of the M-26 hand grenades from his webbing and tossed it into the bunker, then decided for safe measure to toss another one through the exit the VC with the pouch had used.

The hand-grenade explosion was the last sound of the battle. Kenny stood next to the bunker wall and listened to the sounds of the jungle returning. The battle had ended as quickly as it had started.

Gradually conscious thought reclaimed Kenny and he ran as hard as he could back to the trench and slid to a halt when he saw Benjy propped up against the side of the ditch, trying to wrap a field dressing around his chest. Molly lay next to him with a bandage on one front leg. Benjy had seen to the dog before working on himself. He looked up and growled, "Well, don't just stand there. Give me a hand."

CHAPTER 14

SAIGON SAFE HOUSE

September 1968

The conference room was filled with general officers and senior noncommissioned officers from all of the allied armies with units operating in III and IV Corps. Sergeant Major Yates sat in a comfortable leather chair next to the wall behind the long conference table. He was there as an observer, along with a couple dozen other straphangers who weren't a part of the decision-making body sitting around the table. Yates hadn't seen so many stars in one place since he had visited the Pentagon, where it was rumored that there were 136 generals and admirals per acre.

Yates felt someone staring at him and glanced up to catch the only civilian in the room looking directly at him from behind a pair of mirrored sunglasses. The man smiled and slipped over to take the seat next to Yates.

"Sergeant Major Yates?" He held out his hand to shake. "I'm LeBlond . . . we have something in common, I believe."

Yates took the offered hand and proceeded with caution. The man reeked of CIA. "We do?"

"Yes . . . we do." LeBlond touched the frame of his sunglasses and smiled again. He could tell the glasses irritated the sergeant major. "After this briefing, I would like to take you to visit some people."

"I'm afraid not . . ." Yates returned his attention to the battle map that covered the wall behind the conference table. The meeting was about to start. "I have an important meeting to attend right after this one is over." Yates looked at his watch.

"If you check, you'll find that the awards ceremony has been postponed for two hours."

Yates looked directly at the mirrored orbs, giving the impression that he could see the man's eyes. "Are you with the Agency?"

LeBlond nodded.

"Sorry . . . I don't need any of your PRU shit today"

"You're a little confused, Sergeant Major. The PRU isn't a part of the Agency."

Yates raised his eyebrows. "Really? Then who runs it?"

"You'd be surprised, my friend . . . surprised." LeBlond turned his attention to the Army colonel who was looking at General Westmoreland for the signal to begin his briefing. The general nodded and the colonel started talking in the trained voice of a professional staff briefer.

LeBlond leaned over and whispered, "Please . . . I need only an hour of your time."

Yates gave a curt nod. He might as well listen to what the man had to say; someday he might need him for something.

The briefer handed his pointer to the next officer, who replaced him behind the podium and started his portion of the briefing. "As you all know, we have discovered that a major NVA-VC operation is about to be launched in this sector." He used the pointer to locate the infamous Parrot's Beak region of Cambodia, jutting out like a menacing peninsula aimed at Saigon. "The enemy forces are already in place and will be unable to withdraw in time to save themselves."

LeBlond leaned over again and whispered. "Your boys—the Kingston twins—were responsible, I hear, for finding the courier pouch on a dead VC lieutenant."

"They were trained right," Yates confirmed.

The briefing officer gave LeBlond and Yates a sharp look before continuing. "The NVA and the Ninth Vietcong Division have suffered a series of severe defeats recently at Loc Ninh . . ."—he tapped the map—". . . Cu Chi . . ."—another tap— " . . . and in War Zone C." His voice lowered. "Gentlemen, the NVA general in the central office located somewhere near Mimot, Cambodia, has sent a message to the units operating in the Parrot's

Beak that he wants the American Eleventh Armored Cavalry Regiment destroyed."

The Eleventh ACR commander, a puppet who had attained his rank only through debts owed to his father, a high-ranking career officer, smirked and said, "Let them come! The Eleventh needs a good fight."

The colonel on the podium struggled to maintain his composure. If it hadn't been for the capture of the NVA pouch, the poorly commanded Eleventh ACR would have moved right into the trap, and there was no doubt what the outcome would have been. After a moment the colonel continued his briefing. "As you know, General"—he looked at Westmoreland—"the NVA have issued two RPG-7's per infantry squad for this operation, and all of the routes previously selected by the Eleventh ACR have been mined for just this occasion, which tells us that the NVA had copies of the Eleventh ACR's battle plans."

"That's a goddamn lie!" The Eleventh ACR commander stood up and rested his hands on the butts of his mismatched pistols.

The briefing officer ignored the outburst and turned on his Viewgraph. The general officers in the room collectively gasped. Displayed on the wall was the ELeventh ACR commander standing atop of a pile of NVA dead, his hands on his hips. The caption read: "PEACE ON EARTH—MERRY CHRIST-MAS." "This particular Christmas card was air-dropped over major NVA and Vietcong strong-holds in the Eleventh ACR operations area. The

NVA commander has ordered that every one of his soldiers carry one of these pictures into battle with him, thus effectively creating an army of revenge-hungry fanatics."

"You son of a bitch!" the Eleventh ACR commander shrieked until Westmoreland's "Enough!" stopped him.

"Well, that was a little more interesting than most briefings." LeBlond led the way over to his air-conditioned civilian CJ-5. "I thought the briefing colonel did an excellent job setting up that asshole for the kill."

Yates took a seat before answering, "I guess that's how stars are won here in Vietnam—in the staff briefing rooms. Where are we going?"

"To a safe house. I want you to meet someone." LeBlond lit a thin cigar and cracked his window a little so that the smoke would exit from his side of the jeep.

The cigar was half-smoked when he pulled off the road and stopped in front of an ornate wrought-iron gate. He waited until a pair of armed guards unchained and pulled open the decorative barrier. The villa they were approaching had once belonged to a French rubber baron and had been confiscated when the South Vietnamese government discovered that he was personally supporting two Vietcong battalions. The Frenchman had escaped back to his French estate and the government had refused to extradite him to their former colony.

"Nice place." Yates observed the flower garden that lined the driveway to the house.

"The rent is a little high, but the place affords privacy." LeBlond stopped the jeep and got out. "They're waiting for us inside."

The ten-foot doors to the library were closed, and LeBlond knocked and waited for admission. There were three civilians in the room, along with two Special Forces men. Yates recognized the gray-haired chief of SOG and nodded in recognition.

"Well, it looks like we're all here." One of the men wearing a dark gray business suit nodded and another man departed through a different door. He returned escorting a man in his early twenties. "Gentlemen, I would like to introduce Joc Rochambeau, also known as Major Joc Vo Nguyen of the Vietcong's Ninth Division."

Joc recognized Yates from their short meeting at the Special Forces camp at Loc Ninh, but the rest of the faces in the room were unknown to him. He took the offered seat and waited. It had been less than a week since he had been brought back to Vietnam from the surgical hospital in Japan where reconstructive work had been done to repair the wounds he had received in the tunnel.

Yates took the offered seat and waited for the man to continue talking.

"Major Vo Nguyen has a rather low opinion of us right now, but we are hoping that after we present a few *factual* documents, he will understand that we are a very professional organization. I've been led to believe, Major, that you have been told that your father and mother were murdered by members of ex-President Ngo Dinh Diem's tax agency." The man cocked his head to one side as he waited for Joc to confirm his statement. Joc only looked passively at the unknown man. "And that your aunt was assassinated by two Buddhist monks who were actually PRU hit men . . . truc?"

Joc didn't let the hate he was feeling show through his eyes. He thought only of pleasant things, and the tiniest trace of a smile escaped through his mental barriers.

"Wrong, Major Vo Nguyen. True, your aunt was on the PRU list for elimination. She was a Vietcong operative and a very good one, but she was murdered before the PRU could act."

Yates was intrigued.

"Are you familiar with Lieutenant General Bec Sang?" The man smiled. He knew that Joc was quite familiar with the code name for the commanding general of the central office for all NVA and Vietcong forces in the south.

Joc's eyebrows flickered.

"*He* is responsible for killing your parents and your aunt." The man waited for the allegation to sink in.

Joc smiled. He had been through similar interrogations, in which the prisoner was led to believe that the very people he relied on were the ones who had betrayed him. The tactic was basic and unworthy of the man's pathetic attempt.

The briefing agent slowly opened and closed his eyes as if he were reading Joc's mind. "I know it

seems crude and basic, but please bear with me."
A Viewgraph came on and one of the agents started
changing the slides.

"You can see from the name on the bank draft
that a considerable sum of money is being shipped
to that bank in Paris, and all of it is going into the
private account of a Mr. Bec Sang. He's been taking a cut from the drug warlords operating in the
area his divisions occupy in Cambodia and South
Vietnam." The man removed an old ledger from a
nearby table and handed it to Joc. "If you will look
where we have highlighted the page, you will see
that Mr. Bec Sang increased the protection taxes
five times in two years on your family's plantation.
Your father refused to pay the last increase in taxes
levied on him by the *general,* not the Diem
regime."

Joc looked at the entries and the dates. This was
his father's handwriting. He flipped back through
the pages of the ledger and could see that his father
had made huge payments to the NVA general for
protection. Just from his own knowledge of what
the Vietcong collected and of the normal South
Vietnamese taxes, he could see that his father was
operating the plantation at a loss and was trying to
survive until the war was over.

"Sharks, feeding on each other and on an occasional honest victim. General Bec Sang ordered this
ledger confiscated after he had your parents killed."
The man signaled and the Viewgraph was turned
off. "Your aunt found that tax log quite by accident. It was delivered to her by a Vietcong village

chief whose men found it on one of Bec Sang's agents who had been killed by an artillery round in the jungle."

A slight change in attitude flickered behind Joc's eyes and the man caught it instantly. He was very, very good at this tactic and had been flown into Vietnam from Langley headquarters for just this purpose. "Take your time . . . examine everything . . . ask questions, and then we'll talk again tomorrow." He nodded and the guard escorted Joc back through the door.

LeBlond waited until Joc was gone before asking Yates, "What do you think?"

"He was the man who worked at Loc Ninh and disappeared after the dead Vietcong with blue eyes had been discovered." Yates was impressed with the CIA operation.

"Yes, and he also has a younger brother being trained in a Moscow military academy."

"What do I have to do with all of this?" Yates knew he hadn't been invited to the meeting just to watch.

"We would like to break Joc Rochambeau and infiltrate him through your B-Team at Tay Ninh."

"You would waste a catch like him in a B-Team?" Yates couldn't believe what he was hearing.

"Yes . . . you see, we want him to give us the location of the central office in Cambodia and lead a raid to destroy it." LeBlond removed his sunglasses and Yates saw one blue and one green eye staring at him. "We feel that if he knows the truth about Lieutenant General Bec Sang, he'll kill him for us."

"Interesting . . ."—Yates looked at his watch—"but I've got to make it to that awards ceremony."

"I'll drive you." LeBlond replaced his sunglasses. "I like to listen to the music at those functions."

LeBlond took his time driving to the awards ceremony. General Westmoreland had requested that men from each division in Vietnam be present to receive their awards in front of the President of the United States, who was secretly being flown into South Vietnam for a personal tour. There would be three Medals of Honor presented during the ceremony and fifteen Distinguished Service and Navy Crosses, along with more than thirty Silver Stars. None of the soldiers knew that the President would be there to present the awards.

Yates glanced at LeBlond when he stopped for a red light in a congested part of Cholon. "I talked to Specialist James Buchanan over a MARS hookup back to the States, and he had some interesting things to say about our Vietcong major."

"I know . . . I read your report." LeBlond maintained a solemn expression.

"Then you also know that Joc Rochambeau is responsible for saving five of their lives when the Khmer Rouge were going to cut their throats."

"The way I understand it, three of the prisoners already had their throats cut when he shot the camp commander and two of his Khmer soldiers."

"I think we owe him something for that." Yates didn't like the idea of using Joc as a double agent, especially after what he had done for the American POW's.

"We've taken care of that." LeBlond changed gears by double-clutching. "If he cooperates with us, he'll get the vineyard he has always wanted."

"A vineyard?"

"Yes . . . in California." LeBlond smiled. "A *small* one, but who knows, we just might see some good years with a Rochambeau label."

When the jeep arrived at the briefing complex, Sergeant Yates could see the soldiers already lined up in the hot sun waiting for the ceremony to begin. They were wearing helmets pulled down low over their eyes and pistol belts and suspenders. Yates scanned the rows of military men from all of the different branches until his eyes found Kenny Kingston standing next to a huge marine corporal.

Kenny saw Yates the instant he arrived, and smiled broadly at the sergeant major. He was very proud to have won a Silver Star for gallantry in action, and the senior sergeant's presence at the ceremony meant a lot to him. Yates had set things up so that Benjy would receive his Silver Star at exactly the same time back at the Army hospital near Washington, D.C.

Yates returned Kenny's smile and winked. He couldn't be prouder if the young soldier were his own son.

The marine corporal next to Kenny noticed the exchange between the NCO and the soldier standing next to him. He whispered out of the corner of his mouth, "Is that your sergeant?"

"Naw . . . he's my Dad."

The marine did a double take and stared at the black sergeant major. His next question was cut off by the opening bars of "Hail to the Chief" as the President of the United States stepped onto the presenting platform. He smiled and stood until the general officers and members of the ambassador's staff took their positions.

The President took his time presenting the three Medals of Honor. He then trooped the ranks and presented the first rank of troops with the Distinguished Service and Navy Crosses. Sweat was pouring off the President's face by the time he reached the rows of soldiers and marines who were there to receive their Silver Stars. He wasn't used to the heat.

LeBlond leaned over and whispered in Yates's ear, "It looks like the old boy is getting tired."

Yates remained standing at attention while the commander-in-chief rushed down the line of men, shaking hands and pinning on their red-white-and-blue-striped ribbons with the beautiful gold stars attached that had a tiny silver star in the center.

Kenny was so proud when the President shook his hand and attached the valor award to his starched jungle-fatigue jacket that he felt as if he would pass out. The President hardly looked at him, but Kenny didn't mind. It had been a great honor just seeing the famous man up close. It was something he could someday tell his children.

Benjy was propped up on his hospital bed watching the double doors to his ward for signs of the four-star general's arrival. He was nervous about the special attention he was getting in front of the other men in his hospital bay. All of them were recuperating from war wounds, and the chief of staff was going to present all of them with Purple Hearts, with a special presentation to Benjy of the Silver Star.

The Army had invited the news media at the last minute and had briefed them on what was occurring and that the President was presenting the soldier's twin brother with a Silver Star in Vietnam at the same time.

The chief of staff stepped off the elevator, accompanied by his aides and senior staff. One aide carried a velvet pillow upon which lay Benjy's Silver Star, surrounded by a field of Purple Hearts. The general stopped and looked down at the awards before they entered the hospital bay where Benjy waited. "It's a beautiful award. I got mine on the Rhine in 1944."

The aide smiled. "This soldier and his brother really earned these Silver Stars, sir . . ." The aide saw the look in the general's eyes and qualified his statement. "No disrespect intended, sir. What I mean to say is, there's nothing political about this award." The aide balanced the velvet pillow on one hand and reached into his uniform blouse for a piece of paper folded neatly down the center. "Please read this, sir, before we go in there."

"I don't think we have time for that right now, Johnson!" One of the general's junior staff volunteered the comment.

Johnson looked at the senior general. He had been an enlisted man and had won a Distinguished Service Cross during the early years of the war with the First Cavalry Division at the Battle of the Ia Drang. "Please, sir . . . I think you'll go in there with a different opinion if you read his general orders for the Silver Star first."

The chief of staff snatched the paper out of Johnson's hands and flashed a look at his senior aide that told him he wanted the young captain replaced. The general's eyes moved down the paragraph rapidly at first, but Johnson saw the old officer's eyes slow down and then go back to the top of the paragraph to read it over again. "Unbelievable!" He looked up at his senior aide. "Have you read this?"

"No, sir . . . we've been quite busy today." The colonel felt his cheeks turning red. He had served in Vietnam as a battalion commander and knew that Silver Stars were being handed out to company commanders and battalion commanders almost as an end-of-tour present from their division commanders. The Silver Star had become a symbol for an infantry officer's service under fire and had replaced the Combat Infantryman's Badge that had been designed for just that purpose.

"Dammit, man! That's what I have you around for!" He waved the copy of the general orders in front of the staff colonel. "Read it!"

The junior generals standing in a semicircle around the senior officer looked shyly at each other, hoping that he wouldn't ask them if they had read the citation. None of them had.

"That *boy* in there killed thirty-nine NVA soldiers, give or take a few, because his brother is being credited with sixteen! He spent two days underground in a Vietcong tunnel system and killed a couple more Vietcong down there. He killed a Vietcong lieutenant who was carrying a top-secret courier pouch that was the *sole* reason we prevented a major disaster with the Eleventh ACR . . ." The general was now totally angry. He looked at a major general in the group. "Have you replaced that idiot yet?"

"No, sir. His father, sir, was a very famous soldier. We have to move with a little caution to protect *his* family name."

"*General*, I want that idiot out of there before he gets any more men killed while he's waving his nickel-plated guns from the top of an ACAV!" The chief of staff blinked slowly, trying to gain control of his emotions.

"Yes, sir." The major general looked down at his boots. He had been the one to secure command of the Eleventh Armored Cavalry Regiment for the famous general's son.

"We're giving that soldier in there only a Silver Star for all of this?" The chief of staff waved the general orders at his junior aide.

"Yes, sir. That's quite enough sir—he's only an enlisted man, sir."

"*Only* an enlisted man, huh?" The chief of staff pushed the double doors open and entered the ward.

ACTION THRILLERS!